Her Home

"Every journey into the past is complicated by delusions, false memories, false namings of real events."
- Adrienne Rich

Prologue

Annette rushed inside the bedroom and frantically slammed the door shut behind her. Her trembling hands fumbled with the key in the lock before quickly managing to turn it, locking the door. As soon as she heard the latch click, she took a halting step backward, as though she had just touched something extremely hot.

She swallowed through her dry throat and steadied her breathing as she continued staring at the door. Other than the sound of her panicked breathing, silence permeated the air. Annette released a tentative sigh of relief with a trembling breath. Perhaps she was safe after all.

A stampeding batter of footsteps resounded from outside the bedroom, followed by a loud slam on the other side of the door.

Annette recoiled, stumbling backward in the process. She would have screamed, but her voice was stifled by the sheer terror that coursed through her entire being.

Three loud knocks resounded on the door. And then silence.

Annette heard the loud drumming of her heart in her chest, as her legs became wobbly. She fought her body's urge to collapse while she tried to remain as frozen as a statue.

"Anneeeette. I know you're in theeeere," a soft voice called out from the other side of the door.

Hearing her name being called out made the hairs on the nape of Annette's neck stand straight up. Judging by the tinny manner in which the voice came through, it was clear that the person was right on the other side of the door. Annette looked down at the crack under the door, and through the meager hallway light that gleamed inside, saw a shadow standing in front of the door.

"We had a deal, Annette," the voice came through again, still as perky and friendly. "You don't want to break our deal, do you?"

Three more raps on the doors, this time in a much hastier manner. Annette's body refused to budge. All she could do was stare at the shadow under the door as it nonchalantly swayed from left to right, but never disappearing.

"OPEN UP, YOU BITCH!" The knocking sounded more like a battering ram, as it loudly filled the bedroom, effectively snapping Annette out of her stupor.

She turned around and looked around the moonlit bedroom. She ran as quickly as her elderly legs could carry her to the cabinet in front of the window. There, a doll sat on top, staring at her with its vacuous eyes and creepy smile.

"OPEN UP!" the voice said again, the relentless knocking never ceasing for more than a second at a time.

Annette placed her hands on the doll and closed her eyes. For a moment, she couldn't remember the words. The knocking, the shouting, the panic—all of it was putting even more pressure on Annette.

"ANNETTE! DON'T MAKE THIS HARDER ON YOURSELF!"

The first word came to her mind, then the second, and then the rest followed smoothly. Annette chanted the same sentence over and over as quickly as she could, ignoring the knocking at the door. She didn't know what the sentences she chanted meant, but she knew that she had to continue, otherwise it would all be over.

"ANNETTE!" the voice boomed one final time.

And then, just like that, it stopped.

The knocking, the yelling, the threats, all gone. The only sound that remained was Annette's panicked panting.

Annette opened her eyes and was greeted by the doll's face. She did it. She did it. She placed the doll back on top of the cabinet and opened the drawer. She frantically rummaged through it out of fear that she may not have a lot of time left. Just as she was about to lose hope, she found it.

The piece of paper she was looking for. She slapped it next to the doll on top of the cabinet and then looked for a pen in the drawer. As soon as she felt its smooth, oval surface, she fished it out and used her other hand to hold the paper steady. There was a bang somewhere in the house, causing Annette to jump and almost drop the pen in the process.

As quickly as she could, she scribbled one sentence on the back of the paper.

IM SORRY FOR TREATING YOU THE WAY I DID

Before she could finish putting it down on paper, another bang resounded in the house—this time much closer. Annette was frozen in place, and no matter how hard she tried, she couldn't will herself to budge. Somehow, she had the impression that if she did, it would bring the intruder back.

"Found you," the voice said, calmly this time, and Annette felt her blood run cold, because the voice didn't come from the hallway.

It came from behind her.

Her eyes inadvertently moved up to the window for a split second, and there he was, standing right behind her, his silhouette reflected on the glass.

Just as she shot around to face her assailant, she felt a numbness forming on the side of her face. In an instant, that numbness appeared in her leg, and Annette's knee buckled under her weight, causing her to topple sideways. She would have screamed at the painful collapse, but her mouth and lungs refused to cooperate.

As she fell down, she saw the paper she wrote on gyrating left and right in the air before sliding under the bed.

The last thing she saw was a face grinning at her before everything went dark.

Chapter 1

"I know, I know. I don't like it either, but I'll only be gone for a day. Okay?" Jill said on the phone, as she turned the key in the ignition to kill the car's engine.

"I really think I should have come with you," Lee sighed over the phone exasperated.

Jill undid her seatbelt and sighed. She was starting to get a little irked. She'd spent the day working until 3 pm, then drove for three hours, and she barely had enough time to squeeze in one meal for the whole day. It didn't help that her asshole of a boss wasn't very understanding about letting her leave earlier on a Friday. It helped even less that she didn't get to see her son Charlie today.

And now for Lee to be on her back about the things he could have done but didn't—it took everything inside Jill not to snap at her husband. That would do her no good though, and she knew well enough that Lee would end up interpreting Jill's raised tone as hostility, so she instead forced her customer support tone and spoke calmly to Lee.

"Honey, there's really nothing you could do to help me here. Besides, Charlie has his baseball practice tomorrow, and he needs someone to take him there."

"Yeah. Are you sure you can't come back a little earlier? I honestly have no idea how I'm gonna handle all the cooking and cleaning while you're gone."

The thought of not having to cook for the whole family for the next few days filled Jill with comfort. She'd have some work around her mom's house, but at least there'd be no cooking,

She absolutely hated cooking.

"Just follow the things I wrote on the note," Jill said as she exited the car and shut the door.

She was greeted by the orange sky and the chattering of the birds.

"I'll try. But if you come home to a mess inside the kitchen, don't say I didn't warn you."

Jill tuned out halfway through that sentence, when she glanced at the old house in front of her.

The house where she grew up.

The house wasn't lavishly big, but it was two stories, and despite being decades older than Jill, it still looked well-maintained. Jill glanced up at the second-floor window, where her bedroom used to be, and then at the spacious green landscaping surrounding the house.

Memories suddenly flooded her. Her playing in her room with the toys, swinging on the swing behind the house, running in the woods nearby, playing fetch with Kenny, the family dog, etc.

Jill expected the memories to be accompanied by a sort of nostalgic emotion, but she didn't feel anything like that. Not yet, anyway. Maybe once she entered the house, she'd start to get overwhelmed by her childhood memories.

"Are you going to be okay with Cheryl over there?" Lee's voice shook her back to reality.

"Yeah. Yeah, why wouldn't I be?" Jill asked absent-mindedly as she diverted her attention back to the phone call.

She didn't want to enter the house when she was distracted. She would end the call with Lee first, and then give the house her full attention.

"You know, because of—" Lee started.

"Honey, I'm sorry, I need to go. I just arrived," Jill cut him off. "I'll call you and Charlie tonight, okay?"

"Sure thing. Good luck out there, honey," Lee responded.

"Thanks. Love you. Oh, and make sure Charlie tidies his room before dinner."

"Will do, boss," Lee sardonically said. "Love you, too. Talk to you later."

Jill put the phone in the pocket of her slacks and locked the car. She looked around the place. No houses anywhere in sight—just green prairies, bushes, and trees. The chances of someone stealing from her car in a place like this one were abysmal, but you never know.

It was almost night, and now that she thought about it, Jill wondered how her mom wasn't afraid to live here all by herself, with no one in sight—not even a neighbor to call an ambulance or the police for you in case you got in trouble. She trotted towards the house, briefly glancing at the red SUV parked on the lawn.

Must be the nurse, Jill thought to herself, wondering what the person would be like.

As Jill climbed the steps leading to the porch, she felt a sense of familiarity overwhelming her. It was a strange thing to feel like she was here just yesterday, even though years had passed.

She found herself staring at the ancient doorbell next to the door and knowing exactly how firmly to press it in order to make it ring. The house always had trouble with the doorbell, and if not pressed with enough intensity at the right spot, it wouldn't work. Jill remembered her mom constantly yapping to Dad about having to change the doorbell and him promising to do so as soon as he found the time—and then never actually end up doing it.

Jill raised a hand and rang the doorbell. A muffled buzz came from inside of the house. She turned around and stared at the landscape from this point of view. Far across the road was a thicket of trees and bushes. Jill suddenly remembered playing hide and seek with Cheryl over there during summer. There used to be a little boy who joined them as well, but Jill had no recollection of where he came from or what his name was.

"Good afternoon," a voice boomed behind Jill, half-startling her out of her drowsy reminiscence.

She spun around and realized that a woman stood at the now open door. She was a little older than Jill, maybe in her early thirties. She had her hair tied into a bun, and suddenly Jill felt a little jealous over how well she managed to pull off such a simple hairstyle. Jill has always been self-conscious about tying her hair into buns and ponytails because she felt that she had a big forehead.

"Uh, hi. My name's—"

"Jill. I already know. I'm Violet. I've been hired to take care of your mother until you and your sister arrive," the caretaker opened the door wider and stepped aside, revealing the dim interior of the foyer.

Jill nodded and took a tentative step inside, suddenly feeling like she was a guest in her own home. That feeling dissipated as soon as Violet closed the door, and Jill found herself surrounded by the familiar walls of her old home. The outside noises of the animal life instantly disappeared, along with the sunlight that veered inside, leaving only the meager foyer light for visibility.

As she glanced up at the ceiling light, Jill felt a foreboding sense that she couldn't exactly pinpoint. Living in the brightly lit three-bedroom apartment with Lee and Charlie back in Portland, she forgot how depressing the pendant lights in her mom's home were.

To make matters worse, the entire house utilized the same kind of lights. They were bright enough to illuminate the house, but too dim to help with anything like reading as soon as night fell. For the first two years of school, Jill constantly complained about her eyes hurting whenever she needed to do her homework at night.

Well, then finish your homework before nightfall, her mom would always chide her.

Luckily, Jill's dad stepped in and bought her a bright desk lamp that not only illuminated her homework area brightly, but even blinded Jill if she stared directly at the lamp.

"The attorney is not here yet?" Jill asked.

She was about to take off her coat, but she suddenly realized how cold the house was—almost as cold as it was outside. Or maybe it was her own imagination, carried by the memories that accompanied her.

"The attorney said he would be here around 4 pm, but he must have run into some unexpected trouble," Violet shrugged.

"Guess I'll call him later. How's Annette doing?"

"Your mother is in a... less than envious condition," Violet hesitantly said. "Do you want to see her?"

That's exactly what Jill dreaded. From the moment when she got the call from the hospital and throughout the entire week, she couldn't help but imagine what kind of condition she would find her mother in.

"Sure," she simply said, as convincingly as she could.

Violet nodded and started up the stairs leading up to the second floor. Her footsteps were muffled by the old, musty carpeting on the stairs, which made the house seem all the more silent. It was strange to have it so quiet. Growing up, Jill got accustomed to the cacophony of voices permeating the house constantly.

Cheryl playfully screaming, the parents calling to their daughters by shouting, since the house was so big, loud sounds coming from either the kitchen or the garage, etc. To hear it this deafeningly silent was almost unnatural.

Jill followed Violet up the stairs, making sure not to stamp her feet too loudly to avoid disturbing the eerie silence.

"So you've been taking care of my mother ever since the accident?" Jill asked.

"Yes. I've stayed here all day through the week, but now that you're here, I'll be coming once a day to make sure everything is okay. I'm surprised you haven't arrived earlier, to be honest. Usually, when this sort of thing happens, children fly out to see their loved ones within a day."

Jill sensed a hint of animosity in Violet's timbre, but chose to say nothing. The caretaker didn't know anything about Jill's relationship with her mother. She could have just stayed home with her family while Cheryl took care of everything. For a moment, she wondered why she even came here. She concluded that her soft side and faint feeling of love for her mom got the better of her.

Also, Cheryl wouldn't be able to handle everything on her own.

"Is there anything I need to know when taking care of my mother?" Jill asked, ignoring Violet's previous statement.

"I've written everything down, so we'll run through it once your sister arrives. She *is* coming, correct?"

"I think so. I haven't actually spoken to her, but the attorney said that she said she'd be here."

"Hm," Violet chuffed, and this time, Jill heard judgment in her tone.

They reached the top of the stairs and walked past Cheryl's and Jill's old rooms on the right side. Violet stopped in front of the last door on the left side and turned to face Jill.

"I have to warn you that this may not be a pleasant sight," the nurse said solicitously.

"I'll be okay," Jill briskly nodded.

Violet turned around, grabbed the knob, twisted it, and pushed the door open.

Chapter 2

Cheryl fished out her phone and glanced at the clock. It was ten minutes past six. The blaring classical music that played from the car's speakers was jackhammering into her head.

"Dude, can you put on something *normal*?" she remarked stoically.

Tom looked at her from the driver's seat briefly with a frown.

"This is normal. You need to learn to respect *quality*, Cheryl," he sarcastically said.

Cheryl rolled her eyes and leaned forward. She pressed the button to change the radio stations. Rihanna started singing *Umbrella*, while Cheryl raised her hands and began dancing in her seat to the tune.

"Hey! Do not touch the radio, Cheryl!" Tom snapped, as he returned the station to the classical music.

Cheryl stopped dancing and glanced in Tom's direction. He was furious. He had these moments lately where he would get irritated really quickly with Cheryl. At the start of the relationship, it was playful and friendly between them, and she found it cute. Now, whenever it happened, it immediately killed her mood.

"What's your problem, Tom?" she asked, feeling irked at his raised tone.

"My problem is that you asked me to give you a lift to your mom's place, and the entire time, from the moment the ride started, you've been dictating shit!"

"I haven't been dictating anything," Cheryl disagreed.

"Yes, you have. Can we go earlier? Can we stop at this station so I can pee? Can you hurry up? You're driving too carefully. If you don't like my terms, Cheryl, then you can just drive your own car to see your mom."

That came as a gut punch to Cheryl. Had Tom been annoyed with her this entire time and just refused to say anything?

"Well, excuse me for having a small bladder. If I knew that you couldn't stand me so much, I would have found someone else to give me a ride," she retorted, a little more docilely.

She hoped that Tom would refute her statement about him not standing her. He didn't.

Tom sighed and went silent. He pressed the button to turn the radio off, leaving only the sound of the car's roaring engine. With the absence of music, the tension in the air was almost palpable. Cheryl cast a furtive glance at him in time to see him run a hand through his thick hair.

"Seriously, Tom. What's going on with you lately? I feel like you're holding a grudge against me for everything I do."

Tom stared at the desolate road ahead.

"This isn't going to work," he said soft-spokenly, still staring out the front of the car.

Cheryl felt dread building up inside her. A cold shiver enveloped her as she focused her gaze on Tom undividedly.

"I've been thinking about things lately," Tom continued.

He suddenly looked uncomfortable, his face pensive, as if he contemplated how to form a sentence without hurting Cheryl.

"What things?" Cheryl asked confusedly.

"About... about us, Cheryl."

That final word sent another punch to Cheryl's gut. Her mind couldn't comprehend what Tom was saying. And yet, she knew exactly what he was saying, she just refused to acknowledge it.

"What are you saying?" she asked, with a quivering tone.

Tom scratched his cheek.

"I tried envisioning our future together. I really did. But I just... I'm sorry, Cheryl."

"Why are you sorry? I don't understand what you're trying to tell me, Tom," Cheryl was aware of the petulance in her near-the-edge crying tone, but she ignored it.

"I think we should go our own separate ways," Tom spat out in one quick breath.

Cheryl felt dizzy. Where the hell was this coming from? Tom was dumping her? No, that couldn't be happening. When they first met, she was the one who contemplated dumping him. And now, he was dumping her?

Cheryl cleared her throat, "I don't understand. Are... are you not happy with me anymore?"

Tom looked reluctant to say anything, but his silence was answer enough for Cheryl. And then, just like that, she felt anger boiling inside her.

"This is because of Paula, isn't it?" she asked furiously.

Tom's eyes momentarily widened, but he continued focusing on the road. His Adam's apple bobbed up and down. He was about to deny it, Cheryl was sure of it.

"I'm sorry, Cheryl," he finally said to Cheryl's surprise. "Paula and I... we have more things in common."

This definitely couldn't possibly be happening. Her friend Paula? Tom's been cheating on Cheryl with *her*?! For a moment, Cheryl was dumbstruck. But then boiling anger took control of her.

"You cheated on me? With Paula?! Did you fucking sleep with her?"

She wasn't sure if she was ready to hear that answer.

"Cheryl, I—"

"Stop the car," Cheryl demanded.

"What?" Tom asked in confusion.

"I said, stop the fucking car!"

"Are you out of your mind? We're in the middle of nowhe—" before he could finish that sentence, Cheryl started pummeling him with closed fists.

18

She didn't get any good hits, but Tom became disoriented. He cursed and lost control of the steering wheel. Cheryl lolled to the side and then lurched forward before the car came to a complete halt on the side of the road.

Tom let the engine continue running, and before he could recover, Cheryl unbuckled her seatbelt, pushed the door open, and hopped outside, not bothering to close the door behind her. Tear-stricken, she broke into a stride towards the road that ended on the horizon. She heard the car's engine stopping its whirring.

"Cheryl, wait!" Tom called out from behind. "Just let me explain myself at least!"

"Explain what?!" Cheryl spread her arms and turned towards him, continuing her walk backward. "That you've been fucking Paula behind my back? The entire football team has had a go at her, you know!"

"Cheryl, you can't go on foot. You don't even know where we are."

"I'll be dead before I ride with you in the same car where you fucked that whore!" Cheryl shrieked.

"I didn't sleep with her in the car," Tom justified himself.

"Oh, that's a real fucking relief, Tom!"

"Come on, get back in the car, Cheryl."

"Fuck you!"

"Cheryl, get back in the car, or I'll be following you until you change your mind."

Tom's voice was atonal, but still somewhat threatening. Cheryl still had the surge of anger coursing through her. She bent down and picked up a small rock.

"Cheryl, don't!" Tom ducked, just as Cheryl hurled the rock at the car.

The rock landed on the hood with a metallic thud and fell to the side. Tom glanced at the hood and the small scratch that appeared on the surface of the vehicle. Now it was Tom's turn to get angry, and that anger was unmatched by the hostility he displayed back in the car.

19

"You crazy bitch! Fine! I hope you get eaten by a pack of coyotes!"

With that, he jumped back inside the car, started it and made a U-turn, driving off in a cloud of dust. Cheryl watched as Tom's car grew distant until it disappeared behind the rows of trees, along with the sound of his engine.

She was alone in the middle of nowhere.

Chapter 3

The first thing that Jill became aware of was the cacophony of intermittent mechanical beeping and the soft music that played in the room. Violet walked in first and pressed the button on top of the radio on the nightstand. The soft music stopped, leaving only the beeping. Jill followed closely behind.

She suddenly became aware that she was holding her breath. She didn't think that seeing her mother in whatever state she was in would impact her in any way. She was dead wrong. As she stepped inside the room and glanced at the bed, she felt as if she got hit by a ton of bricks.

Her mother lay on her back in bed, eyes closed, face pallid, her temple and eye bruised, her forearms scratched up. She had tubes coming out of her nose, and her fingertips had wires attached to a big machine next to her bed. The other hand was splayed over her chest. The machine had an EKG screen, and right now, it steadily beeped, the chart bouncing up every couple of seconds. Along with everything, there was a distinct redolence inside the room, which Jill likened to the smell of old people and medicine.

She suddenly felt sick. Until now, she had always laughed when someone said that sitting down would be a good idea before receiving bad news. Now as she stared at her mother's comatose body, she felt the strength in her legs waning, threatening to buckle under her.

"Are you feeling alright, Jill?" Violet must have noticed Jill's reaction.

Jill nodded fervently.

"Yeah. I'm fine. I just need to sit for a moment," she said in one quick breath as she slumped into one of the chairs in front of the bed.

"I understand that seeing a family member in this condition is not a pleasant sight. If you want, I can make you some hot chocolate or tea," Violet's voice was more of a whisper now, as if she didn't want to wake up Jill's mom from the coma.

"No, I'm fine, thank you," Jill politely refused.

She averted her gaze from her mother's still body towards Violet. She honestly wanted nothing more than to leave this room—no, this entire house—as soon as possible. She couldn't imagine that Cheryl would insist they take care of Mom themselves when she obviously needed professional medical care.

"So uh, what exactly do I need to do with her?" Jill cleared her throat.

"Right. There aren't many things that you'll need to worry about since I'll be doing most of them. But here are a couple of things to keep in mind."

Violet walked over to the old bedroom vanity and picked up a piece of paper from it. She turned towards Jill and sat on the chair beside her. She flipped the paper over so that Jill could see it, and pointed to the first item on the list.

Over the next ten or so minutes, she went through all the things that Jill needed to do to take care of her mother. There wasn't much to be done, especially since Violet would still be doing most of the work. All she needed to do was make sure that her mom's diaper didn't need to be changed, check the bed for wetting, re-adjust the catheter, if necessary, and talk to her from time to time.

Violet would be doing most of the legwork—feeding her, giving her baths twice a week, checking to make sure that the machine keeping Mom alive was working properly, moving her to prevent her muscles from atrophying and avoid bedsores, etc.

Once all the items on the list were explained, Violet put the paper in her lap and stared at Jill with the look of a discontented teacher.

"Did you get all that?" she asked sternly.

"Yes."

"Good. Then I'll show you how to set up the catheter and work with the machine. You know how to change diapers. You have a child, correct?"

"Uh, yeah," Jill was a bit taken aback by the question, but tried to hide her surprise.

Violet must have really done her homework on Jill—and probably Cheryl—while staying in the house this week. A thought suddenly occurred to her that she should make sure that nothing was stolen from the house. She hated to think that Violet would rob a comatose patient, but Jill had heard of those kinds of things—and worse—happening with RNs.

"Good. In that case, I'll let you have a moment alone with your mother," Violet patted Jill on the knee and stood up.

"Actually, Violet, I'm going to look around the house. If that's okay with you," Jill politely stated.

"Of course. It's your mother's house, after all. I don't know what you're planning to do, but if you intended on selling the house, now would be a good time to go rummaging through the things. This is a big house, and there are plenty of items that may have good value to them. I'll be down in the kitchen if you need me."

"Thank you," Jill smiled courteously.

Violet walked out of the room, leaving the steady beeping as the only remaining sound. Jill felt uncomfortable listening to the EKG machine, and she felt even more uncomfortable staring at her mother. She wondered for a moment if she should expect her to wake up, and if that happened, what she should do. The thought of her mother waking up while screaming and flailing filled Jill with an inexplicable fear.

She quickly followed Violet outside into the hallway and closed the door behind her, instantly muffling the beeping of the machine, much to her elation. She pulled the phone out of her pocket and started towards her old room. She looked through her notifications and realized that she had received no messages.

She'd been expecting a message or a missed call from Dennis Lazarev, the attorney she hired to help her and Cheryl get all the legal affairs in order. She still didn't know what Cheryl's intentions were, but she doubted that she'd want to stay here and take care of her comatose mother.

She had her life, after all. She was in college in California, and there's no way she'd be able to put all her plans on the back burner. Not that she would probably want to, either. Jill didn't see Cheryl as the kind of person to drop partying and hanging out with friends in order to do a full-time job as a home nurse for free. But who knows, maybe some things had changed since the last time she and Jill spoke.

Just as Jill was about to call the lawyer, she heard the doorbell ring.

Chapter 4

Cheryl checked her phone again. Still no reception. She tried making a phone call to her best friend Maddie since she had a car and would come pick her up without hesitation, but the call didn't go through. Even sending messages didn't seem to work out here.

Her only hope was to reach Medford and hitch a ride to Sams Valley where Mom's house was. Cheryl had some cash on her, but she wasn't sure if that would be enough to cover the costs of a cab or an Uber. When she still lived with her parents and Dad brought her and Jill to school, it took about fifteen minutes of driving, but then again, Dad always drove much faster than intended by traffic laws.

Whenever he finished the ride super fast, Cheryl would be exuberant, while Jill would continuously reprimand him for breaking the traffic laws and setting a bad example for Cheryl.

He would always shrug it off, turn to Cheryl and tell her, "Remember, sweetheart. Just because I'm driving like this doesn't mean you should. I'm only doing this because I'm in a hurry. And because I know where the cops are. But I'll teach you everything once you get a driver's license."

Cheryl would always laugh at that, while Jill would sulk from the front seat. Now, as an adult, Cheryl still enjoyed the fast rides, and she thought that she would love driving fast, too, but that wasn't the case. Although she had a driver's license, she wasn't confident enough to put the pedal to the metal.

She always imagined as a kid that she and Dad would go on fast driving road trips together once she became an adult, but unfortunately, Dad wasn't here anymore, so he couldn't teach her all the things he promised.

Cheryl suddenly felt sadness creeping up on her, but the anger from her conversation with Tom still seeped out of her like from a leaking pipe, and it in itself didn't allow the sadness to overwhelm her.

She still couldn't fucking believe it.

Tom cheating on her with Paula.

Cheryl and Paula were good friends, and even though Cheryl didn't exactly have respect for her due to her prurient way of living, she didn't openly judge her about it. All this time, Paula has been fucking Tom behind her back. Cheryl remembered just two nights ago sending screenshots of Tom's and Cheryl's conversations about what sexual things he would like to do to her once they met up. She thought she noticed a change in Paula's demeanor after sending her the screenshots.

The thought of her friend knowing about all of it—maybe even knowing that Tom intended on breaking up with her—and then sending her sexual messages made Cheryl feel sick.

She knew that Paula was a slut, and she knew that the odds of her stealing someone's boyfriend were not low. It had happened before with Abigail and her ex-boyfriend Roger, and then an entire drama broke out before Abigail and Paula stopped talking to each other.

Abigail kept warning Cheryl to keep tabs on Tom because it seemed like Paula took a liking to him some time ago. Cheryl dismissed that. She thought there was no way Paula would do something like that to her, especially since the whole Roger thing was a misunderstanding.

That's what Paula said, at least. That she was the victim in that situation. And Cheryl believed her.

God, I'm such an idiot, she chided herself.

She proceeded to calm herself down. Tom's and Paula's relationship would never work. Paula would end up cheating on him or dumping him as soon as she got bored of him. Happened to Roger, and countless other guys. She changed guys more often than she changed socks.

Tom would end up miserable. He might even crawl back to Cheryl and beg forgiveness—and Cheryl would deny it to him.

As for Paula; she would not have a bright future, Cheryl was sure of it. She'd end up fucking guys until she one day decided that it's time to settle down and then find the first guy willing to marry her—provided she didn't become a single mother before then, which was very likely, due to the fact that she already had one abortion.

Cheryl found some comfort in the thought of such karmic justice. It was enough to calm her down, at least a little bit.

She must have been walking for almost thirty minutes when she heard the whirring of an engine somewhere in the distance. At first, she couldn't tell where it was coming from, but when she turned around, she saw a truck in the distance, slowly approaching her.

No, not slowly. It just seemed that way because it was so far away. The roaring of the truck's engine increased in loudness, slowly, but steadily. Cheryl stopped on the side of the road, outstretched her arm, and stuck out her thumb.

Please, for the love of god, stop and give me a ride.

The truck showed no signs of slowing down, and it would soon drive past her. Just when she decided to lower her arm, she saw the truck coming to a sudden halt. Cheryl got overwhelmed with an intense relief, only just then becoming aware of the thirst and the aching in her feet.

The truck stopped right next to her with a screech, and the door on the passenger's side opened. Inside the truck sat a short, round man with a red cap that clearly hid the balding top of his head.

He ogled Cheryl in a way she didn't like and asked, "Well, what are you doing out here by yourself, girl?"

"It's a long story," she shook her head.

"Where you heading?" the driver asked.

"Sams Valley. But Medford is fine," she smiled.

27

"You're in luck, girl. I'm going through Medford, but you'll have to find your own way to Sams Valley. I would take you there, but my asshole boss keeps a close eye on my routes ever since a recent incident with some missing gas."

"I'm okay with that. Thank you so much," Cheryl said.

"Hop in!" the driver jutted his head to the side.

Cheryl climbed inside the truck and closed the door behind her.

"A little harder, girl, it's an old door," the driver said.

Cheryl opened the door and slammed it shut harder this time.

"Atta girl!" the driver said and stepped on the gas.

Cheryl suddenly felt like she may have made a grievous mistake entering a truck with a stranger in the middle of nowhere. What if he was a serial killer, or a rapist, or something like that?

For a moment, she contemplated if it would have been better for her to stay with Tom in the car and stoically endure the awkward silence until he dropped her off, or risk being dismembered by a serial killer trucker.

If I die like that, at least Tom will forever be haunted by his guilt, she thought to herself.

It became apparent soon that the trucker was a friendly and very talkative fellow. Cheryl still kept her guard up because she assumed that serial killers were exactly that type. Luckily, according to the driver, they were only around twenty minutes away from Medford.

During those twenty minutes, however, the driver talked Cheryl's ear off. He talked about his asshole boss and how he was a cheapskate, about his coworkers and the adventures they had as truckers (which Cheryl didn't find too exciting), about his wife, who he was scared of, and so on.

He never once stopped to ask Cheryl anything back, not even how she got into the predicament she was in, nor did he take the cue that she wasn't in the mood to listen to him talking. He just kept yapping on and on, never taking a break, not even to take a breath.

He must have been really lonely on his long trips, which made Cheryl feel sorry for him, but God Almighty, was she happy to see the sight of Medford after the agonizing twenty minutes of listening to him babble.

As she stared at the town passing by the window, she was overcome by a feeling of nostalgia. It'd been a while since she came back home to visit, and even when she did, she went through Medford in passing and didn't really pay attention to her surroundings.

She remembered spending her childhood in many of the places in Medford, up until she got bored of the small town and then later moved on to college. She saw the elementary school she attended, still vibrant with lively children skipping, chirping, exchanging remarks. Memories—both pleasant and unpleasant—of the days back when she went to school flooded her.

She saw the small dance studio where she went hip-hop dancing for a few years before discovering alcohol and parties. She wondered if Ms. Bennett still taught there. She saw the park where she had her first date and first kiss with a schoolmate named Brian. She also saw a lot of places closed down, but many more new places open—shops, restaurants, even monuments.

Everything in Medford stayed the same, and yet, there was an inexplicable change that Cheryl couldn't quite pinpoint. Maybe nothing had changed at all, and she was just seeing the town with a different pair of eyes now that she was an adult.

As Cheryl watched her hometown, ignoring the truck driver's incessant gawking, she found herself wondering where all her Medford friends and classmates were right now. She had some of them on Facebook, and a very small number of them stayed in the town.

She suddenly came to the conclusion that she would never return to live here again. Coming back to Medford felt like starting a new chapter in an already half-written book.

Being in Santa Barbara gave Cheryl a sense of importance and superiority. Part of her felt embarrassed to say where she was from when asked, because all the girls at college thought of other small-town girls as uneducated hillbillies. So instead, she always lied about being from Portland.

After Jill got married to Lee and moved to Portland, Cheryl visited her there a couple of times before their relationship grew cold. She didn't know Portland as much as she'd like to, so she always tried steering away from the details when asked, but she already devised a story about the part of the city she lived in, the schools she attended, and some favorite spots. People usually didn't go into the details when they tried getting to know her, but Maddie read her like an open book almost immediately.

"Girl, I know a lot of Portland people, and you aren't one of them," she had outright said in private to Cheryl the night they first met.

Cheryl panicked, but at the same time was impressed by Maddie's intuition. The two of them spontaneously became best friends not long after that.

"Alright, this is as far as I can take you, girl," the truck driver said as he pulled the truck to a stop in front of a convenience store.

"Thanks... sir," Cheryl said, suddenly aware that she didn't know the truck driver's name.

She wanted to pay the man, but she was already low on money and doubted she'd have too much left after she paid for a ride to Sams Valley. Despite feeling guilty, she thanked the man and opened the door.

"Don't worry about it, girl. My pleasure. I always say, if a woman commands something, we gotta do it without questioning. That especially goes if you have a wife, you know what I mean? I think husbands these days ain't afraid of their wives enough."

He chuckled at his own remark. Cheryl already stood outside the truck and held the door, ready to slam it shut, but wouldn't do it out of courtesy, since the man was still talking. She flashed him a fake grin and wished him a nice day. He waved goodbye and, as soon as she shut the door, was on his way.

Thank god, she mumbled to herself.

She was equally relieved to be rid of him and just as relieved that he hadn't turned out to be a serial killer. Cheryl took her phone out of her pocket, feeling the explosion of notifications that suddenly vibrated from it.

Ignoring all of them, she called an Uber.

▪▪▪

"Is this the house?" the young male driver pointed to the large, white house off the road to the right.

"That's the one. Thank you so much for taking me here on such short notice," Cheryl thanked the man from the back seat.

Finding an Uber was quick and easy enough, but more expensive than Cheryl expected. She rarely used Uber, and when she did, it was always with her friends, being taken short distances, and they split the costs. The thirty bucks she had to spit out for the ride came as an unpleasant surprise to her. She tipped him three extra dollars to avoid being one of those cheap customers and said goodbye to him before stepping out of the car.

She ignored the sudden squall of the cold wind that wafted into her face and focused on the ancient house. As she stared at the house, she thought she'd feel something— a sense of familiarity, maybe? But nothing like that came to her. Maybe it would occur only after she stepped inside.

She glanced at the two cars parked outside. She guessed that one of the cars belonged to Jill, but she couldn't for the life of her tell which one. For all she knew, one belonged to the lawyer and the other to the nurse.

No, the one on the right was probably Jill's. Cheryl didn't know squat about cars, but the one parked on the righthand side looked more spacious.

Family friendly, Cheryl thought to herself.

She couldn't help but wonder how Charlie was doing. She had last saw him when he was just two. He really took a liking to Cheryl back then, and Jill didn't seem too happy about it. She didn't say anything, of course, but Cheryl could see it on her face.

Charlie would be six now, if Cheryl's calculation wasn't off. Would he even remember her, and run to hug her, screaming *Aunt Cherry!* Like he used to? Or did Jill tell him all the stories about evil Aunt Cheryl, causing Charlie to hate his aunt?

Cheryl dismissed those thoughts. Jill and Charlie were no longer her problem, and Jill made that very clear.

Right now, Mom was the only person that mattered.

Cheryl walked up to the front door and rang the doorbell. She impatiently listened to the chirping of the birds, waiting for whomever to open the door for her.

Who would it be? Her sister? Or one of the hired people?

Her answer came moments later when the door swung open inward.

Chapter 5

Jill stared at her sister standing on the porch. She looked tired. No, not just tired. Jill knew that droopy look on Cheryl's face. Even though years had gone by with them not speaking to each other, Cheryl still hasn't changed. That resting bitch face could fool anybody else, but Jill saw right through it.

"Hey," Jill softly said.

"Hey," Cheryl said back with a vague smile.

There was a sudden moment of awkwardness. Jill felt like she should say something, but she didn't know what, and Cheryl's penetrating stare didn't make things easier on her. Luckily, it was Cheryl who took the initiative to break the ice.

"Mind if I come in?" she asked with a more genuine smile this time that lifted her cheek muscles, "I've had one hell of a ride here, and I sure could use a break."

There was sarcasm in her tone. Typical Cheryl, she hadn't changed one bit.

"Yeah. Sure," Jill said as she opened the door widely and stepped aside.

Cheryl retained the smile as she prudently walked inside. Jill expected her to just waltz in, kick her feet up on the couch, and demand dinner, but surprisingly, Cheryl was quieter than Jill remembered her.

Either she was tired and stressed over the situation with Mom, or she finally matured. Jill hoped for the latter.

"Cheryl, right?" Violet entered the foyer just in time to greet her.

"Hi. Uh, yeah?" Cheryl said with a perplexed stare.

"I'm Violet. I was assigned to take care of your mother until you and your sister decide what to do next."

Jill was glad that Violet arrived when she did. She had already started thinking of conversation starters to avoid the awkwardness between her and her sister. Luckily, she didn't have to do it now, because Violet had stepped in to save the situation.

"Well, then. I understand you had a long ride. Do you want to take a short break before I show you what you'll need to do to take care of your mother?" Violet asked.

"Actually, I'd like to see Mom now, if that's okay," Cheryl smiled.

"I'll go with you, too," Jill added.

She didn't want to, but somehow, she felt that Cheryl would attribute her lack of interest to a lack of emotions, and if that happened, she'd probably never let Jill live it down.

"In that case, Jill, why don't you show her to your mother's room? I'll be upstairs in a few minutes to teach you everything you need to know," Violet said.

Dammit.

Jill really didn't want to be alone with Cheryl, but she tried to think positively about it. Maybe now the two of them could try and reconnect.

"She's in her room," Jill said as she led the way upstairs.

As they neared their mom's room, Jill started feeling slightly uneasy once more. She braced herself for the medicinal and old people's smell as she opened the door and stepped inside. The machine still produced the steady beeping noise. Jill stepped aside and observed Cheryl's reaction.

Cheryl's eyes were slightly wider, her nostrils flared up, and her chest slowly heaved up and down. As she made her way forward and sat on the edge of the bed, she gently placed one hand on Mom's wrist.

▪▪
Her wrist felt cold to the touch, unnaturally so.

"Mom, it's me. It's your Cherry. I'm here now," Cheryl said, suppressing the tears that welled up in her eyes.

There was no response, of course. She thought back to the time when she last spoke to her. It was on the phone, just over a week ago. And when did she last see her? It must have been a few months ago. Mom didn't seem to be doing well then, but she hadn't said anything.

Of course she didn't. She was always so selfless, always doing everything she could to not be a burden to her daughters. That's why ending up in this state was the most ironic thing ever. The doctors Cheryl spoke to said that the chances of her waking up were not optimistic. They told Cheryl that the longer Mom stayed in a coma, the lower the chances were of her waking up. If only Cheryl had been here more often, or at least called more, then maybe this wouldn't have happened. That guilt burned within her like a hot flame.

Now, it was up to Cheryl and Jill to decide what they would do with her.

They had the option of taking care of her themselves— which would be pretty much impossible—or putting her in a nursing home. The problem with that was that it would cost an arm and leg. That's partially why Cheryl and Jill were here. They had to decide if they would sell the house and use the money to take care of Mom.

"It's so strange to see her this quiet, huh?" Jill spoke up.

Cheryl briefly looked at her and nodded.

"She always had something to say. Or a question to ask," Cheryl said.

"When she wasn't shouting," Jill jokingly retorted.

Both of them melancholically laughed at that.

Cheryl looked at Mom's other hand, the one that wasn't attached to the medical things. It was outstretched to the side towards the nightstand, with her palm facing upward. Cheryl pointed and said.

"Jill, do you mind putting her arm in a more comfortable position?"

Jill squinted, and then her eyes widened slightly in terror.

"What's wrong?" Cheryl asked.

Jill opened her mouth and gestured to the arm.

"She... she moved."

"What?" Cheryl sat ramrod straight.

A glimmer of hopefulness surged through her. Jill strode over to the door, opened the door, and shouted Violet's name in a tone that conveyed urgency. Within seconds, the nurse rushed upstairs, visibly winded.

"What's wrong?" she asked as she pushed her way inside the bedroom.

"Mom's arm moved," Jill frantically pointed.

"When?"

"I don't know, it was across her chest, and now it's... like this!" Jill looked like she was losing patience.

That was the sister that Cheryl remembered. If Violet didn't acknowledge her concerns soon, Jill was going to have an outburst and start shouting at the nurse. Violet, on the other hand, just stared at Mom's motionless body. She calmly walked over to her outstretched arm and placed it in a more comfortable position on the side of her body. Both sisters stared at the nurse expectantly, silently asking for an answer. Violet saw it, and with a forlorn grimace on her face, simply said, "Reflexes."

"Reflexes?" Cheryl asked.

Violet looked at her and nodded.

"Yes. Comatose patients usually display signs of activity, but unfortunately, those are only reflexes."

"That was no reflex. Did you see where her arm was?" Jill demanded.

"Yes," Violet calmly answered. "Sometimes, the reflexes tend to be strong. There are reported cases of patients even speaking for brief moments."

"Well, what if she woke up and then fell back into a coma?" Cheryl asked with concern.

Violet shook her head.

"We would have noticed a spike in the EKG machine's activity," she must have noticed the incredulous stares in the sisters' eyes, so she quickly added, "I'll keep a closer watch on her. I suggest you do the same. If you notice anything else suspicious like this, we'll call in a specialist. How does that sound?"

Both sisters nodded almost lethargically.

"Well, then. Let me show you what you need to do to take care of your mother," Violet smiled.

Still feeling somewhat unnerved, but deciding to dismiss Jill's alarm, Cheryl agreed.

■■■

Jill wasn't as good with nurse-related stuff as Cheryl. She was clumsy, while Cheryl managed to do everything calmly and with elegance. Eventually, Violet dedicated more attention to showing Cheryl all the ropes while Jill stood behind and watched, probably because the nurse noticed the disinterest in Jill's demeanor. Once everything was done, Violet smiled and said.

"Well, then. I'm done for the day. We did everything that needed to be done. I'll be here tomorrow around 5 pm to see if everything is going alright, and to feed her. If anything urgent happens, feel free to call me. Oh, and one more thing," she pointed to the radio. "If you're too busy to talk to your mother, I suggest leaving the radio on for a little bit every day. Some patients have been known to react to their favorite songs."

She approached the radio and pressed a button on it. A slow song began playing in the distorted way customary for old radios.

"Thank you for all your help," Cheryl said, and went to see her out.

Left alone in the hallway on the second floor, Jill whipped out her phone to see if the lawyer had sent her any messages or tried calling, yet. It was almost seven-thirty, and Jill really didn't want to be here any longer than necessary. She heard the front door shutting and went downstairs to meet Cheryl.

"Hey, did you get a call from the lawyer yet?" Jill asked.

Cheryl shook her head.

"It's just that he was already supposed to be here, and—" before Jill could finish that sentence, the phone started ringing in her hand.

She looked at the screen and saw the name Dennis Lazarev, Lawyer.

"Speak of the devil," she said and swiped the screen to accept the call. "Hello?"

A stern, male voice came through as a shout.

"Hi, Jill?"

"Yes, it's me. Mr. Lazarev?"

"Yeah. Listen, I'm really sorry, but I ran into some trouble on the way," Jill heard a car driving by in the background, deafeningly loudly for a second before fading in the distance. "I ran into some trouble, and I won't be able to make it today. In fact, I won't be able to make it until Monday."

"Oh," Jill muttered.

She felt immense disappointment overwhelming her. Monday? She was hoping to be out of here by Sunday. Maybe even tomorrow. She looked over in Cheryl's direction and realized that her sister was staring at her with rapt focus.

The lawyer continued speaking.

"Yeah, I'm really sorry about that. Listen, we can take care of all the legal issues on Monday, but until then, what I need you to do is split all the personal property with your sister. She's already there, right?"

"Yeah, Cheryl's already here," Jill said.

"Good. What I need you to do is go through all the items in the house and make a list, and then we'll take care of all the other legal issues on Monday, depending on what you decide to do with the house. Okay?"

"That's fine but, um... can't you arrive earlier than Monday? I mean, I have a family in Portland and work on

Monday, so I can't just cancel my entire life because of this," she chuckled sardonically to mask her annoyance.

She felt Cheryl's judgmental glare on her, but ignored it. Right now, she was too pissed off to care. The lawyer probably ran into a problem, yes, but Jill doubted that the problem would last all the way until Monday. Most likely, he just didn't want to work on the weekend, the son of a bitch.

"I'm really sorry, but there's no way I'll make it before Monday. Listen, I'll be there as early as I can, morning most likely. In the meantime, you and your sister work on splitting all the movable property between each other, alright?"

"Okay, but—"

"Jill, I'm really sorry, I have to run, okay? I'll see you Monday, bye."

Before Jill could say anything else, he hung up. What a son of a bitch. She wanted to hurl her phone across the room, but she controlled her anger as she looked at Cheryl.

"Okay, so um... he said that we should—"

"I heard it all," Cheryl interrupted. "Listen, if you need to go back to your family, I don't mind. I'll take care of Mom, and you can just come back on Monday."

There was a hint of passive-aggressive animosity in her timbre. Or maybe it was Jill's imagination. Still, Cheryl's suggestion sounded heavenly, but she knew that it was a trap.

No problem, you go home and enjoy your time with your family while I do all the legwork around our comatose mother and the house. I'll do it all alone, no problem. I'll always hold it against you, sure. But it's your choice, no pressure.

"Are you crazy? I'm not letting you do all this yourself," Jill forced out on a peal of laughter.

"I mean, it's not that much work, anyway," Cheryl shrugged.

A loud, startling buzz filled the room. It took Jill a moment to realize that someone was ringing the doorbell.

"No, it's fine. We're doing this together," Jill insisted, now on the brink of losing her patience, as she strode towards the entrance.

She wondered what Violet forgot as she opened the door. To her surprise, instead of Violet stood a short, elderly woman at the door, grinning from ear to ear.

Chapter 6

"Oh, hello, sweetie," the old lady chirped in a jovial voice. "My, my, you have grown so much, Jill!"

"Uh, hi," Jill smiled back, trying not to give away that she had no idea who the woman was.

"You don't remember me, do you?" the woman outright asked, the smile still plastered to her face.

"Erika!" Cheryl shouted over Jill's shoulder and skipped to the door.

The old woman made an 'o' shape with her mouth and put her hands together in what looked like a pleasant surprise to her.

"Oh, Cherry, dear Cherry! Come here, let me take a good look at you!"

Jill stepped aside and allowed Cheryl to approach. Erika put her stubby fingers on Cheryl's face and pinched her cheeks.

"Look at you, all grown up. The last time I saw you, you were this small," she motioned below her waist with her palm. "And now you're all grown up. Both of you. Oh, I haven't seen you since you moved in with your Dad, Jill."

She looked at Jill, as if she just remembered that the older sister was there.

Jill gave her a PR grin and crossed her arms. This was pretty much a normal thing. Cheryl would get most of the attention from relatives, friends, neighbors, etc., while Jill would simply get acknowledged briefly out of courtesy.

Jill remembered Erika. She lived nearby, and she used to bring all sorts of homemade cookies to the girls. Even back then, Jill was more of a recluse than Cheryl, so naturally, Erika took a liking more towards the younger sister. Erika did often try to call Jill over and strike up conversations with her—it's just that Jill was scared of adults. Whenever someone came for a visit, she'd go into her room or to the backyard.

Erika lived ten minutes down the street, but she used to visit Annette all the time, almost daily. Those visits dwindled as time passed and Annette's mental health started to deteriorate.

"And you look like you're aging backward, Erika," Cheryl flattered her.

Erika dismissively waved that away from the wrist and then patted Cheryl's hand.

"You haven't changed one bit, Cherry. I bet all the boys at college are just tripping over each other to get in line to ask you out."

Yeah, well. I have a really good job and a family, but whatever, Jill wanted to say, but that would, of course, just confirm her jealousy.

She didn't really want to compete for attention around Cheryl anymore—especially since she knew that she could never win—but it would be nice to get acknowledged sometimes as a successful person.

Erika's smile dropped, and her face suddenly turned grievous.

"I am really sorry about what happened to your mom; I really am," she said.

"Thank you," Cheryl nodded.

"She and I had tea almost every week, you know? But then that blasted dementia started getting to her. It was harder and harder to have conversations with her."

"Oh?" Cheryl raised an eyebrow.

"Yes, it really was. We would talk about something, and she would just space out and forget what we were talking about. Or she'd ask me the same questions multiple times. And sometimes, what she said didn't make any sense at all."

"But I saw her just a few months ago," Cheryl said. "She was fine. I mean, she did have some moments, but she was fine for the most part."

"Yes. Yes, she was," Erika nodded fervently. "And then her mental state began to worsen in just the last few months drastically. It was so sad to see her like that."

Cheryl pursed her lips. She didn't like the sound of that. If Mom ever woke up from a coma, would she even be the same person? Would the coma cause her mental state to worsen even more?

"Well, I won't be bothering you any longer, sweeties," Erika said, and the genuine smile stretched across her face once more.

"You're no bother at all, Erika," Cheryl shook her head. "Do you wanna come in for some tea? I mean, if Mom has tea, that is…"

Erika guffawed and patted Cheryl's hand once more.

"Thank you, dear, but I really should get back home. It's almost dark, and I don't want to be out on the road too late." She briefly looked at Jill and winked connivingly. "But I will be sure to stop by tomorrow and bring you some of my cookies. You remember the chocolate nut cookies I used to bake for you, don't you Cherry?"

"Of course I do," Cheryl's mouth contorted into a grin.

Erika used to bring all sorts of cookies, but the chocolate nut cookies were her favorite. And once she expressed how tasty they were, Erika made sure to bake those primarily. Jill never liked them, and she would only take and eat one, out of courtesy towards Erika.

"Well, then I'll make sure to bring you some tomorrow as soon as I bake them," Erika said complacently.

"No, you really shouldn't bother yourse—"

"Oh, don't worry about it, Cherry, sweetie. It's no bother at all," she looked at Jill. "What about you, Jill? Would you like me to bake you anything? It was always hard to tell what you liked when you were little."

43

"I'm good, but thank you, Erika. Gotta watch my weight, you know?" Jill shrugged.

"I see a lot of young people these days starving themselves to look good. It's not healthy. Not healthy at all, sweetie. You should really put on some weight, you look like skin and bone."

Cheryl suppressed her laughter. When she looked at Jill, she realized that she was staring at Erika with a reticent—and perhaps annoyed—stare.

"I'll keep it in mind, thank you," Jill stated, patronizingly.

Luckily, Erika didn't hear the enmity in Jill's voice.

"Well, I'll be on my way, then," the old lady said. "It was so good to see you both. Please take good care of your mother."

She directed that last sentence at Cheryl with utter seriousness.

"I will. I promise," Cheryl gave her a reassuring smile.

The air felt heavily silent as soon as Cheryl closed the door. But then suddenly, she felt good. She was glad that she got to see Erika, and that she was doing well.

"She was always so kind, huh?" Cheryl asked.

"I guess," Jill shrugged. "We should probably start sorting through things if we wanna get this done in time."

That's Jill. Always focused on the task, never procrastinating or leaving things for later.

"Sure," Cheryl said, as she made her way toward the living room. "How about we order some takeaway first? I'm starving."

Chapter 7

The food arrived faster than Cheryl expected it would. She ordered some chicken wings, while Jill had a salad.

"Are you on a diet?" Cheryl asked with her mouth full of greasy, spicy wings.

"Not really. Just trying not to exceed my caloric intake," Jill shrugged.

"Oh, screw that. Look at your figure. I'm sure you can allow yourself something more sinful than a salad.

Jill had an amazing figure. Her stomach was flat, even when she sat. Even while she was pregnant, Jill seemed to retain her slim structure, despite the incongruity of her bulging stomach. Cheryl was slim, too. But she wasn't as fit as Jill. Jill tried being careful about what she ate, and she did yoga, but Cheryl got lucky with her mom's genetics. She could eat as much as she wanted to without gaining weight. Her stomach was flabbier than Jill's, though, but she didn't care enough about it to start working out or going on a diet.

"So, which room do you wanna start with?" Cheryl asked.

"I was thinking we split the work," Jill said. "How about we start with our old rooms?"

"Works for me."

They continued eating in silence for a while. It felt strange for just the two of them to eat at the kitchen table. It was family tradition to have the entire family eating together. But then Mom and Dad got divorced, and Jill moved in with Dad. That's when Cheryl's and Jill's relationship started growing cold.

"How's college?" Jill broke the silence.

Cheryl tilted her head slightly.

"It's alright. Freshman year was exciting. Now it's all just monotonous."

"You gotta study a lot?"

"Not really. It's a joke, to be honest. The professors don't really care that much."

"Lucky. Back when I was in college, the professors were sadistic. Made us study for hours every day just to pass the exam. Especially the computer science professor. Computer science wasn't even a mandatory term, and he still made us walk through muck."

Cheryl meagerly laughed at that.

"But at least it all worked out well. You got a good job now and a nice family."

Jill continued staring at her salad as she nodded.

"How's Charlie, by the way?" Cheryl asked.

"Good! He's smart. A little too smart for his own good, if you ask me. Just recently, he lost his third tooth, and he devised an experiment to prove if the Tooth Fairy actually exists."

"Oh, yeah?"

"Yeah. He didn't tell us when he lost his tooth and sneakily put it under his pillow. When the Tooth Fairy didn't show up, he realized that we lied to him."

Cheryl guffawed.

"Wow. That is unbelievable."

"Yeah. I dread to think what he'll do when he reaches puberty."

They both laughed at that.

"And what about Lee?" Cheryl asked.

"He's good. Just got promoted recently, so that really helped us financially."

"Did he manage to resolve that elbow problem he had?"

"Yeah. He underwent three surgeries, but now he can finally do things without any pain."

"I guess he learned his lesson not to lift heavy things."

Jill nodded. More time went by in silence before Jill spoke up again.

"So, I thought your boyfriend was going to drive you here? That's what the lawyer said, anyway."

"Uh, yeah," remembering Tom suddenly caused Cheryl's anger to reemerge.

She had gone hours without thinking about him, so she didn't really appreciate Jill reminding her. Then again, she couldn't have known.

"What was his name again? Tom? I saw a picture on Facebook. You two look good together as a couple," Jill continued, further exacerbating the situation.

"We actually broke up," Cheryl blurted out, taking a big bite out of the wings to give herself some time chewing instead of talking.

"Oh, no. I'm so sorry, Cheryl. I didn't mean to poke..."

Cheryl swallowed.

"No, it's fine. He cheated on me with my friend, so..." her voice started cracking towards the end.

She stared at her half-eaten chicken wings, her vision getting blurry from the tears that welled up in her eyes. She blinked them away. She couldn't show her weak side.

Not in front of Jill.

"I'm really sorry, Cheryl," Jill said, almost coldly.

She didn't add anything else. Perhaps she didn't know what to say.

"He actually broke up with me on the way here," Cheryl added, unable to contain the emotions that swirled inside her and inflated to the size of a balloon.

"He broke up with you on your way to visit your sick mother? What a terrible human being!"

Cheryl chuckled.

"I was so upset that I got out of his car and chased him away. And then I hitchhiked to Medford. I guess I should have seen it coming," she said, a little more composed now that the emotions that had threatened to seep through the cracks were held at bay.

47

Jill leaned back and spoke after a moment of silence, "I guess there's some kind of curse on our entire family's generation of girls, huh? Mom's fiancé cheated on her two days before they got married, my boyfriend of three years cheated on me, and now you. I guess you're now officially a member of the club."

Cheryl chuckled at that. It was a stupid joke, but she couldn't help but laugh at it. That laughter almost turned into sobbing, but Cheryl gritted her teeth and pushed the breakdown deeper inside.

■■

Jill suddenly saw herself in Cheryl. She didn't see it until now, but when she stared at her, all sad, pretending to be strong, she remembered the night she caught Rob in bed with a girl she didn't know.

She was twenty back then, and she and Rob had been dating for three years. Rob lived in a one-bedroom apartment, and the entrance of the building was unlocked. She knocked on the door (since the doorbell didn't work), but no one answered. She tried the door, and it was unlocked. She called out to Rob, but there was no response.

She had, however, heard something coming from the bedroom. Giggling. Although she knew already what it was from the knot that formed in the pit of her stomach, Jill proceeded forward, rationalizing the entire time that she wasn't hearing things right.

As she got closer to the door, she heard the bed's squeaking, and soft, effeminate moaning sounds. The door was slightly ajar, and Jill only needed to push it inward slightly to peer inside.

At first, they didn't even see her. The girl, a busty, curvy blonde sat on top of Rob and held her hands on his chest as she bounced up and down. Jill distinctly remembered the expression of ecstasy that Rob had on his face as the girl bounced on him, ground into him, and rammed him like there was no tomorrow—something he never had with Jill

48

Jill let out an uncontrollable gasp and put a hand over her mouth, and that's when they heard her. The girl stopped bouncing, instantly silencing all sounds. Both she and Rob turned their heads towards Jill. The expression of ecstasy that Rob previously had on his face drooped, as if someone had just swiped it off in one steady motion, and was instead replaced with something akin to terror.

He pushed the girl off him and jumped on his feet, covering his private parts with his blanket, but Jill didn't wait around. She was already out of there, crying uncontrollably, ignoring Rob's desperate calling. He didn't follow her, luckily, because it was freezing outside and he wasn't adequately dressed.

When she returned home, Dad noticed the zombified look on her face, so he asked her what was wrong. She told him about it with a straight face. Later she told Mom over the phone, too. Mom was less supportive than Dad. The first thing she said was, 'I told you this relationship was doomed from the start'. Dad, however, sat at the kitchen table with Jill, and only then did she break down in front of him and go into all of the nasty details while he comforted her.

For the next twenty-four hours, Jill's phone buzzed and vibrated with Rob's incessant calls and messages. She never returned any of his calls. She lived in Medford with her dad back then and studied in Portland. Rob lived in Portland, and before the cheating, he and Jill had planned on moving in together, but Rob had seemed reluctant to do so whenever Jill had brought up the topic. Eventually, the long-distance relationship must have made him tired, and he decided to look for comfort elsewhere.

That was all Jill needed to finally move out of Medford. She had only three years left until she finished college, but she already planned what she would do after. Even when she returned to college, Rob kept calling her incessantly. She didn't want to block his number on purpose because it fed her ego to have him run after her.

Eventually, after a couple more unsuccessful relationships, she met Lee, and soon after, they got married. Rob was only a distant memory by then. Jill once looked him up on Facebook and saw that he had a kid now. She had no idea who the mother was.

"I know this seems tragic right now. But in a few years, you'll be laughing at this," Jill said as she looked at her little sister who was silently trying to hide her tears.

Cheryl shook her head incredulously.

"I just hope Tom and Paula end up together and miserable with each other for the rest of their lives."

Jill laughed.

"You know, that's exactly what I hoped would happen to Rob. I used to stalk him online for months after he cheated on me, and I hoped that he'd end up miserable in life and realize what he lost. But you know, once you find your own happiness, you tend to forget about your exes. And I think that's the best form of punishment you can serve them."

Cheryl smiled at that, albeit vaguely.

"I hope you're right."

Jill looked out the window, towards the blackness of the night. Charlie would be going to bed soon. Jill should give him and Lee a call.

"I guess it's pretty late. We should probably start sorting things tomorrow instead," Jill added.

"I don't think I'll be able to sleep, anyway. I'll start tonight."

Jill nodded.

"Alright, then I'll join you."

Cheryl looked up from her half-finished meal.

"You don't need to feel obliged to stay up because of me," she added solicitously.

"I don't. I'm just really interested in the treasure trove we'll find digging through our old things," Jill grinned.

Cheryl nodded.

"Alright, if you say so."

Jill nodded back, complacent that Cheryl believed her lie.

Chapter 8

"Anyway, I'm doing well in college," Cheryl said.

She was sitting next to her mom in the moonlit bedroom, listening to the steady beeping of the EKG machine. She only partially saw her mom's face. In this state, she looked like she was peacefully sleeping. Except Mom never slept on her back. She always slept on her side, covered all the way up to her cheeks with the thick blankets.

"I got a lot of friends there, too," Cheryl continued. "But some of them aren't actually friends. I thought they were, but they aren't."

She shifted slightly in the uncomfortable wooden chair.

"Tom and I aren't together anymore. He cheated on me with Paula. Can you believe it? With Paula," she chuckled. "God, I'm such an idiot. I should have seen it coming a mile away. But it all makes sense now when I think about it. He always asked about her and eyed her up, but I was just too blind to see it."

She sighed deeply, suddenly feeling melancholic.

"I wish you were awake right now so you could give me some words of comfort, Mom. I feel like..." her voice trailed off, cracking a bit in the process, as newfound tears welled up in her eyes. "I feel like Jill and I are strangers. I can't really talk to her about this."

She sniffled. The tears streaked her cheeks, and she wiped them away. The floodgates were cracking, and Cheryl finally gave in to the sadness. She didn't even realize the weight she had on her shoulders until she started crying.

She cried for her mother, she cried for the stranger-like relationship she had with her older sister, she cried for allowing herself to trust and love someone who wasn't worth it—

A sound snapped Cheryl out of her self-pity.

She raised her head, sniffled, wiped the tears from her eyes, and looked at her mom's face. What was that just now? It sounded like a raspy groan, but it was so soft, so quiet, that she barely even registered it.

Cheryl opened her mouth. She tried calling out to her mom, but no sound came out. Instead, she continued staring at her mom, patiently waiting for the sound to come again.

And it did.

But it didn't come from her mom. It came from the corner of the room. Long, raspy, stretched-out groaning, more akin to wheezing. Cheryl pivoted her head, ever so slowly, and focused her gaze on the darkness of the corner.

There was a shape there. A humanoid shape that she couldn't quite discern. Cheryl thought she saw its part of body—shoulders maybe?—heaving up and down with extremely slow motions. It was in fact so slow, that Cheryl refused to blink, just to see if she saw it right.

She did, she was sure of it. Her eyes burned from being held open so widely and without blinking as she watched the figure in the corner and listened to its soft, intermittent raspy breathing. Even sitting next to the obnoxious beeping machine, she could hear the breathing of the figure. And then it produced a clicking sound.

The door opened slightly, letting in a sliver of light, and a bony hand poked through the crack. Cheryl quietly jerked in her seat, unable to produce as much as a gasp. The hand fumbled for the switch, and the room was bathed in a meager orange light.

"Oh, there you are," Jill said, opening the door wider.

Cheryl jerked her head back towards the corner of the room where the rasping figure was just a moment ago.

There was no one there.

Just an old flower table with an empty vase sitting on top of it.

"Cheryl? Is something wrong?" Jill asked.

Cheryl looked at her and noticed the concerned look on her face. She just then became aware of how out of breath she was, but she swallowed and tried to hide it with a fake nod.

"Yeah, I'm fine. You just startled me is all."

"Sorry. I didn't mean to do that."

"It's fine."

"I guess we're both a little jumpy, huh? I don't think we're used to the house being this quiet."

"I guess not."

Cheryl's heart was still drumming in her chest from the imaginary figure in the corner of the room, so she didn't fully focus on Jill. Jill must have noticed this, so she smiled and said, "Well, it's getting kinda late. Do you wanna start going through our things, or...?"

Cheryl looked at Mom, and then back at Jill with a frown.

"You know what, maybe you're right. We should just do this tomorrow morning. It's not like we need to rush anywhere, right?"

"Yeah. Guess not," Jill gave her a reassuring smile. "You gonna go to bed soon? I took a peek inside your room, it's still as tidy as ever."

Cheryl sensed some passive aggression in Jill's timbre.

"Yeah. I'll do it right away," she nodded.

She wanted to be with Mom a little longer, but she suddenly felt uneasy staying in the room. As she stood up and approached the door, she glanced at the corner towards the flower table one more time. She then flipped the switch to kill the light and gently closed the door behind her.

Chapter 9

Jill slept on the living room couch. She wanted to sleep in her old room, the one next to Cheryl's, but she found the room to be too cluttered and too cold. Only one peek inside was enough to tell her that sleeping in there would not be possible.

There were old boxes and toys from Jill's childhood scattered around the room. The bed was stripped of the bedding and covers, so only a musty mattress remained. Books layered with patinas of dust covered the shelves. Essentially, the room looked like an attic storage rather than a room a child used.

Cheryl's room, on the other hand, was as clean and flawless as ever. The walls looked like they had been painted with the fresh pink paint just recently, the bed was neatly made, and all of Cheryl's things seemed untouched—exactly how Jill imagined that Cheryl left her room when she moved out.

Seeing the incongruity in which her mom maintained the two rooms hurt Jill a little bit. At the same time, she wasn't really surprised. Mom always favored Cheryl, and she never failed to show it—whether by announcing it publicly to all the relatives by bragging about the beautiful, smart daughter she had, or with all the attention she constantly gave her.

When Jill saw her room in such a mess, she wanted to just pick up her things and leave. *Screw you, Annette, you have your favorite daughter, let her take care of you, I have my own life.* But something wasn't letting Jill leave. Some pathetic form of compassion she felt for her mom?

All these years living her own life with her husband and son, she thought she was over her mom and no longer cared about her as a human being. But deep down, she still longed for her attention; the attention that only Cheryl received.

And it terrified her.

She reminded herself once again that she had her own life. She had a great husband, and a beautiful son, and she would never treat him the way Annette treated her.

Jill had a short video call with Lee and Charlie after dinner with Cheryl. They were doing okay, even though Charlie spilled the beans about Lee burning the pizza and causing the smoke detector to go off. He retold that story while laughing, and rather than scolding her husband, Jill laughed it off along with them.

Lee wasn't happy about Jill not coming home until Monday, and offered to come there over the weekend. Jill was tempted. She already missed him and Charlie, but ended up saying no. They already had plans for Charlie during the weekend, and they couldn't just cancel all of them to wait at Jill's old home.

With a heavy heart, but feeling immensely regenerated from the short talk with her family, Jill said goodbye and soon fell asleep on the couch.

She had a weird nightmare. In it, she saw herself sleeping on the couch and a figure watching her from the doorway. She couldn't discern any details on the figure since it was dark, but Jill remembered feeling immense dread building up inside her, even though she knew it was a dream. She tried shouting at herself to wake up, but the more she did it, the deeper she seemed to fall into sleep.

And then, the figure looked at her. Not at Jill sleeping on the bed, but at the astrally projected Jill who kept trying to wake herself up.

She suddenly jerked awake on the couch. The first thing she noticed was that it was still dark. Jill looked around the room, even though she knew there would be no dark figures watching her. Eventually, her heart rate slowed down, but she was too awake to go back to sleep. After some tossing and turning, she decided to take a walk around the house, and maybe find something to snack on.

The house seemed even more void of life during the night. The rooms somehow contracted, seeming even more cluttered than they were during the daytime. She was suddenly overcome by a profound sense of sadness. Some of the objects reminded her of her childhood, and more specifically, of the time when Dad was still alive.

He'd have his spot on the sofa from which he'd watch TV, and no matter how enthralled he was with the game on the screen, if Jill ran up to him to tell him about something or ask him a question, he'd immediately give her his undivided attention.

"What's up, Marshmallow?" he'd ask, sometimes before she even opened her mouth.

She didn't remember why he started calling her like that, but it stuck around, even after she grew up.

Jill went into the kitchen and opened the fridge. There was old food in there, some of which had begun to turn moldy—cheese with black and white patches, yogurt with an expired date, a jar of pickles that looked ancient.

Jill found a jar of half-eaten Jif, but upon searching the kitchen cabinets, realized that there was no bread anywhere—at least not one that wasn't older than two days. It didn't matter, she'd just eat it with a spoon. She wasn't really hungry, but she had a strong hankering for peanut butter. She was glad Charlie wasn't here to see his mom being such a bad example.

She opened the kitchen drawer and retrieved a tablespoon. Just as she was about to open the Jif jar, she heard footsteps upstairs. Cheryl must have been awake, too. Jill hoped that it wasn't her kitchen rummaging that woke her up. She proceeded to open the jar and stick the spoon inside. She rarely ate peanut butter. They had a bunch of peanut butter in the apartment, and Charlie ate tons of it, so most of the jars were bought just for him.

More thudding footsteps came from upstairs, going from one end of the kitchen ceiling to the other. Jill had just finished licking clean the spoon, but decided that it wasn't enough, so she stuck it inside the jar for one more round. Just then, more footsteps came from upstairs in the opposite direction, hastier and more aggressive this time.

What was Cheryl doing up there?

Deciding to see if everything was okay, Jill put the lid on the jar, and placed the spoon on top of it before heading upstairs. The hallway was dark, and it took Jill's eyes a moment to readjust. Everything was still and the only sound present was the loud ticking of the wall clock. There was no sliver of light coming from under the bathroom door, so Cheryl must have returned to bed.

Now that Jill was up here, she realized that she needed to use the bathroom. She tip-toed down the hallway, and stopped halfway through. She heard the familiar beeping of the EKG machine in tandem with the clock, sometimes resounding at the same time, sometimes lagging behind. Glancing left, she saw the door to Annette's room slightly ajar. The crack was black, with no visibility into the room whatsoever. Jill approached the door and her hand hovered above the doorknob.

She was tempted to peek inside, to make sure everything was okay, but that permeating darkness didn't allow her to do so. She was afraid that she'd see her mother in a different position again. She looked back at Cheryl's room. The door was closed. Jill turned back to her mother's room. A part of her really, really wanted to peek inside.

Jill grabbed the doorknob and shut the door, before turning on her heel and going to the downstairs bathroom. She hurried back to the couch in the living room. Feeling a little uneasy all of a sudden. However, she fell asleep faster than she thought she would.

She was woken up by the pleasant smell of coffee permeating the air.

Jill opened her eyes and propped herself up on her elbow. She heard clattering and sizzling in the kitchen. The sound of sizzling was accompanied by a distinct and pleasant redolence of eggs and bacon. Jill wasn't hungry, but she could definitely go for some coffee.

She yanked the blanket off her and clambered to her feet. She shuffled her way to the kitchen, where the clattering was much louder, annoyingly so. Cheryl was at the stove, placing strips of bacon into the frying pan, allowing the bacon to cook in its own fat. When Jill walked inside, Cheryl looked at her and said.

"Good morning. Sleep well?"

"Not really. You?" Jill asked drowsily.

Cheryl shrugged.

"Breakfast?" she asked.

Jill looked at the table and saw two plates with scrambled eggs. There was also a mug of steaming coffee next to one of the plates. She suddenly got a warm feeling inside her from seeing her sister making breakfast for her. Despite not feeling hungry, Jill decided to eat out of courtesy to Cheryl, before moving on to the coffee.

"What, no pancakes?" Jill sardonically asked when Cheryl finally finished cooking and sat down to eat.

Cheryl looked at her incredulously for a moment, and Jill feared that her sister wouldn't get the sarcasm. Luckily, Cheryl chuckled a moment later and said, "Sorry. I make terrible pancakes. Not like Dad."

"Dad didn't always make great pancakes."

Cheryl stabbed a piece of the scrambled eggs with her fork and stared at the ceiling, contemplatively.

"Either his pancakes were really good, or they went in the trash. Remember?"

Jill laughed.

"He used to always brag about learning to make pancakes from Nan. He really gave his best whenever he tried making them, didn't he?"

"He did. And then Mom would flip out because he always made a mess in the kitchen. Remember when he stuck the pancake to the ceiling when he tried flipping it?"

Jill almost spat the eggs out of her mouth at that memory. She instinctively looked for the pancake mark up on the ceiling, but realized that it was too moldy and cracked to see it. Jill remembered that day clearly.

She was ten, and Cheryl was four. They were sitting in the kitchen, waiting for Dad to make them breakfast. Mom was out shopping, so it was his duty to feed the kids. He asked both of them what they'd like to eat, and they agreed on pancakes. Dad made the best pancakes in the world.

He had finished making four of them, and had the next one in the pan. At one point, he grabbed the pan and asked the girls if they wanted to see a cool trick. Naturally, they said yes. Then Dad figured that maybe it wasn't such a good idea, but it was too late. The girls were too excited and he had to go through with the trick.

Dad shrugged with an 'oh, what the hell' and flipped the pancake. Except the flip was actually a soar towards the ceiling and before they knew it, the pancake never came back down. Cheryl and Jill laughed hysterically while Dad panicked, muttering 'your mom is gonna kill me' and frantically dragging a chair to get the pancake off.

He was far too late, because Mom walked in the next moment, and when she saw him reaching for the pancake on the ceiling, she dropped her grocery bags and grabbed her head.

The next thirty minutes were filled with all sorts of colorful swear words coming from Mom, while Dad repeatedly apologized. Eventually, he had to get a spatula to get the stuck pieces of the pancake off. That part of the ceiling forever had an oil stain until he and Jill moved out.

It became a part of their lives so much that the family hardly even looked at it. Except for Mom. She glanced up at it pretty often and complained about the ruined ceiling—

mostly in Dad's presence. He would hang his head down, but when she wasn't looking, he would wink at Jill and Cheryl.

"So, I guess we should finally start sorting through our things, huh?" Cheryl asked.

"Yeah. We should probably check up on Mom first, though," Jill added.

She said *we*, but secretly hoped that Cheryl would be the one to do it.

"No problem, I got it," her little sister said, much to Jill's relief.

"Alright. I'll start with my room. Make sure to take notes of everything valuable you wanna keep." As soon as she said that, she felt an overwhelming sense of familiarity.

Don't run off too far away, Cheryl. Don't chase that squirrel, Cheryl. Cheryl, if you walk inside the house dirty like that, Mom's gonna kill us.

"I know, I know," Cheryl dismissively waved at her from the door—just as she always did when they were kids.

Sorting through the items just in her own room was going to be a pain, Jill thought. She didn't even know where to start. She also felt uncomfortable spending too much time in the dust-layered room, so she walked over to one of the boxes on the floor and opened it, eager to get this over with.

The contents of the box were useless, although they did have a sentimental value. Jill found all sorts of toys and dolls from her childhood. They were somewhat protected from deterioration in the box, but some of the plushies had years-old dark splotches on them. Jill rummaged through the box, but she took her time grabbing and examining each toy, because they each had a memory tied to it.

She picked up a doll, and a smile stretched across her face. It was a simple, gray, hand-stitched doll with black hair jutting out of the doll's head, and a crude face drawn on it. The eyes were two black dots, and the mouth was a combination of a black line in the shape of a smile, and red lips. The threads were coming loose on some parts of the doll, the wool stuffing inside it protruding out of the tiny holes.

"Lola," Jill whispered to herself with a rictus.

She had fond memories with this doll. It was given to her by a boy who she used to hang out with. What was his name, though? Jill stared off into space as she tried to remember the boy's name. It was at the tip of her tongue, but she just couldn't recall it.

However, she remembered the boy's appearance clearly. He had neatly combed hair and was really shy. He one day showed up and presented Lola to Jill. Said it was a token of their friendship. Strangely enough, Jill couldn't remember when or why she stopped hanging out with the boy. He must have moved away or something.

Jill put Lola on the bed. She would take her home after all this was done.

She closed the box and pushed it back to the corner of the room. She thought about giving some of the toys to Charlie, but all of the toys were for girls. He wouldn't like them.

As she looked around the room, she sighed in exasperation. There was a lot of work to do, and probably just as much in the other rooms. She decided to check Mom's office. They referred to it as an office, even though it wasn't actually an office. It was just a room where Mom used to store her things, like clothes, shoes, and—

Actually, Cheryl and Jill were never allowed in the room, so Jill had no idea what exactly was in there.

With her curiosity suddenly piqued beyond words, Jill walked out of her room and across the hallway. Mom's office was just across from Cheryl's room. As Jill stopped in front of the office, she heard muffled scraping noises behind her. Cheryl must have already started sorting through her things.

Jill stared at the door disdainfully. She suddenly felt like she was a kid again who had to be careful not to get caught trespassing into the office. If she did, she'd be in a lot of trouble.

How many times do I need to tell you that this room is off limits?! There are expensive things inside, do you understand, you little brat?!

But her mother was in a coma. There was nothing that could stop Jill from sneaking a peek. And besides, she was an adult now.

She grabbed the knob firmly and twisted it. She expected the room to be locked, but surprisingly the door pushed inward. You'd think that someone who treasured their possessions so much would do a better job keeping the room locked. But maybe Annette let her guard down since she lived alone.

As the door opened, it revealed a dark interior, pungent with a musty smell. Jill saw only shapes of objects in the dark. She fumbled for the switch next to the door, and when she felt it under her fingertips, she flipped it upward.

It took the ceiling light a moment to illuminate the room, and when it did, Jill gasped loudly.

Chapter 10

"Come on, you piece of shit!" Cheryl cursed as she slowly and carefully unstuck the two pages of her diary.

She had to be careful about it, otherwise she would damage the pages. She had gotten a little distracted and had been reading the diary that she wrote when she was nine years old. It was full of cringe, and she often winced at some of the things she had written. She wanted nothing more than to toss that diary in the trash bin and burn it until it was all but gone. She wouldn't do it, of course, because this was a gem from her childhood, no matter how cringy it was.

She looked at her phone clock and realized that she had spent the last thirty minutes reading the diary. Her room, although still pretty clean, had some items brought out from under the bed and from the wardrobes. She would spend a little more time reading the diary and then—

"Cheryl?" she heard Jill's voice faintly.

"Yeah?" Cheryl called back.

There was no response.

"What is it?" Cheryl demanded.

When Jill didn't respond again, Cheryl started to get a little frustrated. She clambered up to her feet with a groan and strode over to the door.

"Jill, did you call m—" she didn't finish the sentence because she was greeted by an unfamiliar sight when she looked left.

The door of Mom's office was widely open.

At first, Cheryl couldn't move. But then the excitement began surging through her. The office was *open*! She strode over to it and peeked inside from a safe distance. It was badly illuminated by the hanging ceiling lightbulb, and Jill stood in the middle of the room, frozen and staring at something in front of her. Cheryl wanted to call out to her sister, but suddenly she got a bad feeling. Instead, she tip-toed to the threshold of the office, not daring to cross it.

Going inside felt wrong. Growing up, she never once got to step inside. She managed to peer in a few times when Mom entered or exited the room, but she always had the key in her pocket. And she always kept the room locked.

Now that Cheryl stood in front of the open room, the forbidden fruit within her grasp, and no one in sight to punish her, she still felt uneasy about stepping in. She looked around the room and saw various objects covered in old, tattered sheets, she saw books and notebooks scattered on the floor, and she saw something in front of Jill.

Something on the wall that she was staring at this entire time.

"Jill?" Cheryl asked with a cracking voice.

The entire time, as her sister faced away from her, Cheryl couldn't help but think how this was exactly what went down in horror movies. Jill would turn around now, and instead of her sister, she would see some monstrosity staring back at her.

"Come take a look at this," Jill abruptly turned around and called out, motioning Cheryl to come closer.

Cheryl still hesitated. This was Mom's private room. They shouldn't be in here.

You're being childish, Cheryl. You're a grown ass adult. Nothing bad is gonna happen to you if you step inside, she reprimanded herself.

A part of her also worried about what Jill would think of her for being such a scaredy-cat, so she suppressed all of her brain's warnings and stepped across the threshold.

She expected something—what exactly?—to happen as she tentatively stopped next to Jill. She immediately noticed what she was staring at. On the wall in front of them, painted in crude, black paint, was a symbol of some kind.

"What the hell is that?" Cheryl asked, squinting.

65

The symbol had two long lines horizontally and vertically crossing each other in the middle. On the horizontal line were leaf-like symbols, with stars on each end. The vertical lines had circles that had their own inner lines crossing each other. On the right-hand line was a stick-like shape.

This didn't look like the random drawings of a bored or crazy person. The details were too meticulous, too carefully streaked. In some of the spots, the black paint trickled down where it dried, making the symbol look like it had melted in places. It was also evident from the lack of fading on the black paint against the old wall that it had been painted just recently.

"What in the hell is this?" Cheryl repeated in a perplexed manner.

"I... have no idea," Jill said.

She was transfixed on the symbol, examining each corner of it. It was big and easily took up almost the entire wall. Cheryl saw that the wall paint had faded in rectangular shapes in places, which was evidence that some of the objects or furniture were moved to make way specifically for this symbol.

"Was this Mom's doing?" Cheryl asked quizzically.

"It sure looks like it, but... why would she do it? If this is her way of being artistic, then she's got terrible taste."

Jill took a step forward and ran her hand across the middle of the symbol. The paint had long since dried up and fused with the wall. It made the whole pancake on the ceiling incident seem like nothing in comparison.

Suddenly, Cheryl felt sad for Mom. She knew that Mom had been getting more forgetful as time went on, despite not being what one would call an old person. But was she completely losing her mind, too?

Jill looked somewhere to the left before muttering a quiet 'What the fuck?'.

Cheryl followed her gaze and immediately saw it, too.

A shriveled, dry chicken leg was splayed on the floor next to an open can of black paint. The talons of the chicken leg were coated in black paint, and it too had long since dried. There were black droplets messily covering the floor, and Cheryl just then noticed the trail going from the bucket of paint to the wall where the symbol was.

"Do you think all of this has a meaning?" Cheryl tried rationalizing.

Jill shook her head absent-mindedly.

"I don't think so. I mean, maybe the symbol itself does have a meaning, but I doubt Mom was doing anything with it. Unless she practiced witchcraft without telling us about it."

"I mean, she kept this room secretive all this time. So, it would explain that."

Jill jerked her head towards her sister.

"You really think she practiced black magic here, or something of the like?"

Cheryl shrugged.

"I mean. I don't think she actually cast curses and spells. But maybe she practiced something and, I don't know, thought it worked?"

"Hm," Jill turned back to the symbol. "I think she was just crazy."

Cheryl felt anger forming within her.

"Why are you always so hostile towards her?" she asked.

Jill looked back at Cheryl, this time with alacrity on her face.

"Because, Cheryl," Jill raised her tone slightly. "You weren't old enough to see the shit she put us through. Dad used to say it all the time, too."

"You always bring that up! When are you going to let it go?! And Dad used to say what?!" Now Cheryl raised her tone.

"That she was crazy. That's why he left her and took me with him. Remember? Because he couldn't stand her antics anymore."

"That doesn't mean she's crazy, Jill!"

Jill pressed her lips together. She looked like she was about to say something that she would regret, something hurtful about Mom, perhaps. A moment later, that expression on her face disappeared, and she glanced at the symbol once more.

"You can defend her all you want, Cheryl, but this..." she pointed to the crude symbol in front of them. "This does not really ring normal to me."

She ironically chuckled at that last remark. Cheryl realized that talking about Mom struck a nerve with Jill, so she sighed heavily and decided to drop the subject.

"She lives alone here. Maybe she was scared."

"And then decided to paint this monstrosity?" Jill questioned.

Cheryl shrugged.

"Maybe this is some sort of, I dunno, protection charm, or something like that?"

Jill glanced at her with pursed lips. She didn't look like she was buying it. A moment later, she spun on her heel and exited the room with long strides.

"I don't wanna be inside this room anymore," she said brusquely.

"Jill?" Cheryl called out when her sister crossed the threshold.

"What?" Jill turned to face her.

Jill was leaning on the doorframe, staring at her sister with a raised eyebrow. A moment later, Cheryl shrugged and said.

"We should probably take pictures of this thing."

"Why? It's just something Mom painted in her demented state," Jill squinted.

"So we can find out what it means. We might be able to understand more about the person we call our mother. Learn what caused her *antics*," Cheryl said as she whipped out her phone.

Chapter 11

Jill wanted to go back to sorting through the items in her room, but she couldn't focus after seeing Mom's office. What in the hell was that? Had she completely lost it?

That would be the only viable explanation. But it wasn't just dementia. A person with dementia would forget things and sometimes not make sense, but Mom was higher up on the looney scale. Back when Jill lived there, Annette often spent hours locked up in the office, sometimes even at night. Jill would wake up to go to the bathroom, and she'd hear soft speaking coming from the office.

She once peeked through the keyhole and saw dim, flickering light coming from the room, like a meager candle flame in the wind. Jill heard her mother chanting something softly, almost in a whisper, and she saw her turned away from the door as she fiddled with something that Jill couldn't see.

At one moment, Mom jerked around, seemingly becoming aware of Jill's presence. Jill clasped a hand over her mouth and tip-toed back to bed. She heard her bedroom door opening a minute later, followed by soft footsteps, but she pretended to be asleep, praying that Mom wouldn't suspect anything.

She didn't, and within seconds, she left the room. Jill had no idea if she returned to do whatever she was doing in her office, and Jill was too petrified to get out of bed again.

It wasn't just the office, either. Mom would often speak gibberish, words that made no sense at all. And at other times, she'd flip out at Jill for the smallest things, like going in the woods without telling her, walking too close to the office, being too loud or too quiet when she played in her own room...

Yeah, living with Annette was a nightmare. As a child, Jill constantly felt like she was walking on eggshells, and she never knew what her mother's mood would be like each morning.

With Cheryl, however, it was an entirely different story.

Mom would always talk to her in a soft tone, buy her things that she liked, allowed her to do anything she wanted, and whenever she and Jill got into a fight, it was Jill who got grounded. There were even times when Annette took Cheryl out for ice cream or to the Medford fairs, while Jill had to stay at home.

That was okay, though. At those times, she'd hang out with the boy who came to play with her. She'd often complain and cry to him about Mom when she wasn't there. He would listen, but wouldn't say anything, and for some reason, that was oddly comforting for Jill.

And then one day, Jill's parents decided to get divorced. Dad moved out before that, and he took Jill with him. It was supposed to be a sad day in her life, at least according to what Jill had learned about divorce and parents living apart, but in truth, Jill couldn't have been happier about not having to live with her mom again. The only sad part of it was her separation from Cheryl.

All those memories angered Jill, but now that she was in the house where she grew up, all the painful, long-forgotten secrets started resurfacing. She would look at one object or spot, and she'd remember something from her past tied to it. She remembered some good things, too, but the bad ones were much more potent.

Jill went outside for some fresh air.

The morning was relatively warm, with a soft breeze that gently caressed her face. She glanced at her parked car. It would be so easy to just start the engine, drive off and go back to her family. *Her family.* But she couldn't do it.

Not to Cheryl.

Jill sat on the steps of the porch and stared out front at the thicket of trees far ahead. For some reason, she couldn't seem to get that awful symbol painted on the office wall out of her head whenever she closed her eyes. One part of her kept telling herself that it was just a nonsensical drawing her crazy mother made. But the other half was intrigued and wanted to find out if there was a hidden meaning behind it.

She pulled out her phone and opened the gallery. Back in the office, she took three pictures of the symbol along with Cheryl. As she stared at the pictures, the ugly symbol looked less threatening and obtrusive than in reality, even though it took up an entire wall.

Jill knew just the place to find out what this symbol meant. She opened Reddit and looked for one of the sub-forums where people gave answers about mysterious objects. She posted the clearest picture of it with the caption *Just found this in the house where my mom with dementia lives. Anyone know what it means?*

It would probably be a while until anyone answered her, so she decided to take matters into her own hands and investigate online. She typed into her search engine *magical symbols*. That was too broad, so she tried *magical symbols for protection*, and then *magical symbols for house protection*.

She saw all sorts of symbols in the images section, but nothing that looked remotely close to what she saw in the office. She tried *black magic symbols*, and that was even more off. All of the symbols that she saw were too symmetrical and geometrically aesthetic. The symbol in her mom's room was much cruder than that.

Maybe it wasn't supposed to be crude, and her mom's hand was just too unsteady?

Before she could gain enough momentum for research and input all the words she had in mind, she got a notification from Reddit. Someone had commented on her post. She clicked the notification to open it, and there were already two comments under the symbol's picture.

Looks like some Satanic shit, the first comment said.

Looks like your mom did some voodoo lol, the next one under said.

But then Jill saw a reply to the second comment from a user called *poloniumpoisoning*. It said, *Yes, you are correct. OP, this the Vodou veve used to summon the loa.*

Jill frowned at the sentence. It took her a moment to remember that 'OP' stands for 'original poster'. She didn't know any other words in the sentence the replier wrote. She responded to him with a question, *what does all of that mean?*

While waiting for the reply from *poloniumpoisoning*, Jill looked up the word *vodou* in the search engine. The first result she got said the following:

Haitian Vodou is an African diasporic religion that gradually developed in Haiti between the 16th and 19th centuries. It is a worldview encompassing philosophy, medicine, justice, and religion. Adherents of Vodou are called Vodouisants.

Jill opened the first link on the engine, and lo and behold, she saw a symbol on the right-hand side of the page. It wasn't the one from her mom's room, but it sure looked like the style of drawing was similar. As she scrolled down, she saw more and more of the symbols. And then she ran into the one from the office. Jill went back into her gallery to compare them, and sure enough, they were uncannily similar. Underneath the symbol, it said:

A vèvè pattern designed to invoke Papa Legba, one of the main loa spirits worshipped in Haitian Vodou.

Was her mom trying to summon some kind of Vodou spirit? Jill's head started spinning. She read through the page about Vodou and expected to find things related to sticking needles into dolls, hexes, curses, and similar things. Quite the opposite was true, instead.

Vodou was apparently a peaceful religion that had been wrongfully portrayed by the American media and accompanied by the stigma from the Christian settlers who saw Vodou as Satanic worship. Jill further learned that there are many spirits in Vodou and that each of them has their own *vèvè*.

So that begged the question—was her mom trying to summon this Papa Legba? And why?

"Hey, what's up?" Cheryl's voice behind her caused her to jerk up.

Jill looked at her just as Cheryl sat on the steps next to her.

"I uh... I think I know what that symbol means," Jill reluctantly said.

■■■

Cheryl listened raptly as Jill explained to her about Haitian Vodou, the loa, and the *vèvè*. At first, Cheryl didn't buy it. Her mother practicing Vodou? But when Jill showed her the uncanny resemblance between the symbol in the office and the symbol on the webpage, she started to reconsider her beliefs.

"But, that doesn't make any sense. Why would Mom be practicing Vodou?"

Jill shrugged.

"I still think it's because she was crazy and just drew that in her confused state."

"That didn't look like a confused drawing to me. I mean, did you see that? It looked like it was drawn with precision. And whose *vèvè* is that again? Papa...?"

"Papa Legba. He's the most prominent loa in Vodou."

"What a stupid name," Cheryl scoffed. "And what exactly do these loa do?"

Jill looked towards the trees across the road.

"I'm not sure, yet. They could be good, they could be evil. I don't know anything about Vodou, to tell you the truth."

"I thought it was called *Voodoo*, and it involved—"

"Sticking pins in dolls, yeah."

Cheryl chuckled at that.

The sisters spent a moment in silence. They were probably thinking the same thing. What was Mom trying to do? What if Jill was right? What if she was just crazy and the symbol had no significance? They could be going on a wild goose chase for something that even Mom didn't fully outline.

"We should search the house some more," Cheryl suddenly said as she swiveled towards Jill.

Jill was on her phone, scrolling through a website with books containing symbols similar to the *vèvè* in the office.

"Good idea," she nodded without looking up at her. "And I'll buy some e-books about Vodou."

Cheryl smiled.

"Look at us, collaborating to solve a mystery."

Jill looked at up at her and returned the smile.

"If Mom and Dad saw us now, they wouldn't recognize us."

They shared another glance with each other for a prolonged moment. It was a special moment, a silent, wordless reconnecting of two souls who had drifted apart and now found their way back to each other.

"So, you wanna help me look through Mom's office?"

Jill nodded.

"I do, but, we gotta do one thing, first."

"And what's that?"

"Call Charlie so he can see Auntie Cherry."

Chapter 12

They were inside the living room and sitting on the couch next to each other. Jill pressed the video call button and shoved her hair behind her shoulder. The phone started ringing, and Cheryl felt her heart skip a beat. She wasn't in the frame of the camera yet, and she didn't want to lean closer to Jill to jump into the video call.

After just two rings, Lee answered the phone with a reticent 'hello?' and started talking to Jill. Jill spoke briskly and after making some small talk, told Lee that she was with Cheryl and that she wanted to speak to Charlie.

"Alright, one moment," Lee said with a hint of surprise in his tone.

Cheryl saw Lee disappearing out of view and getting replaced by pixels of something that looked like a wall. She heard voices in the background as if from a barrel, and then the phone moved again.

A little boy jumped into the frame, exposing one missing incisor with a wide grin. Immediately, Cheryl pasted on a rictus.

"Hi, Mommy," Charlie said, waving a tiny hand with fervent motions that made his fingers look blurred.

"Hey, baby! How was baseball practice?" Jill asked.

Cheryl noticed an ear-to-ear smile on her sister's face. She rarely saw Jill expressing such genuine happiness.

"It was good. Our team won," Charlie said. "Jacob got hit in the head with the ball."

He hysterically laughed at that while Jill widened her eyes and fake-gasped. Cheryl let out a quiet peal of laughter, too.

"Charlie, I have someone who I'd like you to meet, okay?" Jill said.

"Okay," Charlie immediately got serious.

Jill leaned closer to Cheryl, so that both of them were in the frame. Now that she saw herself next to Jill, Cheryl realized how much they resembled each other. She smiled at the camera and waved, but Charlie didn't react, much to her disappointment. He continued staring at one spot confusedly as if he were trying to solve a difficult mathematical problem. He must have forgotten who she was. Of course he did, it's been ye—

"Aunt Cherry!" Charlie's voice boomed and his mouth opened into another smile.

Cheryl felt a warm feeling washing all over her, unlike anything she had felt in a long time. The closest feeling to it she had was when she found a stray kitten in front of the dorm one night and decided to take care of her for the night until someone adopted her.

"Hi, Charlie!" Cheryl shouted back, waving more fervently now.

Jill nudged the phone into Cheryl's hand and disappeared out of the frame, giving the two of them a moment of privacy. Cheryl instinctively took the phone, even though she was taken aback by this. By the time she looked at Jill, she was already on the other side of the couch. Cheryl looked back at Charlie and smiled widely.

It was strange to see this child, who she knew as a toddler, now as a much older boy. In her mind, Charlie always stayed a toddler who could barely utter a few words, called Cheryl Cherry, and played with toy trucks.

For a moment, it felt awkward, and Cheryl didn't know what to say, but then Charlie took the initiative and said, "Where have you been all this time, Aunt Cheryl?"

His voice was like a melody to her ears. She again had that warm feeling that had her melting inside.

"I'm sorry, Charlie! I've... I've been busy," she shrugged.

He incredulously shook his head.

"You shouldn't work too hard. Ms. Wilson says working hard can cause burnout."

Both Cheryl and Jill laughed.

"Well, you know what? You tell Ms. Wilson that if I don't study, I'll fail the year, and then I'll be jobless."

As soon as the words left her mouth, she wondered if she used too many big words—she wasn't used to speaking with five-year-olds. To her surprise, Charlie gave her an insouciant remark about having more free time.

Cheryl spent some time talking to him about pre-school and teased him with questions related to girls he might have a crush on. It took Cheryl some time to get used to speaking to him in a more adult tone than the last time she saw him. He was indeed clever, just like Jill said.

The conversation with her nephew was exactly what Cheryl needed to help her forget all about Tom and the ugly *vèvè* in Mom's office. Those things still gnawed at her, like rats slowly nibbling through a concrete wall, but right now, she didn't care.

When it was about time to end the call, Charlie asked her when she was going to visit, which almost brought her to tears. Cheryl did her best not to show any emotions, mostly because of Jill. The two of them were together now, but after everything was done with their mom, they would probably go their own separate ways. This was just a brief moment of bonding they had.

Still, Cheryl foolishly allowed herself to believe that she would be welcome into Jill's life as her sister and Charlie's Aunt.

▪▪

"Say goodbye to Aunt Cherry, Charlie," Jill said when Cheryl gave her the phone back.

"Bye-bye, Aunt Cherry!" Charlie waved frenetically, stretching out each word.

Cheryl waved back. For the first time since they arrived at the house, Cheryl seemed genuinely happy.

Jill walked towards the kitchen, still speaking on the phone, "Charlie, let me talk to Da—"

But Charlie ended the call.

"He hung up on me," Jill groused aloud.

Cheryl laughed at that remark. Jill called back and waited for the video call to connect. She walked into the kitchen and, with her free hand, poured a glass of water for herself from the tap. She glanced at the tap, and when the glass was almost full, she pulled it away from the stream and turned off the tap.

She brought the glass to her mouth and looked at the phone, and almost dropped the glass on the floor.

The call was already connected.

The screen was glitchy, green pixels shuffling from corner to corner, and Jill saw Lee in the frame. He was standing horizontally, indicating that the phone was splayed on its side. Lee's entire figure was in the frame, hunched over something, facing away from the camera, but it was dark from the sunlight that peered directly at the phone's camera.

"Lee?" Jill called out.

She took a sip of water and placed the glass on the kitchen counter. The phone made glitchy noises, something akin to short electrical bursts with the sound perpetually cutting out. Jill saw Lee swaying left, and then right, frame by frame.

"Lee, can you hear me?" Jill asked, now suddenly feeling a little uneasy.

Lee turned his head sideways and froze like that, along with the entire phone. His face was pixelated and dark, and Jill saw one white square for an eye. She tried pressing the 'end call' button, but the phone wouldn't respond. She tried holding the power button to restart it, but still nothing.

"Come on, you piece of shit," she said as she smacked the phone against her palm out of frustration.

She repeatedly pressed the end call button, forced to stare at Lee's frozen figure. And then she just stopped pressing anything at all and continued staring. But then she started to notice more and more details on Lee's frozen figure. The more she stared, the less the figure actually looked like Lee.

The arms that hung to the side were too long, too thin, and too incongruous compared to the rest of the body. The legs were just as slim, and the shape of them was strange. There weren't any wrinkles or bagginess notable for clothes—especially the kind of oversized clothes that Lee often wore.

The figure in the frame moved its head slightly more to the side, revealing a noseless (and lipless?) black face and pearly white teeth. From the pixelated image, it looked as if the person was baring its teeth like a dog.

The video suddenly went entirely black. The call was still on because the big red button to end it was there, but the screen on Lee's end was pitch black. A soft, raspy growl escaped from the phone's speakers.

Jill jumped, dropping the phone on the floor in the process. It thudded against the kitchen tiles with a dull sound, thanks to the rubber case.

"You okay?" Cheryl called from the living room.

Jill glared at the phone. The call had ended. She looked towards the door leading to the living room and was about to shout to Cheryl not to worry when a vibration caused her to nearly jump out of her skin again. When she looked down, the phone was ringing. Lee's name was on the screen.

"Jill?" Cheryl shouted with a more solicitous timbre this time.

"Yeah, I'm fine. Just dropped my phone," Jill shouted back.

The phone continued vibrating intermittently, each vibration giving Jill a foreboding feeling. Nevertheless, she bent down and picked it up, reprimanding herself for being so silly. She pressed the green button to accept the video call and waited.

The screen was glitchy again, little squares of various colors flying across the video. The pixels started decreasing, and a shape appeared in the middle of the screen. It said something indiscernible in a robotic tone.

"Jill, can you hear me?" the screen suddenly cleared up and presented Lee's head and shoulders in the frame.

Jill sighed in relief—a little too deeply, she noticed. She wasn't even aware of the breath she'd been holding up until now.

"Jesus, Lee, where have you been?" Jill asked.

"Sorry, hon. I didn't hear the phone. Everything okay over there? You look like you've just run a marathon."

Jill laughed that off.

"I'm fine."

"Are you sure? Maybe Charlie and I should come help you there."

"No, no. It's fine, really," Jill replied quickly.

She didn't want Charlie to be anywhere near this house. It was bad enough that his grandmother was comatose in the house, but to see the crazy stuff like they found in the office would probably raise a lot of questions with a kid his age.

"It's really no problem, Jill. We could be there in just a few hours."

"No. Really, Lee. It's fine. Besides, I wanna do this on my own."

Lee glowered at Jill.

"Okay, fine," he conceded a moment later.

"I'll be back before you know it," Jill smiled. "Honey, listen. I got a lot of work to do here, so I'll talk to you later, alright?"

"Sure, sure," Lee nodded.

"Don't forget to—"

"Pick up the clothes at the dry cleaner's, I know," Lee rolled his eyes.

"Love you," Jill sent Lee a kiss.

"Love you, too, babe. Have fun with your sis."

81

The call ended and Jill put the phone back in her pocket.

She walked out of the kitchen in a stupor, the image of the glitchy black figure still etched in her mind.

Chapter 13

Cheryl really didn't want to go back to the room with the *vèvè*, but she had to get some answers. Mom was doing something, and she was determined to find out what. Maybe she was crazy just like Jill said, but Cheryl couldn't let it go. There was a missing piece of the puzzle here, she was sure of it.

As she entered the office, she suddenly became aware of just how cold the room was. Or maybe it was just her overreacting. She always had an overactive imagination, even from an early age.

Before she got her own room, she and Jill shared a room. Whenever Cheryl would get scared of the monsters hiding under her bed and in the closet, Jill would tell her that there are no such things as monsters. Sometimes, she'd encourage her with some words of comfort, and by allowing her to keep her flashlight on through the night. But as they got older, Jill would get frustrated and tell her to quit being a crybaby. Eventually, Cheryl ignored any sounds she thought she heard from the closet because she didn't want Jill to think of her as a coward.

At the age of six, Cheryl got her own room, but her imagination was still active. The monsters under her bed seemed even scarier and bolder now, so she often had to call her parents to check the room. Dad checked the closet and under the bed while she was there, but she was usually too upset to continue sleeping on her own. Mom would then get soft and tell her that it's okay for her to sleep with them that night.

Now that Cheryl entered the office, the same sense of unease crept up inside her, making her feel small as she was as a child.

No, that's stupid. There are no such things as monsters and ghosts, Cheryl, come on.

With that thought, Cheryl broke into a more confident amble, ignoring the gnawing feeling of fear at the back of her mind. Once she was deep inside the room, the feeling of dread was gone, and she instead felt brave.

"Now, where do I start?" she muttered to herself.

She looked around the office for anything that could harbor any secrets. There was a dusty, cobweb-covered bookshelf on the left side of the room. Cheryl hoped there would be no spiders. She hated spiders.

There were tattered books messily thrown on the shelves, most of whose spines had no titles. Cheryl saw a small cardboard box on the top shelf next to the pile of books. It was small enough for jewelry, so that's what Cheryl thought she'd find in there—not that she would wear or keep anything from this horrid room.

A sudden thought of finding a cursed earring ran through her mind. She'd put the earring on and have really bad luck financially and in relationships. She suppressed hysterical laughter at the thought that she might already be cursed when it came to love. When Cheryl grabbed the small box, opened the lid, and peered inside, she didn't find any jewelry.

Instead, she found a picture.

It was an old picture of a middle-aged woman. The picture had a symbol across the face of the woman, painted in black. It wasn't the same symbol as the *vèvè* on the wall. It was something simpler, with only three lines streaked across each other and some circles around.

"Is that... Barbara?" Cheryl squinted, mumbling to herself.

She turned the picture over in various angles as if she'd be able to get a better look through the paint, but the face was still half-covered. There was no mistaking it, though. Cheryl knew the woman in the picture.

■■■

"Find anything useful?" Jill asked from the office entrance, which accidentally startled Cheryl.

"Sorry," she apologized a moment later.

She looked at the box Cheryl was holding and tilted her head slightly.

"Whatcha got there, Cherry?"

Cheryl looked down at the box with her mouth slightly ajar, but said nothing. She looked up at Jill and outstretched her arms to present the box to her. Jill put the phone in her pocket and approached Cheryl.

She didn't even need to take the box from her to see the contents inside. Still, what she saw in there was so bizarre that she inadvertently squinted and stared at the photograph for a long moment.

"Is that Barbara?" she asked and looked at Cheryl, expecting a more sensical answer from her, but Cheryl was just as flummoxed as Jill was.

Her little sister stood with tense shoulders and lips tightly pressed into a thin line.

"Why the hell would Mom have a photograph of Dad's second wife here?" Jill repeated the question, staring at the grotesque photo of the middle-aged woman with the black painted symbol across the face.

She already knew the answer, she just refused to admit it to herself.

"Well, it's obvious, isn't it?" Cheryl asked.

"Yeah, it is," Jill nodded.

She returned the box to Cheryl, suddenly feeling disgusted by it. Cheryl promptly returned the box to the shelf on the left side of the room and stared at it for a moment with a wrinkled nose, while wiping her hands on one another.

"I cannot believe this. She must have really lost it," Jill said.

"We don't really know that," Cheryl made a grimace. "I mean, maybe all of this has a rational explanation."

"Oh, yeah, definitely. The rational explanation was that Mom tried to use black magic on Barbara because she couldn't stand the thought of Dad remarrying."

Jill became aware of how she raised the tone, but this newfound discovery of their mom was too much. It was one thing to be a narcissistic control freak and ruin your child's life, but to be so petty as to ruin another person's life just because they were happy and you weren't? That was even lower than Jill thought her mother was capable of.

Cheryl didn't object. She must have realized that Jill was right about whatever was going on here not being normal. Cheryl cleared her throat and crossed her arms, glancing at the box on the shelf once more.

"Let's leave this room for now," she suggested when she saw how visibly uncomfortable Cheryl was.

Once again, Cheryl didn't object to that and turned to follow Jill.

"Did you find anything out from the books?" she asked as soon as the door of the office was closed.

"Oh, right," Jill snapped a finger and pulled out her phone. "I finished reading one book about Vodou and started with the second one, and there's some good info in there."

"Wait, you finished reading an entire book?" Cheryl raised her eyebrows so high that her forehead wrinkled.

"Yeah," Jill nodded.

"You downloaded it just two hours ago."

"I'm a fast reader," Jill shrugged.

Cheryl opened her mouth in shock and amazement.

"Doesn't matter, listen," she waved away Cheryl's reaction dismissively. "I learned some good information about Vodou."

"Okay, I'm listening."

"Well, apparently, the loa, or the spirits of Vodou can be summoned when you need a favor. And I'm not talking about wash your dishes kind of favor."

"I figured."

"Apparently, you can do favors for the loa, and if you do them right, the loa have an obligation to serve you just as you served them."

"That sounds like a commitment. I'm too lazy to even unsubscribe from promotional emails."

Jill guffawed at that. Cheryl's humor hasn't changed much, it only got more advanced as she got older. Out of the two sisters, Jill was always the more serious one, while Cheryl was the type who broke the rules and didn't take anything seriously.

"Okay, so, you think Mom summoned one of these loa to do her bidding?" Cheryl asked.

"I am almost one hundred percent sure."

"Almost?"

"Yeah. Loas in Vodou each have their own *vèvè*, and depending on what you need, you summon the corresponding loa."

"How do you know who the right loa is?"

"That's the thing. You can summon any loa to help you, but you'd be better off asking an agricultural loa to help with your garden than a loa in charge of love. You need to really know Vodou by either being a *houngan* or a *mambo* to know who the best loa is to assist you."

"A what now?"

Jill knew that the words would confuse Cheryl, but she just couldn't help but throw around the Haitian terms that she just learned.

"*Houngans* and *Mambos* are Vodou priests and priestesses. They spend years and years studying Vodou and serving loa."

Cheryl looked down for a moment with a frown before asking.

"So, if our investigation is on track, then we can assume that Mom was trying to summon a loa to serve her?"

"Exactly," Jill complacently snapped her fingers.

"But why?"

"We already know why. You've seen the picture in the box."

Cheryl shook her head. She refused to believe what Jill was telling her—what all the evidence was telling her.

"Mom wouldn't want to hurt someone like that. I know her."

"Do you really, Cheryl?" Jill lowered her chin slightly. "She was always really good to you. But you didn't see some of the things I saw."

Cheryl bit her lip uncomfortably.

"There's no denying it," Jill shrugged matter of factly. "Mom was trying to summon a loa to hurt Barbara."

"No, that can't be right."

"Cheryl, think about it," Cheryl sensed the frustration in Jill's voice. "All the things we found in that room so far, all of them, they point to that and nothing else. I mean, what other explanation do you have? Casting a blessing on Barbara?"

She laughed at her own zinger. Cheryl swallowed since she had nothing to say, but she still shook her head defiantly.

"You think she managed to do it?" she asked.

"Do what?" Jill scowled.

"You know... summon a loa?"

Jill put her hands on her hips and looked up at the ceiling pensively with a frown. At the back of her mind, Cheryl hoped that Jill would say that Mom did manage to summon a loa. That way, she wouldn't need to worry about telling Jill about her fears of the supernatural.

"No, I think it's a load of bullshit," Jill shook her head a moment later.

Cheryl suddenly felt like they were kids again and that she was the scaredy-cat who was afraid of the imaginary monsters in her closet.

"Yeah, you're probably right," she agreed with Jill.

"Okay. Maybe we're overthinking this. We should probably just let it go. We're not going to understand what happened to Mom by deciphering all this Vodou bullshit. I mean, Mom was—"

Her sentence trailed off.

"Mom was crazy, that's what you want to say," Cheryl scoffed, ready for another conflict with her sister.

Jill gave Cheryl a vague smile and sighed.

"How about we get some lunch? We still have a lot of work to do, and it's already Saturday afternoon."

She didn't wait for Cheryl's answer and instead turned around and broke into a gait towards the stairs.

Cheryl cast one final glance at the door of the office before following Jill downstairs.

Chapter 14

"Stop it!" Cheryl shouted.

She was a child again. Tears welled up in her eyes as she spun in circles and repeatedly shouted at the kids to stop mocking her. There were five of them, and they were running in circles, singing 'Cheryl the barrel'.

Cheryl didn't even know how it came to that. One moment, they were all playing together in the woods, and the next thing she knew, one of the kids called her fat, and then another added that she looked like a barrel, and they started singing the mocking song.

She tried to break out of the circle and run, but the kids held hands and wouldn't let her leave. She clasped her ears with her hands to block out the noise. And then one of the boys screamed in pain, which in turn, caused everyone to stop singing and spinning. When Cheryl looked at him, she realized that his lip was busted and bleeding.

Everyone looked in one direction, and Cheryl followed their gazes. Jill stood there, with two more rocks in her hands, ready to hurl them at the bullies.

"Ow! You hit me!" the boy said.

"And I'll do it again!" Jill raised her hand with the rock.

"No, no, wait!" the boy pleaded.

"Get out of here before I throw this rock at your teeth!"

"Okay, okay!" the boy said and immediately, the bullies ran off.

With the threat gone, Jill dropped the rocks and approached Cheryl. She wiped the tears off her face and hugged her.

"It's okay, Cherry. The bad kids are gone. I'll always protect you," she said.

The forest dispersed along with Jill, leaving a black, swirling mist that surrounded Cheryl. It was so thick that she couldn't see anything except it. She turned in circles, but all she could see was the fog. She moved in one random direction, listening to the soft thudding of her shoes on the carpet. She also became vaguely aware that she was no longer a child, but back to her adult self

She had no idea where she was, so she decided to just go in one direction until she stumbled into something. But what if she didn't stumble into anything, and just kept walking on and on forever?

That thought caused her to panic, so she broke from a trot into a jog. Her panting was muffled in the air, the sound barely leaving her mouth before getting drowned out by the oppressive silence.

And then, just as she stopped, the mist started clearing up. At first, she thought it was just her imagination, but as she spun around, she saw the gigantic wisps of fog retreating all around her, like snake-like coils.

Cheryl saw the pink carpet on the floor, and then more and more objects began revealing themselves around her. A bed, a closet, walls, a door, a window...

It was Cheryl's room.

The mist was still present, but now it was in the form of a transparent smoke that caused the entire room to slowly dance along with the wisps, almost like staring through the smoke above a fire.

Cheryl spun around and saw herself sleeping in her old bed. She was on her back; her head lolled to the side, one arm above, the other at her side, the cellphone clutched in her hand. The bed was barely long enough for Cheryl, and her feet dangled off the end of it.

It was surreal, staring at herself sleeping, and for some reason, Cheryl knew that this was a dream, and yet, something more. She remembered that she decided to take a break after lunch. She remembered slumping into bed and being on her phone scrolling through social media. She remembered—

Movement under the bed caused her to jerk her head towards it.

There was a shadow obscured by the darkness under the bed, but undeniable movement was there. Cheryl froze and stared at the spot without blinking. Nothing happened. For a moment, she convinced herself that she just imagined it, but then it happened again.

Ever so slowly, something slithered and crawled towards the bottom of the bed where Cheryl's feet dangled. Cheryl felt her heart beginning to race. Simultaneously, the Cheryl in bed began stirring. Her head turned from one side to the other, and her face contorted into a painful grimace.

Wake up! Wake up! Cheryl tried to shout to her asleep body, but for some reason, she couldn't even open her mouth.

The black mass seeped into the light and slowly climbed towards Cheryl's foot. Cheryl saw pointy fingers protruding at the end of the arm-like mass, but they looked anything but human. They were elongated and tendril-like.

The fingers clutched the edge of the mattress, causing a low scratching sound. Cheryl wanted to scream at herself to wake up, but her figure on the bed just slightly tossed and turned, as if having a bad nightmare.

"We had a deal," a raspy, croaky voice said from under the bed, almost in a whisper.

Cheryl widened her eyes, feeling like she was going to lose her mind from the fear that enveloped her. All the hair on her body stood straight up and she felt shivers running down her spine.

"We had a deal, Annette," the voice said once more.

Cheryl saw another clawed hand appearing in the light at the foot of the bed, and then the top of a black, shapeless head. And then another limb—a foot maybe?—and for a moment, Cheryl thought that there were multiple figures under the bed. That, or there was one, but it was extremely elastic.

The hand that gripped the mattress grabbed Cheryl's ankle.

She felt icy cold on the spot where she had been grabbed, but at the same time, it was as if the touch burned her. The Cheryl in bed now tossed more violently and moaned, but still refused to wake up.

"WE HAD A DEAL!" the voice came through again, guttural and deep this time.

Cheryl shot up in bed so explosively while scooting backward that she hit her back against the wall. She was covered in a cold sweat, trembling like a leaf in the wind from head to toe.

She didn't even register the knocking on the door until it came again more loudly.

"Cheryl?" It was Jill and she sounded concerned.

"Yeah, I'm awake," Cheryl said, aware of how brittle her voice sounded.

"Alright. Violet is here for her daily checkup on Mom. Do you wanna join us?"

"Yeah. I'll be there in a minute," Cheryl said absent-mindedly.

Her eyes were fixated on the foot of the bed. There were no black hands reaching for her there, even though Cheryl expected them to. For a while, she couldn't move. What if that black figure was still under the bed and just waiting for her to step off so it could grab her?

Even after a full minute, she still trembled violently, as if suffering from hypothermia. After some time though, she managed to compose herself enough to start moving.

Cheryl got on all fours and crawled towards the foot of the bed, hand by hand, foot by foot. When she got close to it, she veered over the edge towards the floor, inch by inch.

There was nothing there.

She got a little bolder and leaned further forward. There was noth—

No, there *was* something there.

Scratches on the carpet. Four parallel, two-inch long white scratches, contrasting against the pink floor, as if someone clawed at it with their nails. Cheryl felt her heart rate quickening once again. She took a few deep breaths, and without thinking, plunged her head down to glance under the bed.

A pair of eyes floating in the darkness stared back at her.

No, just her imagination. There was nothing there. No black figures. No monsters. As she raised her head, she sighed in a mixture of exasperation and relief. She hopped off the bed, much calmer now.

And that's when she became aware of it.

The steady pulsating of her right ankle. Cheryl looked down, but the sweatpants she wore covered her ankle. She prayed that it was her imagination as she bent down to pull the pant leg up. She hesitated. She wasn't sure if she wanted to see what was causing that pain. Blocking out those thoughts, Cheryl yanked the cloth up.

There was nothing there.

Cheryl rotated her foot to scrutinize the ankle from various angles, but there was nothing there. No finger-shaped bruises, no scratches, no markings. At the same time, the pulsating she felt began subsiding. Did she even feel the pulsating in the first place, or was it just her imagination?

Another knock on the door caused her to jerk her head back up.

"Cheryl? Are you asleep again?" Jill's muffled voice came from the other side.

"Sorry! I'm coming," Cheryl pulled her pant leg back down.

The pulsating in her ankle was gone, even though a faint coldness remained present around the area that she imagined was grabbed in her dream. She shook her head, scolding herself for letting herself get scared so easily.

The scratches on the floor? They were there before, they must have been.

And the black figure? That was just a stupid nightmare, that's all.

Despite telling herself that over and over, Cheryl couldn't get the horrid voice that she heard in the dream out of her head, and with that, she wondered about one thing.

What kind of deal did that thing have with my mom?

Chapter 15

"Everything okay?" Jill asked Cheryl as soon as she opened the door.

Her little sister looked distressed. She took a nap, that much was evident from her bedraggled hair, but her eyes portrayed anything except drowsiness. They were wide and alert, and they confusedly darted in various directions.

"Yeah, why wouldn't it be?" Cheryl asked with a grin before turning to Violet. "Hi, Violet. Sorry for making you wait."

Violet nodded aloofly, "Not a problem, Cheryl. Shall we?"

The sisters followed Violet into their mom's bedroom. The room had rays of orange gleaming in from the setting sun through the window and falling on Annette's pallid face. Jill was overcome by the familiar sense of sickness as soon as she heard the machine's beeping and the medicinal, old people smell. The first thing Jill did when she entered was to observe her mother and make sure she hadn't changed positions again.

That was so weird yesterday, to see her arm in a different position. Jill spaced out and thought about everything she had experienced since she arrived to the house.

The Vodou *vèvè* on the wall, the chicken leg and Barbara's picture, the nightmare of the black figure staring at her, the glitchy call she had with Lee... she started to get a bad feeling about all of this, but the rational part of her refused to believe that something out of order was happening here.

You just spent too long in the house, and it's starting to get to you. That's all.

But it wasn't just that. The longer Jill spent in the house, the more she started to imagine a figure standing in the corners of the house. She'd see it with her peripheral vision, but whenever she turned her head, it was gone.

She saw it just before Violet arrived, too.

Jill was sitting in the living room, reading a Vodou handbook, when she thought she heard something on her right. She didn't respond to it immediately. This house was old, and it made noises from time to time. But then, when it abruptly came again a few minutes later, accompanied by just-barely visible movement, she froze.

She refused to look in that direction because if she did so, the figure would disappear. So instead, she tried to discern what it was by using just her peripheral vision. She pretended to read off her phone while focusing intently on the figure in the corner of her eye.

At first, she just saw an outline of... something. But then that outline started to get more and more defined. Jill saw something that looked like an arm hanging limply next to a body with a twitching hand.

A few times, Jill inadvertently moved her eyes slightly towards the figure, but the harder she tried to look at it, the more it seemed to retreat out of her line of sight. She decided to continue focusing on it with her peripheral vision instead.

After just a few minutes, the figure seemed to be much closer. It must have been moving so slowly and gradually that Jill didn't even notice it until she was able to see the twitchy, rigid, and elongated fingers with sharp nails on the bony black hand.

She still refused to look. She wanted to let it get just a little closer, and then she would jerk her head towards it. But before she could do that, a noise startled her.

A low, raspy groan sounded, just barely loud enough to be heard over the silence hanging in the air. When Jill swiveled to look at the figure, it was gone. What stood there instead was just the tall lamp next to the wall, its shadow making an oddly humanoid shape. Jill pivoted around but found herself to be alone in the room.

She massaged her temples and convinced herself that she was just tired. But then another scary thought occurred to her; that she may have been losing her mind instead—just like her mother.

That terrified her more than any demonic shadow. She spent her entire life trying to be the exact opposite of her mother, and she would be damned if she'd start going crazy like her.

"You really don't need to be here," Violet's voice pulled Jill back to reality. "If you'd like to assist, I don't mind, but I can take care of everything without your help. You don't need to bother yourselves."

Jill was about to agree when Cheryl interjected.

"No, it's fine. I think we should probably know how to do these things."

Violet looked at Jill for confirmation.

What could Jill do then? Say that she won't stay? Her relationship with Cheryl was wobbly at best, and she didn't want to exacerbate it further by alienating her mother, no matter how indifferent she was to her.

She nodded with a fake smile and allowed Violet to start with her work. The nurse placed her handbag on the edge of the bed and began taking out various medical items, including syringes, vials, alcoholic swabs, etc.

The entire time, Cheryl stood next to Violet, basically invading her private space, while Jill stood at the back, allowing her little sister to take the lead—but still watching to show that she was at least somewhat interested in the process.

Violet was quick and efficient. Everything that needed to be done around Mom was done with finesse and calmness. Jill reckoned she would need triple the time that Violet needed in order to just prepare the syringe and injection.

Once the nurse finished moving Mom around for her daily exercise, she pulled the covers over her. She accidentally knocked the empty syringe and vial off the bed and onto the floor. The vial rolled under the bed.

"Oh, I'm such a klutz sometimes," Violet complained.

"It's okay, I'll get it," Cheryl knelt down.

She prudently grabbed the syringe, careful not to touch the needle, even though it still had the plastic cap on top. She reached under the bed, her arm and head disappearing out of view. She stayed like that for a solid ten or so seconds before pulling herself out.

"You got it?" Jill asked.

Instead of the vial, Cheryl was holding a piece of paper.

"What's that?" Jill asked.

Cheryl held the paper with both hands and had already started reading the message that was written on it. Even from here, Jill could tell that the note was scrawled, rather than written. It looked like the handwriting of a child who just learned the alphabet.

Or an old person who forgot it, Jill thought to herself, wrinkling her nose.

Cheryl flipped the paper, revealing a wall of printed text. She darted her eyes across the lines of text, ignoring Jill.

"Cheryl!" Jill said, more sternly this time.

Cheryl stood up and turned to Jill, pale as a piece of paper.

"What is it?" Jill asked, awkwardly chuckling to suppress the knot that she felt in the pit of her stomach.

Cheryl handed the note to Jill with a blank look in her eyes. Jill took the note and glanced down at it, already certain that she wouldn't like what she was going to read.

"It's... it's Mom's will," Cheryl said soft-spokenly.

Jill read the document speedily. She then reread it once. And then twice. And then three times. No matter how many times she reread the document, it didn't change. And still, Jill couldn't believe it. She thought that this was probably a prank, a cruel joke played by her mother on her less favorite daughter as a final fuck you to her.

"It says in the will that she left the house to me," Jill said timorously as she looked up at Cheryl and then at Violet for silent confirmation.

Chapter 16

Cheryl looked as perplexed as Jill, so she simply shook her head incredulously. Jill looked down at the document once more. She had to read it one more time, word by word, to make sure she didn't miss anything important. It seemed legal enough, and it even had Annette's name signed under, along with the signature of a witness and an attorney.

"I don't understand," Jill said as she flipped the paper.

On the backside was a scrawled sentence.

IM SORRY FOR TREATING YOU THE WAY I DID

Jill frowned. Is that what this was? Her mother felt guilty for mistreating Jill her whole life, so she wanted to make up for it by making her the sole heir of her property? Jill had mixed feelings about all of that.

On the one hand, she didn't want the house—and she wanted it even less just for herself. Jill never thought about the inheritance she'd receive from her mother because she always assumed that Cheryl would be the one to get the house.

On the other hand, selling the house could get her a lofty amount of money for the family. Even if she gave half of it to Cheryl (which she would do without hesitation), she would have more than enough to pay off her own mortgage.

"Good for you, Jill. Looks like you were wrong about who Mom's favorite daughter was after all," Cheryl forced a smile.

She was aware of the hostility in her voice, but she couldn't help it. Jill was to receive the house. The entire fucking house. Mom could have left half to her, the daughter in college who had student loans to pay off, but no, she decided to give it to the one who already had her own apartment and was financially stable.

Fucking thanks, Mom.

101

She suddenly became furious. She imagined unplugging the goddamn machine keeping her mom alive, and hearing the beeping turn into a flatlined tone. She would never do it, of course, but fantasizing about it helped assuage her anger slightly.

Jill, Cheryl, and Violet stood in silence for a long time. Cheryl didn't even hear the beeping of the machine in the background anymore.

"We need to figure out if this is even the real thing," Jill said.

"Sure it is. Why would she have a fake will in the house?" Cheryl asked, doing her best to suppress the audible frustration in her voice.

Jill glowered at her for a prolonged moment, perhaps sensing that enmity.

"She has dementia, remember?" Jill asked with an impatient timbre.

"Yes, it was so sad to see your mother becoming more and more like that," Violet forlornly said.

Both Cheryl and Jill looked at Violet.

"Wait, you knew our mom before the accident?" Cheryl asked.

Violet nodded with a facial expression that indicated that it was the most obvious answer in the world.

"Of course. I've been assisting your mother for the last few months now. When her mental health started to deteriorate rapidly, she decided to hire me because she couldn't deal with everything on her own."

Cheryl and Jill exchanged glares with each other.

"I don't understand why she didn't tell us anything," Cheryl looked at her mom's comatose body.

She suddenly had so many questions. What was going through Mom's head in those last few months since Cheryl's last visit? Was she trying not to be a burden on her daughters? What was it like for her in those last hours when her mind was already devastated by dementia? Was she scared? Confused?

"Unfortunately, I never had those conversations with your mother," Violet said. "I came once a day to make sure everything was okay and give her her meds, and that was all."

"Violet, did you see anything... strange happening with our mother?" Jill asked.

Violet squinted.

"I'm not sure I understand the question," she said.

Jill scratched the back of her head.

"I don't know. Did she do anything suspicious? Something not normal for patients with dementia?"

Violet looked down for a moment with a focused stare. When she looked up, she shook her head.

"Come to think of it, there may have been some things that your mother was doing, but I attributed those things to dementia."

"What kind of things?" Cheryl asked.

Violet walked past the sisters and around the bed to the nightstand. She opened a drawer and bent down to grab something from it. When she turned around, she was holding a stack of papers.

Her head was down as she sauntered towards Cheryl. She handed the papers to her with a stoic expression. Cheryl hesitantly took them and glanced down. Jill moved to her side immediately to see what the big deal was.

The first paper on top had a pencil drawing. It was a *vèvè*, similar to the one they found in the office. The one on the paper was much cruder, with jagged lines jutting out and circles drawn unevenly.

"Is that the *vèvè*?" Jill asked.

Cheryl grabbed the paper on top and put it at the back of the stack. The next paper had some writings. It was scrawled so badly that Cheryl had to bring the paper closer to her face and read slowly. As soon as Cheryl read the first

103

line, she realized that the rest of the lines on the paper were the same sentence.

Papa Legba, grant me protection against the evil in my house.

Papa Legba, grant me protection against the evil in my house.

Papa Legba, grant me protection against the evil in my house.

The lower the sentences went on paper, the more they seemed to have been scrawled in a hurry, and with more mistakes. Some of the sentences were missing punctuation or letters until the final two sentences at the bottom of the paper, which became entirely unintelligible lines of gibberish.

"Oh, it's what you need to say to invoke Papa Legba," Jill said.

Cheryl flipped the paper to the back and looked at the next one. More writings.

"Is that French?" Cheryl asked.

"Haitian Creole," Jill said.

Cheryl glanced at her momentarily, amazed by the profound knowledge of Vodou Jill learned in just a few hours of reading. Cheryl looked at the writing, and although she couldn't discern what it said, she assumed that it was the same as the first page because she recognized the words 'Papa Legba'. She was about to flip the page to the bottom of the stack when she saw something written on the backside.

HES AFTER ME

"Who is? Papa Legba?" Cheryl asked.

"That doesn't make sense," Jill shook her head. "Papa Legba is not an evil loa. Unless Mom did something to piss him off."

For a moment, Cheryl wondered if Jill talked about all of this hypothetically or if she truly believed that there was a Vodou loa in the house. She chose not to share her own thoughts, mostly because she was still angry about the will. She instead flipped to the fourth and final page.

A pencil drawing covered the paper.

There was a wide circle covering a big portion of the paper, as if whoever drew it did so dozens of times over, making it thicker, denser, like a swirling void. Lines jutted out at the edges of both the interior and exterior, like a child's drawing.

In the center of the circle was a figure—a tall, faceless, featureless figure with elongated arms and legs, a thin head, and a hunched back. Sharp fingers protruded from the bony hands, and where the eyes should have been, instead, there were two black orbs from how the pencil was pressed harder against the paper.

Cheryl felt her breath catch in her throat.

"I don't know what exactly plagued your mother's mind," Violet broke the silence. "But whatever it was, it drove her farther into insanity."

Cheryl looked at Jill, who retained a studious glower at the paper.

"What do you think?" Cheryl asked, hoping against hope that Jill would give her an answer that would confirm the presence of something metaphysical and that Cheryl wasn't losing her mind.

Jill shook her head, and for the first time today, Cheryl thought she detected confusion on her older sister.

"I don't know. Dementia must have really gotten to her badly," she said at last.

Cheryl turned to Violet.

"Violet? What do you think?"

Violet slightly cocked her head.

"I think what happened to your mother was unfortunate. If you're asking me if there's something... supernatural happening here, I really cannot say."

"But do you think it's possible?" Cheryl insisted.

She avoided looking at Jill in case she stared at her judgmentally. Violet inhaled deeply through her nose and slightly raised her chin. She clasped her hands together in front of herself and gave a once-over to Cheryl, as if testing to see if she was screwing with the nurse.

"You have to understand, Cheryl, I am a nurse. Whenever something unusual happens—and there *are* a lot of bizarre things happening in my line of work from time to time—my first assumption is never that it's something out of this world."

Cheryl's cheek twitched at the disappointment of Violet's sentence.

"But this house," the nurse continued. "It's unlike anything I have ever experienced before."

"What do you mean by that?" Jill asked.

Violet looked at Annette's motionless body in bed before facing Jill again. The nurse looked like something was on her mind, and she weighed her options if she should talk about what troubled her or not.

"It's an old house, and I can see how someone could go crazy in it."

"How so?" Cheryl interjected.

Violet shrugged.

"I don't know. I'm not a religious person, and I definitely do not believe in ghosts, or anything of the like. But lately, whenever I step inside this house, something doesn't feel quite right. Now, I honestly think that this is just my own paranoia because I've listened to your mother raving on about it for a while, so it must have gotten to me."

"But what if it wasn't just the ravings of a person with dementia?" Cheryl asked.

Violet retained the focused stare for a moment, and then grimaced at Cheryl.

"As I said, this house is old. There are sounds coming from the walls, especially at night. Objects take up strange shadows under the dim light. And your mother used to read and watch things related to it. I think it only exacerbated her condition."

"Mom's in a coma, and somehow her dementia got to us so much that we're discussing spiritual and otherworldly things," Jill scoffed.

Violet laughed uneasily at that.

"Well, it's easy to be influenced by this," she said. "Especially if you spend more time than necessary surrounded by it. There was even similar research done which explained that spending too much time listening to radical radios or watching radical TV can cause us to become like that."

Jill thought about that for a moment. Violet was right. Carried by what happened to their mother, Cheryl and Jill had started to succumb to a form of mass hysteria that there was something going on in the house.

"You're right, Violet," Jill said. "Whatever did happen here was logical. Our mother had dementia, that much we know for sure. She started going crazy living alone in the house, and eventually began concocting rituals that she thought would protect her from whatever she thought wanted to harm her. And then one night, she got scared by something she thought was there so much that she literally fell into a coma. Case closed."

Silence fell on the room.

Cheryl didn't look like she bought that theory, and it was impossible to tell what Violet thought.

"What happened doesn't matter anymore," Jill added. "What matters is that we need to decide what to do next."

"I'll leave you two to take care of your matters. I will be here Monday around the same time," Violet nodded.

"Thank you, Violet. I'll see you to the door," Cheryl smiled politely.

As the two of them exited, Jill was left alone with her mother in the room. She looked at the will that Cheryl found under the bed and then at her mother. Jill tried to imagine what her mother would be like if she woke up right now.

Would she apologize to Jill for mistreating her? Or would she retract what she wrote in the will once she realized that she might live for another few years? Jill strode out of the room and grabbed the doorknob. As she closed the door halfway, she glanced at her mother one last time.

This is a small price to pay for the hell you put me through, Mother, she thought to herself and closed the door.

Chapter 17

The knocking on the door came less than a minute after Cheryl saw Violet out.

Must be Erika, she thought to herself with exuberance.

She could already practically taste the chocolate nut cookies. But it wasn't just the cookies that Cheryl looked forward to. Erika didn't just bring amazing cookies whenever she arrived. She brought an aura that filled the entire house with a contagious positivity—and Cheryl desperately needed a little bit of that right now.

Sure enough, when she opened the door, the kind old lady stood at the entrance, holding a tray of cookies.

"Hello, Cherry, sweetheart!" she excitedly exclaimed.

"Erika! Come on in!" Cheryl matched her tone.

Whenever Cheryl was in a bad mood, she wasn't very enthusiastic about someone visiting, and she made no effort to mask that, but with Erika, it was impossible to stay indifferent.

As soon as Erika stepped inside, the smell of freshly baked cookies wafted to Cheryl's nose. The pleasant redolence was more than just the fragrance of a tasty dessert. It was a reminiscence of Cheryl's childhood, of the days when she was carefree and happy.

"I'm so sorry for not arriving earlier, sweetie. Here are the cookies I promised," Erika said, as she pushed the tray into Cheryl's hands.

"You carried this tray all the way from your house?" Cheryl raised her eyebrows. "What if you tripped and fell?"

The road between Erika's and Mom's houses was not difficult, and there was a sidewalk connecting them, but for Erika to get here, she would need to go down a slight gradient.

"I'm more agile than you think, Cherry. I used to run some sprints back in the day before I broke my hip," Erika winked.

"Hi, Erika," Jill had come downstairs to greet the old woman.

"Hello, dear. I baked some cookies for you and your sister. Would you like to try some?"

"No, thank you. I wouldn't want to eat Cheryl's favorite cookies," Jill sardonically said.

There was a moment of silence in the foyer. Cheryl started to feel awkward, so she spoke up.

"Well, how about we all go to the living room and eat some of these magnificent cookies? I could also make us some tea or coffee."

"You're very kind, sweetie," Erika said warmly. "But if it's okay with you, I would like to go see Annette."

Her face turned stern when she said that.

"Of course. Do you need a moment alone with her?" Cheryl asked as she held the cookie tray from the bottom with one hand.

She used the other hand to grab one of the warm cookies and took a bite. The savory taste of nuts and chocolate was as heavenly as she remembered it to be. Over the years, Cheryl often tried various products with nuts in them, including bagels, pancakes, cakes, etc., and only a few of them managed to get close to replicating (but not surpassing) the recipe that Erika made.

"No, no. I have no dark secrets to share with your mother," Erika chuckled. "So you girls feel free to join if you like."

Jill nodded with a sour expression on her face. It was clear to Cheryl what that look meant—*No, I'm good, you guys go ahead.*

"Okay. I'll go with you," Cheryl said. "Jill, would you mind putting these in the kitchen?"

"Sure," Jill said with a blank look, and took the tray.

Cheryl noticed her giving a subtle, pitiful glare to the cookies before turning around and disappearing through the door leading to the living room. Erika followed Cheryl upstairs towards Mom's room.

For once, Cheryl was glad that she managed to grab a moment alone with Erika because she wanted to ask her some things related to Mom, the house, and perhaps Vodou. But she would take it slow—she didn't want to scare Erika off, especially if she already suspected that something was going on.

From what little information Cheryl had about Erika, the old woman was somewhat superstitious, and if she really visited Mom weekly or even monthly, then there's no way she wouldn't notice if something was wrong. Cheryl just hoped that she'd be able to keep the conversation a secret from Jill. If her older sister heard Cheryl asking Erika about anything paranormal, she would surely make fun of her for it.

Cheryl opened the door to her mom's room and stepped aside, allowing Erika to walk in first. As soon as she did, the old woman began speaking in a soft tone.

"Annie, hi. It's me, Erika. How are you today?"

She took up a seat on the chair next to the bed. Cheryl walked in and closed the door. Erika continued whispering softly to Annette. She told her what wonderful daughters she has and how much they look like her. She also gave her words of encouragement, telling her that she was sure she'd wake up soon, and that she's lucky to have such caring daughters to be here for her.

If only Erika knew how false that was. Cheryl and Jill haven't discussed it yet, but the choice was pretty obvious. Mom would have to be put in a place where she would get full-time medical care. As for the house, that was no longer on the table for negotiation. The house now belonged to Jill, and she could do whatever she wanted to with it.

After Erika was done softly speaking to Mom, she and Cheryl remained silent for a few minutes. The low and steady

111

beeping of the EKG machine was intoxicating, and Cheryl felt her eyelids becoming heavy with sleepiness. She didn't have much time before either Erika decided to leave, or Jill barged in. She had to talk to the woman now.

"You knew my mother well, didn't you?" Cheryl asked.

"I would hope so. We knew each other for years, even before you and your sister were born. I would even go as far as to say that we weren't just neighbors, but really good friends."

"It's kinda interesting how you two became so close despite the age difference," Cheryl smiled.

"Annette and I clicked right away. She is smart, really smart. Even when she was young and just moved here with your father, I felt like I could always talk to her at the same level as I would to some women my age."

"Were you also good with my dad?"

Erika lolled her head from left to right.

"Kind of. We were never exactly close, but we didn't have a hostile relationship, either."

Erika looked at Annette.

"If you came to visit my mom every week, then you must have noticed some weird things going on in the house," Cheryl blatantly said.

Erika continued staring at Annette, but Cheryl noticed her gaze freezing. The old lady raised a hand to scratch her cheek, and her fingers trembled violently. It could have been from old age, but it also could have been from something else.

"I have," she finally said and locked eyes with Cheryl.

"You have?" Cheryl widened her eyes in surprise.

"Yes. Of course I have. Anyone who remotely knew your mother would have noticed it, let alone someone like me."

Cheryl waited with bated breath. She had no idea if she and Erika were on the same page, and she was impatient to find out. Erika looked at Annette once more with a forlorn smile.

"Your mother and I went on a vacation together once, you know? It was a ladies-only vacation to Haiti a few years after Jill was born. Your dad insisted that Annette take some time for herself to relax while he took care of Jill. She didn't even want to hear about it at first, but with my help, your dad managed to convince her."

Cheryl nodded.

"It was supposed to be a nice trip. It was supposed to last for just a week, but we returned only four days later."

"Why?" Cheryl jumped in, far too impatient for Erika's slow manner of speaking.

Erika turned to face her. She shifted in her seat momentarily and placed her hands on her lap. Her face suddenly turned dark and serious, which was even more exacerbated by the lack of light in the room.

"Your mother started to behave strangely. Back when we were on that trip in Haiti, we went to visit an ancient cave. Ancient spirits supposedly inhabited the cave, but it was all just an urban legend. The cave was open for tourists, and for a small fee, you could enter."

Cheryl stood ramrod straight, her arms limply hanging next to her body as she listened with rapt fascination. Erika continued.

"It was a rainy day, and despite that, the temperature was very high. I remember it like it was yesterday. Your mother and I were the only tourists that day who went to visit the cave. We paid the man at the entrance, and he warned us not to leave the marked paths while inside."

Erika raised one hand to her face once more, and Cheryl noticed that it trembled even more violently now.

"The cave was strange. Some people would describe it as beautiful, but to this day, I can't think of any other way to describe it except 'strange'. It had these unnatural-looking shapes, drawings, symbols... Annette was especially fascinated by the place, and driven by her enthusiasm, I suggested we disobey the rules and go outside the marked areas," she shrugged with an expression that simply said *'whoops'*.

Cheryl knew that this was the moment when something bad happened in the story. She brusquely nodded and continued listening to Erika.

"The cave got even weirder there. The drawings we saw in the tourist section were more complex, and the symbols more detailed. Now, it was a large cave with wide passages, mind you, so there was practically no way to get lost or anything like that. At least we thought not. I honestly don't know how it happened, but all I remember is staring at one of the wall drawings one moment, and then turning around and seeing your mom gone," Erika's voice took on a brittle timbre. "I shouted after her, but all I heard was my own echo. I panicked, and ran through the cave, but the deeper I went, the more I seemed to run in circles. I ran like that for what seemed like ages, calling out for Annette, and then... then I saw her."

Erika's eyes were wide now, and her hands which were still on her lap, trembled like a dog trying to shake off the rain. She also spoke in a much quieter tone, barely louder than the beeping of the machine.

"She was standing in front of one of the walls with the drawings. Just standing there. I remember thanking God that she was okay and telling her that she gave me a good scare. But she didn't respond; just kept staring at the drawing on the wall. It was as if she was hypnotized," Erika took a moment to compose herself. "You have to understand, Cheryl. I didn't think this cave was really possessed by anything otherworldly, but when I stood there behind Annette in front of that gigantic, unnatural-looking drawing, I wanted nothing more than to run."

Cheryl swallowed. It felt as if she had sandpaper in her throat.

"But I didn't run. I couldn't leave Annette there. Something was wrong, I could tell that much, I just didn't know what. You also need to realize that there was no reason for me to get so scared. I had a fright losing her for a few minutes, yes, but I was so scared when I found her standing there, more than I've ever been in my life."

"What happened?" Cheryl found herself asking breathlessly.

Her eyes started to sting from a lack of blinking.

"I approached your mother from behind, the entire time calling her. I said, 'Annie, come on. Let's go back, Annie.', but she ignored me. Even as I stopped right next to her, she continued staring at the wall, even as I called out to her over and over. I did so in a whisper. It just felt wrong to speak loudly there. And I couldn't look at the drawing on the wall. I only glanced at it briefly, but every time I did, it felt like it was staring right back at me."

Cheryl felt her blood turning to ice. The way Erika described everything made her feel like she was really with her in that Haitian cave. Erika clasped a hand over her mouth for a long moment. It looked like she was about to vomit, but she then put her hand down and continued speaking.

"As soon as I touched Annette's shoulder, she screamed. And I don't mean screaming because she got startled. No, this was shrieking at the top of her lungs, as if someone attacked her. She fell on the floor and writhed and screamed, and I tried calming her down, but she was inconsolable."

Erika put a hand on her neck and cleared her throat. She cast a furtive glance at Annette before facing Cheryl once more.

"She must have screamed for some five minutes or so, because at one point, the man at the entrance showed up. He yelled at us that we shouldn't be here, and tried chasing us out. When he saw the condition your mother was in, he instead decided to help us. He spoke some words in a language I didn't recognize over and over, and over, for minutes. Gradually, Annette's screaming stopped, and she lost consciousness. We took her to the hospital right after that."

Erika put a hand over her mouth once more and shook her head. Cheryl saw the glimmer of tears forming in her eyes.

"She was never the same after that happened. When she woke up in the hospital, she had no recollection of what happened to her. She didn't even remember that we planned on going to the cave. We decided to go home earlier because we were obviously distressed—I more than her. On our way back, she kept looking around, like... I don't know... like she was on the run from someone. A few times, she even asked me if I heard something. I never knew what she meant, but she swore that she heard something that wasn't really there."

"Is that when her dementia started?" Cheryl asked.

Erika shook her head.

"No, the dementia didn't come for years. It was the paranoia that took over her life."

"Paranoia?"

"Yes," Erika nodded and wiped the tears from her eyes. "Like I said, she wasn't the same ever since that cave incident. I thought that it was maybe just trauma and that she would return to her old self soon, but as time went by, it became obvious that Annette as we knew her, wasn't coming back. It was like a completely different person took her over, and yet, it was still her. I could see my old friend resurfacing sometimes, but those moments were so, so rare. Your dad noticed it, too, of course."

"What did he do about it?"

"At first, he ignored it. Just like me, he thought that the paranoia would leave in time. But it only got worse. Annette spent more and more time in her office, read up on ancient religions and spirituality, and even engaged in some sort of rituals. Your dad ignored all of it, figured it was a coping mechanism for whatever scared her in that cave," Erika sighed. "But when all of it became too much, he tried fixing

116

her. Took her to all sorts of doctors and such, but nothing worked. Eventually, I think he just decided to live with her. In the meantime, you were born, and both your father and I thought that this would fix Annette's paranoia. It only got worse after that."

Cheryl nodded and crossed her arms.

"Eventually, your dad got fed up with it all and decided to leave. He took Jill with him because Annette treated her badly."

"So, you knew about the Vodou rituals that my mother conducted in the house? But why? Why did she do it? What did she see in that cave that scared her so much that she couldn't recover for years?"

A knock resounded on the door, startling both Erika and Cheryl. Erika hastily wiped the remainder of her tears away and forced a smile.

"Hey. Everything okay in here?" Jill asked softly.

"Yeah. We were just remembering stuff about Mom," Cheryl quickly lied.

Jill softly smiled and nodded.

"Sorry for interrupting. Cheryl, I just wanted to let you know that I made some calls, and um..."

"The will is the real thing?"

"Yeah," Jill nodded. "But I don't plan to have the whole house to myself, so I wanted to see if I could talk with you a bit later about what we should do with it."

"Come on, Jill. You don't owe me anything," Cheryl scoffed. "Mom left the house to you, so you should do whatever you want with it."

Right now, Cheryl didn't care about anything as insignificant as a stupid, old house. She was eager to find out what happened to her mom, and Jill's interruption wasn't welcome.

"We'll talk about it later," Jill dismissed Cheryl's last sentence.

Erika stood up.

"Actually, I should get going, too. I'm feeling kind of tired," she said.

Dammit.

"I'll see you out, Erika," Cheryl said, hoping that this didn't mean she was done talking about what happened to her mom.

Jill went down to the living room, while Cheryl saw Erika to the front door. On the way there, Erika's mood returned to her usual jovial one, and she talked about what a nice day it was and how Jill and Cheryl should eat all the cookies and put on some weight.

Once she was outside, she grabbed Cheryl's wrist—not gently this time, but with a trembling, and yet somewhat firm grip as much as an old person could muster—and spoke, "Come by my house tonight, Cherry. And I will tell you everything I know."

Cheryl thanked her and said goodbye. As she closed the door, her mind raced a million miles an hour. She wanted to rush into the living room and tell Jill everything that Erika told her. But Jill was a skeptic, and she wouldn't believe a word of it. In the best-case scenario, she'd dismiss Erika's story as an old person's paranoia.

She could hardly wait for tonight.

Chapter 18

Jill still couldn't believe it. Her mother left the house to her! Even after she verified the information with the phone call, she still didn't believe it. Why would Annette do it? Her mother never showed any regret for treating Jill the way she did, so why the sudden change of heart?

Probably because she knew that her time was almost up, and she wanted to fix things before dying.

Jill never knew whether her mother was religious or not, but she knew that people never really thought about fixing their mistakes until the threat of death started looming over their heads.

The front door closed, and moments later, Cheryl walked into the living room. She looked exhausted, as if she had spent two nights partying without a break.

"Have a good talk with Erika?" Jill asked.

She was sitting on the couch, and Cheryl took a seat on the sofa across from her. Her little sister shrugged.

"Nothing special, I guess."

Jill leaned forward.

"Listen, um. I know that this thing with the will is not small news. I just want you to know that—"

Cheryl grimaced and shook her head to interrupt Jill.

"Let's just drop it, Jill. Okay? You got the house, it's yours. Now you can finally stop complaining about how Mom always loved me more than you."

That came as a gut punch to Jill. She narrowed her eyes, flabbergasted at what Cheryl just said. It caught her off guard so abruptly that she didn't even know what to say back in response. Cheryl whipped out her phone and frantically started scrolling through something.

"This has nothing to do with that, Cheryl," Jill finally added.

"Oh, yeah? Then what?" Cheryl lowered her phone and looked up at Jill with a hostile expression.

Suddenly, Jill got angry, too.

"You're a spoiled brat, you know that?" she said. "All your life, you got used to being in the center of Mom's attention while I had to fight for it. And now, for once, you're not Mom's favorite, and the whole world stops because of it!"

"Well, excuse me for making a big deal out of not getting a portion of the fucking house I grew up in!"

"You think I wanted this house?! You think I even wanted to be here in the first place?! I hate Mom, you understand?! I *hate* her!"

The final sentence pierced the air and was followed by a deafening silence. It felt liberating to say that. Jill thought it many times, but she never actually vocalized it. Cheryl's face contorted into a grimace, but then she returned to the assault with that same alacrity from before.

"You say that I'm a spoiled brat. But you know what? You are one ungrateful bitch!"

Jill shot up to her feet. She was pretty much ready to pull Cheryl's hair out.

"What should I be grateful for, Cheryl?! For being treated like an unwanted child all my life?! For always being the one who got in trouble while you got off the hook easily?! For having to dread coming back home from school because I didn't know if Mom was gonna have one of her mood swings?! You have no idea what it was like for me, and how could you?! You were always pampered, and you got everything you always wanted!" Jill had to fight to suppress the tears that threatened to well up in her eyes. "Well, guess what? You're not in the center of the world, Cheryl! Nobody has to conform to your whims like Mom did when you were a kid!"

Cheryl clambered up to her feet, red in the face.

"You think you're so much better than me!" she said. "Because you have a family and a good job?! Is that it?! Well, go on, keep the fucking house! If Mom was so horrible to you, then I don't understand what you're doing here in the first place!"

She spun on her heel and started towards the door. But Jill wasn't done spewing vile words towards her. No, no. Cheryl started this war, but Jill was going to finish it.

"You're right, I do think I'm better than you! And you know why?! Because I'm not so self-centered! Why do you think Tom left you?! Maybe stop and look around you for a moment instead of just focusing on you, you, and only y—"

A booming sound from upstairs caused Jill to stop speaking. A song on the radio from their mother's room began playing. Cheryl looked how Jill felt—terrified. Both sisters instinctively looked up towards the ceiling, listening to the distorted, muffled music upstairs.

Jill silently gestured for Cheryl to follow her upstairs, instantly forgetting about the heated argument. Cheryl nodded timorously. Jill took the lead, and as soon as they approached the stairs, the song got louder. Jill recognized it as *'I want to know what love is'* by Foreigner.

Tentatively, Jill started climbing the stairs, step by step, her eyes fixated on the top. She heard Cheryl's terrified, trembling breath right behind her. The moment Jill set foot on the second floor, the song that played from her mother's room started stuttering, repeating the same few words over and over.

Face it aga—
Face it aga—
Face it aga—

Jill noticed something else, too. She turned to Cheryl, whose face was now drained of all color.

"Did you leave Mom's door open?"

Cheryl shook her head incredulously. Jill glanced back at the door. It was slightly ajar, just barely a crack. There was an intruder in the house. And he was in Mom's room.

"Stay here while I check it out," Jill said.

She didn't look at Cheryl to see if she would agree with her. She tip-toed across the hallway, never once looking away from the door or blinking. As she approached the door, she peeked through the crack, expecting to see some sort of movement in the room.

Nothing, and if there was, it was too dark to see.

Jill grabbed the edge of the door and opened it. The door luckily produced no creaking noise. She gave the room another once over before stepping inside.

She barely had enough time to take a step forward when she heard a loud thud.

Cheryl stayed at the top of the stairs. Her arms were crossed, but she had her phone ready in her hand to call the cops if necessary. Somehow, however, she felt that the police wouldn't be able to help them with whatever was going on in the house.

Jill disappeared into the room and then—

A muffled thud and a scream pierced the air.

"Jill!" Cheryl shouted.

"Cheryl! Get over here, quick!" Jill shouted from the room in what sounded like sheer panic.

Cheryl sprinted across the room and ran inside, looking around, the adrenaline pumping through her giving her the boost of courage she desperately needed to fight whoever was inside. She saw Jill standing in front of the bed with tense shoulders, her back straight as an arrow. Mom was no longer in bed.

"What the fu—" Cheryl started, and then her voice disappeared when she looked on the floor to the left.

Mom was lying on her back on the floor next to the bed. She was in the exact same position as she was when sleeping, and the first thing that came to Cheryl's mind was that she rolled off the bed and continued lying in a coma.

But everything was still attached to her, and the machine and the covers on the bed were neatly pushed to the side, so it looked like someone had gently picked her up and placed her on the floor.

Cheryl looked around the room once more, just to make sure Jill didn't, in her shock, miss seeing any intruders. It must have been almost a whole minute of Cheryl and Jill just staring at their mother's body in a stupor, with *Foreigner* repeating the same lyrics brokenly when Jill finally broke into a gait forward.

She stepped around Mom's body like it was contagious and furiously slammed the radio's power button. The stuttering song stopped, leaving the room in silence. The sisters shared a terrified glance with each other. Jill rarely looked scared, but right now, Cheryl saw palpable fear in her eyes.

"What the fuck?" Jill asked with a hint of frustration.

Cheryl broke out of her trance and looked around the room one last time, just in case Jill had missed a potential intruder in her shock. She knelt down and looked under the bed. She expected to see a face staring back at her, but of course, no one was there.

■ ■

Jill ran a hand through her hair. What the fuck was going on here? Was someone really in the house? Where did they go?

She glanced at the window and realized that it was closed. They didn't escape through there. There were no other hiding spots in the room. Jill jerked her head towards Cheryl, causing her hair to fall into her face.

"We need to check the rest of the house," she said.

Cheryl agreed. Together, they went from room to room until they checked every nook and cranny in the house. Eventually, they came to the conclusion that no one was there. Once they were sure that they were safe, they lifted their mom back on the bed and covered her with the blankets.

"Shouldn't we call the police?" Cheryl shrugged.

Her current docile mood was incongruous to her usual volatile personality, Jill noticed. She thought about Cheryl's suggestion to call the cops.

"We shouldn't jump the gun here," she shook her head.

"There could be someone dangerous in the house, Jill!" Cheryl exploded, returning to her normal self.

"We just checked the house. For all we know, Mom just rolled out of bed on her own."

"And turned on the radio in the process?" Cheryl raised an eyebrow.

Cheryl wasn't going to believe her, Jill knew that right away. She pulled out her phone and said.

"Let's call Violet and see what she says."

Cheryl crossed her arms expectantly. She nervously shifted her weight from one foot to the other. Jill dialed Violet's number and waited. It started ringing, and after a few rings, Violet answered.

"This is Violet. Please leave a message and I'll get back to you as soon as I can," the voicemail said in Violet's frigid tone.

"Hi, Violet. It's Jill. Listen, something strange is going on with Annette. So um, would you mind getting back to me when you find a moment? Thanks," she stated on the voicemail, and then ended the call.

She was disappointed that she couldn't get Violet on the line right now to prove to Cheryl that this sort of thing was possible with comatose patients. A part of her also wanted Violet to reassure her as well, and not just Cheryl.

When Jill looked up at Cheryl, she saw her staring at her with a stern expression.

"I know what you're suggesting, Cheryl," she said.

"I'm not suggesting anything."

"Ghosts aren't real."

"I'm not suggesting that!"

"Yes, you are. And that's fine. But let's be rational for a moment here. Both the front and back entrances were locked before Erika arrived. All the windows were closed. There was no way that someone just snuck inside without us knowing about it. So that eliminates the possibility of an intruder pushing Mom off the bed. And why would they do it in the first place?"

Cheryl looked nowhere in particular. Jill could tell that she wanted to believe her, but she was just too unnerved after what she saw.

"I think... yeah, maybe you're right," Cheryl looked back at her and pressed her lips together into a thin slit.

She said that in a patronizing tone. It was the tone she used whenever she dropped the ball and agreed with the other person just to get the argument over with.

"Alright," Jill simply nodded, following her lead and also dropping the line of conversation.

"Listen, um... I'm gonna go to Erika's for a bit. I need a moment away from this place."

"Yeah, sure. Just call me if you need anything," Jill solicitously remarked.

Cheryl nodded. Without a word, she left the room, stampeded down the stairs, and a moment later, the front door opened and slammed shut so loudly that the window rattled.

Jill suddenly felt uneasy standing in her mother's bedroom. She exited and closed the door behind her. She suddenly felt a strong urge to check the one room she and Cheryl still didn't check for any intruders—the office.

As Jill approached the door and grabbed the knob, she felt a knot forming in her stomach. For some reason, she knew that she would not like what she would find inside, and yet, she was unable to just leave the room be. She pushed the door open and peered inside.

She screamed at what she saw.

Chapter 19

Erika fumbled for the keys of her house and unlocked the door. Her hands still violently trembled, even five minutes after leaving Annette's house. For the duration of her walk home, she contemplated whether telling Cheryl about the cave was a good idea.

She hadn't planned on saying anything at all—ever. Annette made her promise once Cheryl was born that she would never tell a soul. At first, Erika didn't even know what it was that she wasn't supposed to tell anyone. All she knew was that Annette was convinced that something otherworldly was after her and that she was trying to protect herself.

But just like everyone else, Erika dismissed Annette's paranoia as just that—paranoia.

She entered the house and closed the door behind her. She locked the door for the first time this early in years. As Erika made her way towards the kitchen, she held a hand over her mouth, reprimanding herself over and over for opening up to Cheryl.

Now the poor girl might go down the same path as Annette. And what if that leads to the same madness that Annette went through? Cheryl would surely visit later, and then Erika would fix the mistake she made. She will tell Cheryl that she was just scared and confused, and that her ravings shouldn't be taken seriously.

Erika walked over to the kitchen sink and poured a glass of water for herself. Her legs suddenly felt wobbly. She had to hold the glass with both hands to stop the water from spilling. As soon as she took one sip, she felt much better. She turned around with the glass still in her hands and placed it on the counter. She sighed deeply as she glanced towards the living room. A low bang upstairs startled her.

Erika recognized that sound. She knew it all too well after living in this house for almost forty years. It was the window in the hallway upstairs. It had faulty hinges, and whenever it was left open, it would often slam shut from the draft, only to reopen on its own. Erika's late husband Shane promised he'd fix it, but he never did. Erika must have forgotten to shut it before leaving.

She climbed upstairs, scolding herself for becoming so senile. Old age, after all. Every day, she left that window open for an hour or so a day to let some fresh air in, but she would put a rag or an old shirt on the windowsill to keep it from slamming into the frame. Maybe she forgot to put the rag there today in a hurry, when baking the chocolate nut cookies.

It wouldn't be the first time it happened. But the solution was simple. Erika would just need to stop opening that faulty window. The last thing she needed would be a shattered window.

The bang came from upstairs louder this time, almost causing Erika to jump out of her skin.

She placed a hand on her chest, feeling the drumming of her heart. She climbed upstairs just in time to hear another startling bang from the window. When she finally reached it, she realized that the sound was indeed, coming from the window slamming.

She breathed a sigh of relief. A part of her thought that maybe it was something else, something... unnatural, but she dismissed that thought, telling herself that she was just influenced by Annette's paranoia.

It happened in the past, too. She would visit Annette and listen to her talking about dark figures that visited her in the night. Erika would nod and listen, and then she would go home and start to feel like someone was standing just behind her all night long. On those nights, she would sleep with the lights on and a Bible next to her bed.

Erika approached the open window handle just as it was about to slam shut in full force. The glass rattled even at the slightest movement from the years of damage it sustained.

"Shane, Shane," she said to herself melancholically with the shake of her head. "Maybe it's about time I fix this stupid window myse—"

Something caused Erika to stop speaking. Did she hear that right just now? She jerked her head to the right and observed the hallway. The spot where Erika stood was illuminated by the moonlight, but the hallway was enveloped in gradual darkness, the end of it not even visible through the blackness.

Erika stared into the dark, squinting through her thick glasses. She couldn't tell if there was anything there, not just from the dark, but from how dirty her glasses were. Erika raised a hand and took the glasses off, lowering them to her shirt in order to wipe them.

Everything was so blurry without her glasses. Blind as a bat, she'd always say.

A dull thud came from the end of the corridor, causing Erika to jump. The glasses slipped from her hand and fell to the carpet with a muffled sound.

"Oh, blast it!" Erika said as she knelt down, ignoring her aching back and knees.

She felt the carpet with her palms and fingers while focusing her gaze at the end of the corridor, even though she couldn't see a thing. She clapped the floor on all sides, but the glasses were nowhere to be found. This is what always happened to dropped items—they somehow end up on another continent.

Erika clapped her palm on the floor in frustration and then stopped. Her clap echoed. It echoed? Was that right? She slammed the floor with her other palm harder this time, and it echoed again.

Erika waited.

Silence.

"Hello? Is anybody there?" she squinted harder, but to no avail.

Her eyes were starting to hurt from exertion. Convinced that it must have been her imagination, Erika continued searching for her glasses—with gentler motions this time.

Even so, the sounds of her hand shuffling against the carpet echoed. What was going on here? Erika brought her palm down on the carpet abruptly. It echoed once more. She clapped twice in a row. Both claps echoed. Erika held her breath as she stared at the blurry corridor in front of herself.

She raised her hand and brought it down, just above the carpet, but didn't touch it.

Clap.

The sound came a foot in front of Erika. The old woman screamed and scooted backward. She clambered up to her feet as quickly as her frail bones and muscles were willing to cooperate, ignoring what she thought was a blurry figure standing in front of her in the hallway.

She grabbed the railing of the staircase and felt the first step with her toes without stopping. In the end, this turned out to be a mistake because Erika missed the next step and felt herself stumbling forward and losing balance.

Through a blurry vision, she saw everything around her spinning and felt immense pain exploding all over her body each time she landed on a step. She forgot all about the pain in her body when she felt something hard and sharp colliding with her neck.

Her tumbling came to an end, and Erika's neck pulsated with an intensity that she never felt before. It took her a moment to realize that she couldn't inhale or exhale.

As she lay there, motionless and scared, she forgot all about the sounds she heard upstairs and instead wondered where she would end up once she was dead.

Chapter 20

It was already night when Cheryl stepped outside. It was somewhat chilly, despite summer almost being here.

The house is barely warmer, Cheryl thought to herself.

She was glad to be out of the house for a bit. It didn't even hit her how choked she felt inside the house until she stepped outside. And it wasn't something that she was already used to by now. Usually, she'd have the feeling of needing her own space whenever she visited a small place filled with people, but that wasn't the case here.

Mom's house was huge, and only she and Jill were inside. It felt as if the walls themselves were closing in on Cheryl. No...even worse than that. Like someone—*something*—was in there and sitting on Cheryl's chest, twenty-four seven.

She couldn't believe how Jill didn't notice it. Maybe she just wasn't that attuned to negative energy. Or maybe she was so attuned to it that it felt normal to her. It didn't matter. Once Cheryl got the truth out of Erika, she would go back to Jill and tell her everything, and then the two of them were going to get to the bottom of this.

Maybe Mom could still be saved? Maybe she was in a coma because that malevolent presence was keeping her imprisoned, kind of like in that horror movie? It was far-fetched, but right now, it was the only thing she got. She had to hope that Mom was not lost.

Cheryl had so many things to say to her. To tell her that she loved her, and that she grew up to be the woman that she is today thanks to her (even if Jill thought she was a brat), to tell her that she'd gladly take her into her own home to take care of her, if she had one...

To ask her why she gave Jill the house.

That thought infuriated Cheryl, but she tried not to think about it. She tried telling herself that Mom probably had a good reason to give Jill the house. She just wished that Mom had explained to her why she did it so that Cheryl didn't feel so excluded and estranged.

Cheryl walked up the path towards Erika's house, enjoying the soft breeze that blew around her face and exposed arms. She glanced back towards Mom's house. The lights were on in most of the windows, and despite the surrounding darkness of the night, the house barely glowed with a meager, orange radiance, like a Jack-o-lantern on a porch for Halloween.

I would never want to live there, even if I got the house. Not after these last few days.

Come to think of it, she didn't want anything to do with the house, after all. If she could help it, she'd never step into it ever again. Even if Mom stayed in a coma, Cheryl would not take care of her there. Maybe she would be able to get her transferred to a hospital in California (since Jill wouldn't care about her being in Oregon), but that would probably be really expensive.

Cheryl ogled Erika's house. The lights in the living room were on, but the rest of the house was engulfed in darkness. Cheryl hoped that Erika didn't have second thoughts about sharing some more information with her.

As she approached the house, she was overcome with a meager nostalgic feeling—meager because the dread of the impending conversation loomed just above her. Had it not been for that, she would have remembered with relish all the times when she visited Erika's home for some cookies or the other treats that she used to bake, when Cheryl took a break from playing.

Right now, all she saw was a lonesome house of an old woman, segregated from everyone else. And yet, the people in Sams Valley were always good to each other. Neighbors often helped those in need, invited each other for meals, etc.

132

There was more distance between each house, but there was no distance between the people.

Cheryl walked up the walkway leading to the enormous house and rang the doorbell. A loud *ding-dong* carried through the house. She waited, feeling like she was on eggshells. She nervously looked around herself, cradling her arms and listening to the loud chirping of the insects.

When Erika didn't answer the door after a whole minute, Cheryl rang the doorbell again. Still nothing. She tried knocking on the door, but there was no answer. That was weird. Maybe Erika just didn't hear it. She was old, after all. The lights were on, so she must have been home.

Cheryl decided to try the back door instead.

She waded around the house, her shoes rustling through the tall and long, rarely-mowed grass. Why didn't Erika hire someone to cut the grass for her? She obviously took care of her front lawn, but the side and back of the house were horrendous. Cheryl decided she would do it for her first thing in the morning. It's not like she had too many things to do around her mom's house, anyway.

Cheryl stopped in front of the back door leading to the kitchen and rapped on the door.

"Erika?" she called out, peering through the pane of glass.

She could clearly see the kitchen from here. A glass of unfinished water on the counter, and literally nothing else. It was evident that Erika kept her kitchen clean. Of course, that's probably where she spent most of her time.

Cheryl knocked on the door three more times.

By now, it became clear to her that Erika probably wasn't home, or if she was, that something was wrong. A part of her told her that she was just firmly asleep, but Cheryl refused to believe that.

That feeling of fear and panic only intensified when she twisted the knob and found the door to be unlocked. Cheryl gently pushed the door open, allowing it to creak loudly until it stopped moving.

"Erika?" she called out once more.

Her voice sounded muffled in the enormity of the kitchen. She glimpsed towards the living room, which was only partially illuminated by the strong kitchen light. Cheryl began ambling forward. She suddenly felt like she was intruding; like she was somewhere where she wasn't welcome. But that was silly, right? Erika always told her to let herself in when she was a kid. She wouldn't get angry for finding Cheryl inside her home, right?

So then, why did she have this feeling of dread building up at the pit of her stomach, so potently that it was almost debilitating?

"Erika?" Cheryl called out again, but her voice was just a whisper now.

She stepped onto the carpet of the living room. It was too dark to see anything, even with the partial radiance coming from the kitchen. She took out her phone and turned on her torch.

She wished she hadn't.

Chapter 21

Jill couldn't believe what she was looking at.

The *vèvè* was still there, on the wall. If anything, it only seemed to become more prominent, as it brightly glowed with a black color, even in the darkness of the room. But that's not what caught Jill's eye. What made her scream was the message written in a crude, black paint above the *vèvè*.

WE HAD A DEAL

At first, Jill was frozen. She held a hand clasped over her mouth to further suppress the scream building up in her lungs. Someone was inside the house. Someone—

Crash!

Something in the room fell and broke. Jill only saw a sliver of something toppling from the shelf and disappearing in the darkness, but the shattering sound was unmistakable.

"What the fuck!" she shouted.

Or at least, she thought she did, but the sentence came out as a frightened whimper. She swiveled one hundred and eighty degrees in one quick motion and started dashing towards the stairs.

She was in great danger and had to get out of the house right now. She raced down the stairs and towards the front door. She grabbed the doorknob and yanked it backward.

The door wouldn't budge.

Jill rattled the doorknob violently, not understanding why the door wouldn't open. Cheryl left it unlocked when she left just five minutes ago, there was no doubt about that.

"Come on, open up, open up!" she squealed in terror.

A loud pop exploded above Jill, and she was immediately plunged into darkness. She screamed and turned around, slamming her back against the door. No, it wasn't darkness. It was complete and utter blackness. For a moment, Jill couldn't see a finger in front of her nose. Her eyes may as well have been plucked out of her sockets.

She hyperventilated and stared ahead, fumbling with one hand for the knob. She continued rattling it, but the door refused to cooperate.

Crack.

The sound came from somewhere near the top of the stairs, like a joint snapping from hours of not being used. Jill stopped moving. She gasped, panting louder before calming down her breathing into shallow, panicked breaths.

Thud. Thud. Thud.

The footsteps descended the stairs, getting closer to Jill with each step.

Thud. Crack.

The sickening bony sound almost made Jill scream, but she kept her mouth closed. She breathed in and out deeply through her nose, probably giving away her position not just to the intruder in the house, but to the whole fucking neighborhood.

Thud.

The step resounded at the bottom of the stairs. Jill kept her eyes fixated in front of herself, but she couldn't see a thing. No, there was something there. A short silhouette, standing and... twitching? Its head convulsed violently, but it made no sound.

Crunch.

The step came on the floor in front of Jill, right where the foyer ceiling lightbulb shards probably fell after popping.

Crunch. Crunch.

Two steps closer. And then they stopped.

"Who are you?!" Jill shouted. "What do you want from me?!"

Crunch.

The sound was more muffled this time, like eating cereal with a closed mouth. Jill couldn't see the twitching figure anymore. If it remained there, then it was too dark to see it.

And despite logic telling her that it was right in front of her, Jill couldn't budge. She hadn't realized that even her breathing had stopped almost entirely.

Something touched her hair.

Jill screamed and shoved at whoever was in front of her. She felt her hands connecting with something soft and fleshy, but she didn't stop to think about what it was. At that moment, only one thought raced through her mind—*I have to live for Charlie.* The thought of never seeing her son filled her body with a boost of energy that she never experienced before.

Jill rushed into the living room and, from her memory of years living in the house, slammed her palm against the light switch without looking. She didn't really think at that moment, she just knew that she couldn't stand to be blinded like this in such everlasting darkness, stuck with whomever broke into Annette's home.

The living room was instantly bathed in meager lights, even though right then, to Jill, they seemed like they were sent from heaven. She barely had enough time to turn around and look at the figure stalking her.

Chapter 22

Cheryl's phone torch jerked in various directions from her uncontrollable trembling. She screamed at the top of her lungs, and when she was out of breath, she screamed again. And then again.

And then her rational thinking returned. She pointed the torch at the bottom of the stairs one last time, just to make sure she didn't see things wrong in her terror.

Erika was at the bottom of the stairs, her body splayed upside-down, her arms in unnatural positions that the human body was not capable of without injuring itself immensely. Her neck was craned sideways almost ninety degrees, with a neckbone jutting prominently against her skin. Her eyes were open, vacantly staring directly at Cheryl with wide eyes. Her mouth was slightly agape, as if trying to say something but unable to, due to the broken neck.

Cheryl sobbed and screamed some more, but she was aware that she needed to get out of here right now. She could still be in danger.

Jill!

She had to get back to her sister and warn her. She never should have left her alone in that fucking house. She turned around, sprinted across the kitchen and out of the house.

She didn't even care if there were potential witnesses who would later testify to seeing her run away from a crime scene.

There were moments in Jill's life when she felt really scared. The most terrified that she'd ever been in her life was when she was seven years old and got stuck in a log. She was exploring with the boy who gave her Lola, when they found a hollow toppled log. He suggested they crawl through it. Jill

138

inspected it first to make sure there were no bugs or other creepy crawlies inside.

Once she deemed it safe enough, she crawled inside first, just to try to go through to the other side like the special agents from the cartoons she saw. It was a tight fit, but she pushed forward. The other end was just there, a few feet away.

But when she made it halfway through, she could no longer move. She tried going backward, but she couldn't move there, either. No matter how she tried moving—rotating, pushing, pulling—she couldn't budge. The boy tried helping her, but he couldn't do anything to move her.

Eventually, she realized that she was stuck in that log, in the woods, with no one close by capable of helping her. That caused a panic to jolt through her so abruptly that she began hyperventilating. This caused the tight space of the tree trunk's interior to press against her chest even more, until she thought she was going to suffocate in there. The boy told her that he'd go fetch help and ran off, leaving her alone. Minutes went by, maybe even hours, but Jill lost track of time.

Dad heard her screaming eventually and came to the rescue. He couldn't pull her out, so he told her to calm down because that way, her chest would deflate a little bit. It took a while, but eventually, she listened to him. Once she was calm enough, Dad grabbed her by the feet and pulled her out of the tree.

He carried her home in his arms and made her hot chocolate to calm her down. Her mom, of course, scolded her and told her how she knew Jill would get in trouble in the woods, but her words were nothing compared to the terror she experienced that day.

Jill never experienced anything in her life even remotely as scary as getting stuck in that hollow tree.

Until tonight.

Now, as she stared at her mother standing in the doorway between the foyer and the living room, the fear that she felt inside the tree trunk faded in comparison.

Annette's head twitched violently, and the corner of her mouth was contorted into a stroke-like grimace. Her wrists and fingers were rigid, twitching just as violently as her head. In one of her hands was Jill's doll, Lola. The only part of her body that seemed stable were the perfectly still legs that she stood on, in a somewhat spread-out stance.

Jill wanted to call out to her mom, but she knew that the monstrosity that stared back at her through her mother's eyes was not actually her mother.

An eternity of being locked in a staring contest passed, even though it was probably just a few seconds, and then the thing embodying Annette moved. It arched backward with impossible flexibility, causing another loud, bony crack to fill the air. It planted its palms on the floor, going into a bridge position, and then scuttled up the stairs.

It was gone within seconds.

Jill looked down and saw Lola on the floor next to the bloodied carpet and the shards of glass from the busted ceiling bulb. The doll was in a sitting position, her black orbs for eyes staring right at Jill. Jill couldn't take it anymore. She ran into the kitchen and dashed towards the backdoor.

She heard a muffled *thud-thud-thud-thud* coming upstairs from her mother's footsteps. Jill yanked the door open so violently that it slammed against the wall. The cold air that wafted into her face had never felt so refreshing, as she rushed through the thick grass around the house, towards the road.

As soon as she reached the paved path, she bumped into a figure, causing her to lose balance and fall backward. Jill screamed, and the figure screamed back.

"Cheryl! Cheryl!" it took her a moment to realize that the shrieking figure was her sister.

She was tear-stricken and hysterical, even more so than Jill. They hugged each other tightly, and Jill hastily tried to convey what just happened. The words came out incoherent and disconnected, just like Cheryl's. If someone saw them, they probably would have thought they were two lunatics, screaming like that into the night.

Eventually, they calmed down, and Cheryl was able to utter one sensical sentence.

"We need to call the police!"

Chapter 23

"And you just found her like that?" the older of the two police officers asked as the younger one took notes.

"Yes, I already told you, she was dead when I entered," Cheryl said in frustration.

She was standing in Mom's room along with Jill, Violet, and two of the police officers. It took a lot of convincing to get Jill to go inside, but Cheryl had to know what had happened. She had never seen her sister so distressed, so whatever happened must have been terrifying. Even when the cops entered the room and Cheryl behind them, Jill refused to budge.

After some convincing, she peeked inside, and only when she saw for herself that Mom was really in bed and comatose, she entered—hesitantly. Jill explained over and over that Mom was awake and running around the house. She even pointed to the foot sole where the shard of glass from the broken lightbulb was embedded, along with fresh trickles of blood. Everything she said pointed to it being the truth, but for some reason, Cheryl still couldn't believe it.

She saw all sorts of scary things in the past few days, but for Mom to just wake up, run around the house in a gymnast-like position before returning to bed? She wanted to believe Jill, but she just didn't see that happening. Or perhaps, her brain was just trying not to imagine it, to protect her from the fear that would drive her insane.

"So, she didn't open the door for you, and you decided to just let yourself in?" the cop asked again, this time with a hint of animosity.

Cheryl started to think that she might become a suspect in Erika's death.

"Are you suggesting I did something to Erika?" she outright asked.

"I'm not suggesting anything, but—"

"Is my sister a suspect, officer?" Jill asked, and crossed her arms.

She had a protective tone, and despite being hysterical earlier, she almost seemed to be back to her normal self now that she had to protect Cheryl. The police officer shook his head defensively.

"Ma'am, I'm just doing my job. I need to make sure nothing is amiss here."

"I think you should focus on the bigger picture and do a better job, then," Jill raised her tone.

Violet gently put a hand on Jill's shoulder and stepped slightly in front of her.

"Officers, Cheryl and Jill are going through a lot. Their mother is in a coma and they need to decide what to do with her, as well as with the property. They are already under too much stress. And now to discover that their neighbor died in her home..."

"Alright, alright, I get it," the officer raised one hand dismissively. "A proper investigation will be conducted anyway, so we'll see if there's any foul play involved in your neighbor's death."

He glowered at Cheryl.

"And what about our mother?" Jill insisted.

The cop scratched his head and looked at the comatose body in the bed. He looked at Jill and said. "So tell me again what happened."

Jill looked at Mom, and then shook her head.

"You know what? I already told you everything. I'm not gonna repeat myself because you're too lazy to pay attention."

"Whoa, calm down, lady. I'm just trying to help."

"But you don't believe me!"

"I never said that."

"You didn't have to, I can see how you're looking at me, like I'm a crazy person!"

The police officer sighed in exasperation. The junior cop stepped forward.

"Ma'am, I'm really sorry for what you two have been through tonight. I know it must have been tough seeing something like that," he glanced at Cheryl, but she looked away. "My partner and I are going to do what we can to help you with this, but right now, we need to focus on the case of your neighbor."

Jill probably noticed the cop's patronizing tone, but she didn't say anything. The cop wrote something on a blank piece of paper in his notepad before saying, "Tell you what. Here's my number. If you see anything suspicious in the next few days—anything at all—you just call me, and I'll be here."

He tore off the piece of paper and handed it to Jill. She reluctantly grabbed it and stuffed it inside her pocket. Cheryl didn't even need to guess if Jill was going to keep the cop's number or recycle it. The two sisters silently exchanged glares with each other, and it was obvious what they were thinking—the cops can't help.

The policemen excused themselves, stating that they were needed at Erika's house with the other police officers. Cheryl pulled the drapes at the windows aside long enough to see the two cops walking towards their cruiser and talking to each other. She heard the senior one chuckling about something and wagging his forefinger in small circles next to his temple. They entered the cruiser and drove off. Cheryl glanced toward Erika's house and saw the flashing red and blue lights in the distance.

Poor Erika...

She felt like crying. All her life, she's known that woman, and now, just like that, she was gone. She didn't even care that much about the information she was supposed to get from her. Her last words resonated in her head over and over.

Come by later, and I'll tell you everything.

144

Cheryl tried not to think how scared she was in those last moments before she died. What did she even see that scared her so much?

■■■

Jill hadn't moved, even after the cops had left. Violet stood in the middle of the room with her hands clasped together in front of herself while Cheryl stared out the window. The room was eerily silent, save for the machine's beeping.

"Violet, please tell me you have an explanation for this," Jill said.

Violet grimaced and looked at Annette's body briefly. Earlier, she performed a full check on her to make sure nothing was amiss.

"We should probably admit her to a hospital, first thing Monday," Violet finally said.

"But what about what I saw? How the hell did she do that?"

"I'm afraid I have no explanation for what you saw," she reticently shrugged.

"That's it?" Jill took an almost aggressive step closer to Violet.

The nurse didn't even change her facial expression, let alone flinch, as Jill violently gestured to her mother's body in bed.

"I literally saw her standing in the foyer!" she shouted.

"Yes, I heard your story when you told the policemen the first time."

Violet's calmness pissed Jill off even more. She wanted to grab her by the shoulders and violently shake her until she got into her head what Jill was telling her.

"And you don't believe me?!" she asked in an offended tone.

Violet didn't say anything. She didn't have to. It was clear that she didn't believe a word Jill said. Jill may as well have been trying to talk to a wall.

"We'll have her taken to a hospital for a full checkup," the nurse diverted Jill's answer. "But Jill, you have to understand. Your mother has been in a coma for a whole week. That means she hasn't moved in seven days. She would not be able to stand up on her own, let alone run in the manner you described."

"Then, what the hell did I see?!" Jill started, nearly becoming hysterical again.

By this point, Cheryl had returned from the window and was watching Jill. Out of the two sisters, Cheryl was supposed to be the impulsive one, and yet, the roles were now reversed. Jill assumed that her little sister was simply too traumatized to be as volatile as Jill.

"I'm sorry," Violet shrugged once more.

The urge Jill had to shake her by the shoulders morphed into an uncontrollable desire to slap her. Before she could entertain that thought, Cheryl spoke up.

"Come on, Jill. Are you really going to ignore what you saw? Even when it's right in your face?" Cheryl's voice had an impatient timbre.

"What are you talking about?" Jill swiveled her head towards her sister and frowned.

"You know well enough what you saw. And you know damn well that no doctor can explain it. You saw Mom standing in the foyer. Even though she's in a fucking coma."

Jill exhaled through her nose and slightly tilted her head. The thought of that horrible moment of standing in the living room and seeing her mom standing there in front of her, twitching and staring, sent shivers down her spine.

"Whatever I saw down there," Jill finally said soft-spokenly, "It wasn't our mother."

Silence fell on the room for a moment. Eventually, Violet was the one who broke it.

"I'll be leaving you two for now. I will be here Monday to make sure everything is okay. I will try to be here earlier, in case you need anything from me," she said.

She elegantly turned on her heel and wished Cheryl and Jill a good night before exiting, leaving the sisters alone and in silence. They stood there for a while before Jill ended the silence.

"I'm sleeping in the car tonight. No way am I staying in the house," she said.

Cheryl looked at her brusquely.

"I can understand that."

More silence.

"I'm sorry for what I said earlier," Jill said.

"Me too," Cheryl reciprocated.

She awkwardly looked at Mom and then Jill.

"Is it cool if I sleep with you in the car tonight?"

Jill smiled. For a moment, she saw that kid on her sister's face who was afraid of the monsters hiding under her bed back when they lived together. Reflecting back on those times, Jill felt immense regret for not being more supportive to her sister. Maybe if she did, their relationship would have been better right now.

She remembered once hearing someone say that a bond between siblings is built and strengthened in youth, and once you reach a certain age, all you can do is have an aloof relationship with your siblings. That pained her, but she wanted to believe that it wasn't too late for her and Cheryl.

"You don't even need to ask me that," Jill said. "But, we gotta take care of one thing first.

"And what's that?"

"Lock Mom's door."

Chapter 24

Five minutes later, Cheryl and Jill were in Jill's car. Jill was in the driver's seat, while Cheryl sat behind. As soon as they entered the car, Jill called Lee to tell him what happened. Even though Cheryl told her to be careful with her wording, Jill had to tell her husband what had happened.

The thought of getting killed and leaving Lee and Charlie alone to fend for themselves scared the living crap out of her, and she just had to talk to both of them to calm herself down.

They had a video call, and Cheryl joined in, too, even though she wasn't very talkative. Eventually, Lee noticed that Charlie was getting sleepy, so he told him to go to bed. As soon as Charlie was away, Lee suggested coming to the house.

Jill adamantly objected to that suggestion, but Lee was pushy. In the end, when Lee insisted on coming, Jill downplayed the danger that she told him about and managed to convince him not to come because she'd be home in just two days. Lee was reluctant, but finally agreed.

By the time Jill ended the phone call, a metallic pitter-patter of the rain had started echoing off of the car's rooftop. Jill and Cheryl must have sat in silence for at least ten minutes—Jill reclined in her seat, and Cheryl lying on the backseat, covered up with the blanket she brought from the house.

From this position, Jill could see the lights in the window of her old room. It was pale, and she couldn't help but imagine opening her eyes and seeing a figure—her mother?—standing there. Or even worse, waking up to see her right outside the car window.

With that thought, Jill pressed the button to lock all the car doors.

She covered herself with the blanket up to her neck and tried to find a more relaxed position. She closed her eyes, but she found that keeping them open was much easier, with the fear still racing through her veins.

With nothing better to do, Jill started to replay the night's events in her mind, reel by reel. She couldn't get the disgusting cracking sounds that her mother's body had made out of her head. She couldn't get the sounds of glass crunching under her bare feet out of her head. But what disturbed Jill the most was her mother's face.

When she stood in the foyer, staring at her, it was Annette's face, and yet, it wasn't. The face was too pallid, corpse-like in color, and the facial expression... Jill couldn't quite put her finger on it until now, but now that she was calm enough, she could process the whole event more clearly.

The corner of Annette's mouth was stretched into a grimace of some sorts, and her eye was twitching, if Jill remembered correctly. Her eyebrows were rising and dropping, and the muscles in her neck bulged and relaxed intermittently. It was like a person just learning how to use their face for the first time in life. Jill felt the hairs on the nape of her neck stand straight.

"You were right all along, Cheryl," she said, her voice cracking slightly.

The drumming of the rain had increased slightly, giving Jill a sort of tranquil feeling.

"About what?" Cheryl asked.

"About everything. The house. Mom. Everything."

She heard Cheryl shifting in the backseat.

"You think there's something ghostly going on in the house?" she asked.

Jill frowned. She didn't like thinking in that direction because she found it to be outlandish. She mostly wanted to avoid going down that path because she was afraid that it might lead her to become like her mother. In the end, however, her mother was not crazy after all, was she? She was right all this time.

"Jill?" Cheryl called out.

"I do," Jill brusquely said. "I didn't want to think that way, but we can't ignore it anymore. Something weird is going on in this house. And I think if we get to the bottom of it, we might be able to save Mom."

Cheryl adjusted into an upright sitting position.

Cheryl's heart started to race a little faster. Maybe there was a chance to save Mom after all. That thought filled her with painful hope. She leaned forward so that her head was next to Jill's.

"Earlier, when Erika visited us, she said she had something to tell me about Mom," she said.

Jill turned her head to the side to face her sister. Her face was gaunt and battered, a testament to the difficult night she'd had.

"Oh, yeah?" she asked sleepily.

"Yeah. Here's what she told me."

Cheryl proceeded to tell Jill everything that Erika communicated to her. She told her about the cave in Haiti, the trance Mom fell into, the paranoia that took her over, the books she read about relating to Vodou, the entity she believed was after her.

The entire time, Jill listened attentively. She went from looking sleepy to sitting ramrod straight in her seat and staring at Cheryl with a penetrating gaze. When Cheryl was done speaking, the only sound that remained was the rain. It had increased in intensity somewhat, and the metallic pitter-patter had grown louder as a result.

When Jill didn't say anything for a whole minute, Cheryl broke the silence.

"Well? What do you think?" she asked.

Jill inhaled deeply through her nose and continued to maintain the silence.

"I think we need to hire a houngan or a mambo," she finally said with alacrity.

"A wha— oh, you mean the Vodou expert?"

"Vodou priest or priestess, yeah," Jill confirmed.

She had already reached forward to grab her phone from the compartment in the door. Cheryl saw the screen of Jill's phone lighting up against the contrast of the night so brightly that she had to turn away for a second.

Jill was apparently bothered by it, too, since she reduced the brightness of her phone a moment later. Cheryl saw hasty typing as Jill's fingers flew across the phone's touchscreen keyboard. The first search result that came up for her was *Voodoo Doughnut* from Portland.

The two of them exchanged a look with each other before bursting into laughter. Jill tried a different search term. She browsed something that Cheryl didn't have enough time to read over Jill's fast scrolling, but she saw what the website she entered was about as soon as she glanced at the huge *'Mambo for Hire!'* title on the top.

"Here's one. And she lives in Springfield," Jill said with excitement in her voice.

Cheryl leaned closer to see what the fuss was all about. Jill was scrolling through a page filled with particularly interesting images, including African people participating in what Cheryl assumed were Vodou activities. The people in the pictures wore traditional attire, most of them white, and some of the members had white face paint. There were historical drawings of the loa, too, along with the *vèvès*.

Jill clicked on the button that took her to the about info. There were no pictures, but there was a paragraph called *About the Mambo.*

My name is Fabiola, and I have been practicing Haitian Vodou since early childhood. Born and raised under Haitian Vodou influence, I have extensive knowledge when it comes to the loa, including how to summon them, serve them, and ensure you live a long, prosperous, and healthy life.

I also teach those who are interested in how to serve the loa, as well as which loa suits them best for their needs. I help over one thousand people every year, and all of those who have committed to practicing Vodou using proper techniques have reported good results.

See my clients' testimonies below.

Under the biography were various quoted sentences from satisfied customers who Fabiola had helped. At the bottom there was an email address and a phone number. Jill clicked the phone number. It took her to her dial screen.

"You're gonna call her now?" Cheryl asked.

"Yeah," Jill nodded, like it was the most obvious answer in the world.

■■■

After the fourth ring, Jill realized that she was calling too late. It was almost 10 pm, after all. But then, in the middle of the fifth ring, the line connected, and a strong, female voice spoke up in an accent that Jill couldn't quite place.

"*Bonswa.* This is Fabiola. What can I do for you?"

Each word sounded connected and atonal, and Jill wondered who wrote the biography for the woman.

Sounds like French, Jill thought.

"Good evening. I'm really sorry for calling you this late."

"No problem, *cheri.* I can hear that you are scared. What is wrong?"

Jill was taken aback by that. Was the woman really able to tell that something was wrong just from one sentence, or was she just playing polite?

"Well, um, I don't even know where to start," Jill said.

"You need help cleaning evil from your home, *wi?*" Fabiola asked.

Her voice pierced like a spear through the speaker, but her authoritative and motherly tone was exactly what Jill needed right now.

"Yes," she simply responded.

"No problem, *cheri.* Where do you live?"

"We're in Sams Valley, Medford."

"Medford?"

The way she asked that sounded like she never heard of the town before.

"Yes, Medford. It's a small town just a couple hours away from—"

"Send me the address in text. And I will come tomorrow afternoon. Okay?"

"Okay, but—"

"I will come tomorrow, and I will see what the problem is. Then we will fix it together, *wi*?"

"*Wi*," Jill instinctively said.

"*Byen.* Send me the address in text. Okay?"

"Okay, I will."

"*Byen. Bòn nwi.* Bye-bye!"

Before Jill could say anything, Fabiola disconnected the call. Jill was flabbergasted. She glanced at Cheryl to see if she heard that, too.

"I guess I should send her the address," Jill shrugged and then entered the messaging option on her phone.

"Are you sure we want to hire her?" Cheryl wrinkled her nose.

"We don't have a choice. She is the only one who can help us with this."

"Maybe she didn't understand you well. Springfield is about two hours away from Medford."

"Maybe she travels. I mean, the website said she helps thousands of clients, and I doubt all of them are from Springfield," Jill shrugged.

"How about hiring a priest instead?"

"A priest wouldn't be able to help us understand what loa Mom was trying to summon. We have to try this."

Jill sent the address to Fabiola. She replied five minutes later with a text.

Okay, I will be there tomorrow 6 pm, cheri. The cost is $900.

153

"Geez, she's expensive," Jill scoffed.

"No wonder she's willing to drive out, huh?"

"For nine hundred bucks? I'd do the same.

Jill leaned on her seat and pensively stared at the dimly lit room on the second floor. Cheryl curled back up into a sleeping position.

"Let's just hope she isn't a fraud," she said through a yawn.

Chapter 25

Cheryl was woken up by the obtrusively bright rays of sunlight gleaming in through the window. She tried to ignore them as much as she could, but not only were they visually annoying, but the car was getting too hot to sleep in, too.

After some unsuccessful attempts to fall back asleep, Cheryl pulled herself into a sitting position. Jill was not in the car. The first thing that came to her mind was the traumatic event from last night. She remembered seeing Erika all broken at the bottom of the stairs, her eyes staring blankly into nothingness. It made Cheryl feel sick.

Last night, she had trouble falling asleep because of it—among other things.

Jill had already fallen asleep by then, by Cheryl was still tossing and turning, thinking about Erika, Mom, and all the creepy stuff Jill told her about. Eventually, she decided to browse social media a little bit.

That turned out to be a mistake, too, because she saw something that she shouldn't have. She was scrolling her feed on Instagram when she came upon a picture posted by Tom. It was a picture of Tom and Paula hugging and smiling at the camera. Underneath the picture was the caption "Love this woman so much" and a bunch of heart-shaped emojis.

Cheryl thought she'd feel anger or sadness. She thought she'd go hysterical for the knife she had embedded in her back. She was surprised at how calm she actually was. Not only calm, but little she cared seeing it.

When she further tried to click on Paula's profile, she realized that she couldn't.

She must have blocked me, she thought blankly.

She entered Tom's profile instead, but realized that that was his only new post recently. She also noticed that he removed all the pictures he had with Cheryl. At first, Cheryl just stared at his latest picture. She kind of expected this to happen sooner rather than later, so she wasn't even surprised.

The only thing that bothered her was how people would be talking behind their backs because Tom, up until recently, posted pics with Cheryl. In the end, she deduced that she would be the victim here—Paula was the slut who stole someone's boyfriend.

Eventually, she just thought to herself sardonically that she hoped the two of them were happy before blocking Tom on all social media. As soon as she did it, she felt an invisible stone drop from her heart.

Cheryl fell asleep almost immediately after that.

Now that she was awake, she took a moment to ponder whether she felt anything regarding the picture she saw last night. Maybe her emotions were blunted from the trauma she went through last night, but if things stayed like this, then she could safely say that she was free of Tom's toxic influence.

When Cheryl entered the house, she saw Jill's childhood doll still sitting on the floor. She's been in that position since last night, facing the living room, creepily staring towards it. Cheryl went around it in a wide arc and loped through the living room.

"Sleep well?" Jill asked her as soon as Cheryl walked into the kitchen.

The sound of something sizzling came from the pan on the stove. A savory redolence which Cheryl instantly recognized as pancakes filled the air, causing her mouth to water. Cheryl was surprised to find Jill in here, especially given how timid she was yesterday about entering the house. She supposed it was because the house was much less unsettling in the daytime.

"I guess so. You?" Cheryl asked as she sat at the kitchen table.

"Fine. I noticed you couldn't fall asleep," Jill said as she flipped a pancake on top of the already finished ones on the plate next to her.

"No, I guess I couldn't," Cheryl opened up.

Jill grabbed the plate with the stack of pancakes and walked over to the table, where she promptly placed the food in front of Cheryl. The syrup was already there.

"The whole thing with Erika?" Jill asked as she sat down.

"Some other things, too. But mostly Erika, yeah," Cheryl said as she picked up the syrup and pulled the plate of pancakes closer to herself. "Thanks for the breakfast, sis."

Sis.

She hasn't called Jill that since they were kids. The word accidentally left her mouth, but somehow it felt natural to utter it. Jill seemingly noticed this, too, because she smiled when she heard that. She visibly tried to hide it, but it was too late.

"Is it Tom?" Jill cleared her throat and asked.

Cheryl nodded and poured the syrup over the pancakes in abundance. It slid all the way down to the bottom of the plate, creating a moat-like puddle.

"Wanna talk about it?" Jill asked.

"It's nothing major. He just posted a picture with his new girlfriend," Cheryl said.

"I'm so sorry, Cherry," Jill reached across the table and gently put her hand over Cheryl's. "How do you feel about that?"

"To tell you the truth, liberated," Cheryl chuckled.

Jill leaned back in her chair and smiled.

"Really?" she asked.

Cheryl stabbed a piece of pancake on her fork and nodded.

157

"Really. I didn't even realize how toxic our relationship was until he left me."

She stuffed the pancake from her fork into her mouth and chewed a few times. The pancakes were good, really good. She'd even go as far as to say they were as good as Dad's.

"For example," Cheryl said as she swallowed. "He tried to convince me not to go home after Mom fell into a coma."

"Why?"

"He said that she didn't have much time left anyway, and I'd be wasting the weekend traveling."

"Jesus. He said it in those exact words?"

Jill probably thought that Cheryl twisted Tom's words, but she didn't. She remembered him saying it very clearly.

Babe, I'd hate to be the bearer of bad news, but your Mom's probably going to be gone soon. Why don't you just come over to my place for the weekend and try to relax?

"Yeah," Cheryl said. "He was probably too lazy to drive me all the way out to Medford. And he made it very clear how much he hated the fact that he had to cancel the plans with his buddies to give me a ride."

"What piece of shit," Jill shook her head.

"Yeah. But, then again, Tom just had a tendency to say the stupidest things ever, just out of the blue."

"It sounds like a lot of stuff had been piling up with you guys."

"Yeah," Cheryl nodded.

Jill had no idea exactly how much had piled up between Cheryl and Tom. Their relationship was doomed from the start. Now that Cheryl was out of the relationship, her eyes were wide open, and she realized just how much bad stuff she turned a blind eye to.

When they first met at a dorm party, Tom was so kind and compassionate. Cheryl had a lot of guys hitting on her in college—mostly because they thought she was easy—and although she may have seemed like she was only looking for one-night stands, she wasn't the kind of girl who would sleep around (courtesy of Mom's upbringing).

That's why she fell for Tom almost immediately. He was polite, he wasn't pushy, and he attentively listened to Cheryl as she talked about herself—not like the other guys who would nod and pretend-listen and then invite her to their room.

Cheryl and Tom fell in love with each other pretty early on in their relationship, but Tom's side of emotions seemed to burn out rather quickly. The kindness and compassion he had at the beginning of their relationship was replaced by indifference, and then later, hostility. He stopped telling her that he loved her and showed less affection, criticized her for everything she did, got irritated quickly...

It happened so gradually that Cheryl couldn't pinpoint when exactly it started. And now that she was finally out of the relationship, she couldn't help but wonder why she tolerated all that. She wasn't a saint herself, she was aware of that. She took Tom for granted and was self-centered, but she didn't deserve to be cheated on.

"I see you finally managed to perfect Dad's secret recipe," Cheryl said as she took another bite of the moist pancakes.

"It's about time. I make these pancakes for Charlie from time to time, and he loves them," the look in her eyes turned sorrowful as she mention of her son.

Maybe she was wondering if this was all going to end well.

"You don't have to do this," Cheryl said.

Jill looked at her in bafflement.

"Do what?" she asked.

"All of this. You can get back inside your car and drive home to your family. It's that easy."

For a moment, Jill looked like she was tempted to do just that, but a moment later, she smiled forlornly and shook her head.

"You think I'd let you take care of this alone?"

"No, I assumed not. But you probably need to think about this. You have a husband and a son. You need to take care of them."

"I also have a sister. And I don't plan on letting you face whatever's in this house alone. Not this time."

That almost brought a tear to Cheryl's eye. The knowledge that Jill still cared about her meant the world to her. Cheryl smiled. She was mostly playing with her pancakes by this point.

"You think this woman... Fabiola... is going to be able to help us?" she asked.

"I did some research on her today."

"Of course you did."

Yup, that was Jill. Ever the vigilant sister who made sure nothing went wrong. Jill ignored Cheryl's remark and continued.

"A lot of people vouched for her. Lots of them claimed they had problems similar to ours and that Fabiola managed to fix them in just one or two visits."

"Did they have problems as severe as ours?" Cheryl asked, taking another bite of the pancakes, now mostly out of boredom.

"No. But there were some creepy encounters that other people had."

"Do tell."

Jill shifted in her seat and leaned on the table with her elbows.

"Well, this one guy said that his wife used to talk in her sleep. When I first read it, I thought he was joking, but things started to actually get really freaky. She'd sleepwalk and talk about all sorts of scary, incoherent things. And one night, he woke up to find her standing with her face against the wall and walking sideways while feeling it with her palms. When he asked her what she was doing, she shushed him and said *'they are in the walls'.*"

Jill made quotation marks with her fingers.

"Who was?" Cheryl jerked her head back in confusion.

"No idea," Jill shrugged. "Anyway, it got so out of control that he ended up calling Fabiola. And according to Fabiola, the wife was haunted by some malevolent spirits. She did some stuff to the wife and cleansed the house, and apparently, everything's been fine ever since."

"Any negative experiences from other people?"

"A few, but they were minimal in comparison to literally the hundreds of positive ones that were there."

"What did they say?"

"One of them complained that Fabiola talked too much and too fast."

Cheryl raised an eyebrow. She had long since placed her fork down and stopped eating pancakes. She offered them to Jill, but she politely declined, stating that she wasn't hungry.

"But what about her paranormal problem? Did she resolve that?" Cheryl asked.

"They didn't say. They just wrote one sentence that Fabiola talks too much."

"Some people..." Cheryl rolled her eyes.

Jill stood up from the table, pushing the chair backward with a loud scraping noise.

"Well, I'm gonna go through the things I still haven't seen in my room. What are you gonna do?"

"I think I'll..." she wanted to say that she'd do the same, but then she remembered the nightmare she had in her room yesterday. "I think I'll be lazy, and then I'll go check on Mom later."

Jill glanced at her momentarily. There was caution in that glare, and rightly so. Cheryl didn't want to step inside Mom's room, either.

"I'll be fine, don't worry, Jill," Cheryl chuckled.

Jill nodded and gave her a fake smile.

"Alright. When you decide to do it, I'll go with you."

Chapter 26

As soon as she stepped out of the living room, Jill stopped dead in her tracks.

Damn, I forgot all about Lola, she said as she looked down at the doll. It was in a seated position, facing the living room. Up until yesterday, Jill found her charming. Now, she saw the doll as the embodiment of creepy. Still, a part of her felt attached to Lola, and she couldn't throw her away just because of what happened last night, no matter how distressing it was.

She bent down and picked up the doll. It felt cold to the touch, but not unnaturally so. She's been in the shade, away from the rays of sun all morning, and the house was already cold as it was, even in the spots where the sunlight landed. Jill turned Lola over in her hands, examining it for any sustained damage. She looked as good as the day the boy gave it to her.

The boy.

Who was he? Jill tried remembering more about him over the past few days, but she just couldn't remember anything more than blurry snippets of her and the boy playing as kids.

Maybe Cheryl would remember. She was very young back then, but she would surely remember any boy that Jill would have played with. It's not like that many people visited them back then, anyway.

Jill took Lola upstairs towards her old room, not letting the door of her mother's bedroom out of sight. She touched the pocket of her jeans and felt the outline of the key there, much to her relief. The house was silent right now, unnervingly so, but Jill preferred it that way.

Last night, at some point, she was sure she heard the radio playing from her mom's room.

Shoving those thoughts out of her mind, Jill went into her bedroom and placed Lola on the nightstand into an upright sitting position. She was on the fence about bringing the doll back home, but after everything that happened in the house, she was sure she wouldn't be doing that.

Even though she didn't want to actively admit it, a part of her feared that she'd bring some evil with the doll into her home, and that the same things might start happening. That suddenly got her thinking about the whole thing.

Why was her mom holding Lola last night in the first place? It's not like the doll was in her room, so she picked it up off the nightstand and ran outside. The doll was in Jill's room, which made Jill think that her mom—or whatever possessed her—went out of her way to grab it.

But why?

Jill scrutinized Lola once more. Was there anything on her that she was supposed to see? She flipped her around in various positions, expecting to see a small, hand-drawn *vèvè*, but of course, there was nothing. Determined not to bash her head around a mystery that may not have been a logical mystery at all, she put the doll back down and exited her room.

Sometime later, the sisters decided to check up on Mom. Jill had the key in her hand, which she clutched so firmly that veins bulged on the back of her hand.

"Are you sure you want to check up on her?" Jill asked.

Cheryl nodded. She actually wasn't sure, but she had to ensure that Mom was okay.

"Just a quick glance, and we're out," she said.

Jill furrowed her brow. The creases on her face were more prominent from this angle, with her head only partially illuminated by the sun. Jill approached the door and bent down, leveling her eye with the keyhole.

As she peered inside, Cheryl went silent. She heard the muffled beeping of the machine inside the room. Suddenly, she felt a foreboding sense building up inside her. She couldn't help but imagine some Vodou ghost on the other side of the door and sticking a sharp, elongated finger through the keyhole.

She wanted to tell Jill to move away from there, but at the same time, she didn't want to panic for nothing. What if she was just exaggerating? Jill wouldn't trust her as she used to. But what if she wasn't, and something really was in there? What if it poked Jill's eye out and—

"It seems okay," Jill said a moment later, straightening her back—much to Cheryl's relief.

She stuck the key inside the keyhole and slowly turned it. The lock clicked in an overly loud manner. Jill pushed the door and allowed it to open on its own, revealing the dim interior of the room.

Cheryl suddenly felt like they were walking into hostile territory. She'd been apprehensive from day one, but that was a different kind of apprehension. Now, she was scared of Mom's comatose body, no matter how much she hated that thought.

Jill was the first one to step inside, and that gave Cheryl a much-needed boost of courage. They stood in front of Mom's bed for a little while in silence. Cheryl noticed Jill glancing at the radio on the nightstand.

"You're thinking of what we heard yesterday, right?" she asked.

Jill glanced at her briefly and gave her a terse nod.

"Yeah. And there was music playing last night, too. We should probably unplug the radio."

Cheryl agreed, ignoring the hairs that stood straight up on the nape of her neck. She noticed that Jill didn't actually do anything about the radio. She also noticed that she stood close to the door, almost as if ready to make a quick exit in case something—what?—happened.

"You're right," Cheryl said and walked over to the radio.

A part of her wanted to impress her big sister, but another part wanted to avoid hearing the radio turning on on its own again. With one swift motion, she yanked the plug out of the wall socket (right after making sure she wasn't unplugging the machine instead) and lifted the radio by its handle.

As she turned around, she froze, her heart suddenly starting to race. She glanced down at her mother's hand. It was hanging off the edge of the bed.

No, wait, it wasn't. It was just the blanket shaped that way. Cheryl felt the scream that had been building up in her slowly abating, and she did her best not to show those emotions to Jill. She resisted the urge to break into a quick stride as she returned to the door, now standing even closer to it than Jill.

"There. Now we're at least safe from the evil radio," she said, once again trying her best to hide the quivering in her voice.

Her heart rate was starting to slow down finally, and Jill didn't seem to notice Cheryl's gaffe. They walked out of the room and closed the door, neither of them uttering a word or showing in any way that they wanted to spend more time inside. Cheryl placed the radio on the floor next to the door and straightened her back just as Jill locked the door.

■■

Jill breathed a silent sigh of relief as soon as the door was locked. She steadied the trembling in her hands as much as she could before stuffing the key in the pocket of her jeans. Cheryl started towards her old bedroom without a word.

"Cheryl?" Jill called out to her softly.

For some reason, whenever they were upstairs—and especially when they were close to their mother's room—Jill felt compelled to speak quietly. Moreover, the house was unnaturally quieter upstairs than downstairs, and up until today, Jill didn't chalk any of that up to supernatural entities, but rather psyche.

"What's up, sis?" Cheryl called out.

Jill got a warm feeling inside whenever Cheryl called her 'sis'.

"You remember my doll, Lola?" she asked.

Cheryl nodded and smiled widely.

"Of course I do. You used to be really protective of her. It's one of those things I remember clearly from when we were kids."

Jill smiled at that, too. She suddenly remembered the moments Cheryl mentioned—eating dinner and pretending to feed Lola, speaking to her during the tea parties, not wanting to go to bed without her and other things like that.

"What about her?" Cheryl asked.

She crossed her arms and leaned on the door of her room with her back.

"Do you remember the boy who gave her to me? What was his name?"

Cheryl frowned and looked up at the ceiling pensively.

"What boy?" she finally looked down and shook her head in confusion.

"You know, the one who used to play with us all the time. I think he lived close by."

Cheryl looked even more confused.

"Oh, come on, you must remember him!" Jill exclaimed, now a little frustrated. "He was always quiet, and he and I used to play. We called you over many times, but you always refused."

Cheryl slowly shook her head from left to right.

"He made Lola for me, don't you remember?!" Jill shouted.

Cheryl raised both hands in a stop sign.

"Jill, what are you talking about? You got Lola from Mom!"

Jill opened her mouth, but found herself speechless.

"What?" she asked, the word barely leaving her throat.

"There was no boy. No kids lived anywhere near for miles, don't you remember?"

Jill raised an eyebrow and scratched the back of her head.

"You probably don't remember since you were only four or five back then. I specifically remember the boy giving me the doll."

"And I remember Mom doing so. She came back from the marketplace one day and bought both of us toys. She gave me a Barbie doll, and she gave you Lola."

"Maybe you're thinking of another doll. That boy gave me Lola."

"No, it was from Mom, I could bet an arm on it. I remember because you looked so happy to get her, and Mom asked you what you would call her, and you gave her the name Lola right away."

Jill's head started spinning.

"Well, what about the boy?" she asked.

"It was your imaginary friend."

That angered Jill. How in the hell would Cheryl be able to remember from such a young age if Jill had an imaginary friend? She opened her mouth to protest, but Cheryl interrupted her to speak again, and as if reading her thoughts, said, "Mom mentioned it many times later on, don't you remember? She used to always talk about how you had an imaginary friend. Dad even talked to some specialists about it because he wasn't sure if having an imaginary friend was healthy."

Jill leaned on the wall with the palm of her hand. She felt like she was going to collapse. The harder she tried to remember the boy, the more he seemed to fade from her memory.

Was there ever even a boy at all? Now that Cheryl mentioned it, Jill felt like her entire reality was questionable.

Did she play with the boy in her room, or did she play alone and pretend that there was someone there? Was she really with that boy in the woods when she got stuck in that log or was it all just a figment of her imagination?

You're going crazy, Jill. Just like your mother. You're losing your goddamn mind.

Before she could entertain that thought, she heard a car pulling up in front of the house.

Chapter 27

The pink creature that pulled up in front of the house couldn't really be described as a car. Partly subcompact, partly SUV, and kind of convertible, the car looked like a kid's drawing of what a car should look like, brought to life.

Jill looked at Cheryl to see if she noticed the same thing, but if she did, then she didn't show it in any way. The roaring of the engine stopped, and the miniature car door swung open.

Out stepped a woman, but not the kind Jill expected. She was black, that much she assumed rightly, but she expected to see a round, elderly woman with lots of jewelry, a bandana over the head, maybe even an animal's foot hanging around her neck.

The woman who stepped out was slim, enviously so, which could be seen even through the thick, white robes that she was wrapped in. She was young, around Jill's age, maybe only a few years older than her—or maybe younger. It was hard to tell, really.

As soon as the woman slammed the door of her car shut, she looked at Jill and Cheryl and her mouth contorted into a welcoming rictus.

"Hello, *mezanmi!*" she spread her arms widely for what seemed to be an inevitable hug.

She hugged Cheryl first, and kissed her once on both cheeks with an exaggeratedly loud 'mwah'. Then she moved on to Jill with the same gestures. Jill felt the strength of the woman's rock-hard grip momentarily. The kisses were also pretty strong.

"You're Fabiola?" Jill asked when the woman finished greeting her.

"*Non.* Who is this Fabiola you speak of?"

Jill opened her mouth dumbly, just as silence ensued.

"I joke!" the woman said, and started cackling a moment later.

Jill and Cheryl exchanged a furtive glance with each other before they, too, started laughing hesitantly.

"*Wi*, I am Fabiola," the woman said.

"My name's Jill. And this is my sister, Cheryl."

Fabiola nodded, and then her face turned slightly more serious.

"You have a problem, *wi*? Inside the house?" she asked.

"Yes, with our mother," Cheryl interjected, pointing to the window upstairs.

She enunciated every word. Perhaps she thought that Fabiola's English wasn't so good and that she would need word-by-word explanations.

"I will help you. I will look at the house. But first, you make me tea, *byen*?"

Jill slowly nodded. She was starting to become a little skeptical about hiring her. What if she was a fraud who preyed on people who had this issue, pretending to have a solution, and then robbed them?

Don't be ridiculous, Jill. There's two of you, and just one of her. And she drove out all the way from Springfield.

Yes, but maybe she has a gun, another voice in her mind said.

She ignored that voice as she invited Fabiola inside the house. Jill hawkishly observed Fabiola as she stepped over the threshold to see what her reaction would be like. Her facial expression didn't change one bit.

"Do you uh... sense anything in this house?" Jill asked.

"*Non*, I am a mambo, not a medium, *cheri*. If you ask me, mediums are scammers!" there was a hint of anger in her voice, and Jill guessed that Fabiola probably had some run-ins in the past with fake mediums.

"Feel free to take a seat anywhere you like," Jill gestured to the couch as they entered the living room.

"*Non, mèsi,*" Fabiola shook a hand. "I will sit in the kitchen, okay?"

"Oh, okay," Jill said, slightly taken aback by Fabiola's strange mannerisms.

Maybe she had special rituals as a mambo that she needed to follow before each house cleansing or whatever. They went into the kitchen, and Cheryl began boiling the water for the chamomile tea.

Jill and Fabiola sat from across each other at the kitchen table. Fabiola leaned her elbows on the table and stared at Jill with a half-smile. It made Jill feel uncomfortable, and she barely even registered that she had retreated into her seat and crossed her arms—a sign of a protective body language. When Fabiola's gaze didn't abate even after a whole minute, Jill decided to break the silence.

"Can you like, not stare at me like that? It's kind of creepy," she chuckled, trying to shrug it off as a joke and hopefully not offend Fabiola.

"*Dezole, cheri.* I am trying to see something," Fabiola grinned.

"I thought you said that was for mediums."

"*Wi,* I look for how upset you are. Last night, you were upset, yes?"

"Yes," Jill nodded.

Cheryl had finished the tea and put it on the table in front of Fabiola.

"*Mèsi anpil, mezanmi,*" the lady said and smiled at Cheryl.

Cheryl nodded in confusion, but said nothing. She was as confused about Fabiola using half-English and half-Haitian Creole as Jill was. Fabiola cupped the mug with her hands and looked at Cheryl.

"Honey?"

Cheryl raised her eyebrows in apprehension.

"Yes?"

"Honey," Fabiola pointed to the mug.

172

"Oh, you want honey in your tea," Cheryl chuckled in embarrassment. "Sorry, no honey in the house."

"Okay. Not a problem," Fabiola smiled briskly.

She grabbed the mug by the handle and raised it to her mouth. Despite the steam billowing in the air from the heat, Fabiola loudly slurped. She proceeded to smack her lips, as if tasting the tea and exclaimed a loud *'Ahhhhh'*.

Jill saw Cheryl putting a hand over her mouth to suppress her laughter. This almost caused Jill to start laughing as well, but since she was right in front of Fabiola and not behind her like Cheryl, she had to show respect to the mambo. Luckily, Fabiola didn't seem to notice this because she continued slurping and *'ahhh'-ing,'* never lowering the mug from her mouth.

"So, about our mom—" Jill started, but Fabiola raised a finger while still drinking.

She proceeded to do this for a few minutes, not bothering even to lower the mug from her mouth, until it started to become annoying. The entire time, Cheryl and Jill were silent, impatiently waiting for Fabiola to finish her tea. Once she was finally done, she set the mug down firmly on the table and intertwined her fingers with a complacent smile.

"Now, I will listen. Tell me where the problem is, *cheri*," she said.

Chapter 27

At first, Cheryl tried to jump in and say a million things at once, but it ended up with her and Jill talking over each other. Fabiola silenced them with a raise of the hand and a brisk *'pst'*. She then gestured to Jill, "You go first, *cheri.*"

Jill proceeded to explain everything that had transpired in the last few days. Her speech was quick and connected, with no pauses in-between. She spoke like an excited child who was telling a story to her parents, although instead of excitement, Jill spoke with fear.

The entire time, Fabiola listened and nodded fervently with a patronizing smile, muttering *'wi'* from time to time. This made Cheryl think that the mambo didn't understand a word of what Jill was saying due to the language barrier. Jill seemed to think this as well because she stopped and asked Fabiola if she understood everything.

Fabiola nodded and repeated the gist of what Jill said, like a child who was forced to repeat what the parent just said. Both Jill and Cheryl were surprised—and impressed.

"Okay?" Fabiola asked once she was done summarizing Jill's story.

"Okay," Jill nodded confusedly.

Fabiola rotated in her seat towards Cheryl.

"Okay, now you," she grinned.

Cheryl cleared her throat. She suddenly didn't know where to start. Fabiola's penetrating stare didn't help her feel less pressure, either.

"I, um..." she started and glanced at Jill for support.

"We have a lot of work, *cheri, prese!*" Fabiola clapped her hands together to urge her to hurry.

This kickstarted Cheryl, and her tongue began rolling, pretty much as quickly as Jill's was a few moments ago. She spoke about the bad dreams she'd been having, the things she'd been seeing in the house and Erika's death. She then retold the story of the radio turning on and Mom being on the floor next to her bed...

The entire time, she had to fight the urge to break down and start crying. Much like with Jill, Fabiola nodded and muttered in her language, and once Cheryl was done speaking, the mambo continued staring at her, as if expecting more.

"That's all," Cheryl said.

"Okay. You started to see bad things here when you were little?" Fabiola asked.

"No," Cheryl said, before reconsidering if that was the truth. "At least I think not."

"Okay," Fabiola said as she stood up. "Your mama is in the house?"

"Yes, she's upstairs," Jill mirrored Fabiola's gesture and stood up. "Do you want to see her?"

"*Wi,*" Fabiola nodded.

"Alright, let's go see her," Cheryl impatiently took the initiative.

■■■

Of the three, Fabiola was the bravest, and Cheryl wasn't sure if that should be attributed to her lifelong experience handling this sort of thing or the lack of knowing what lurked in the house.

Either way, as soon as Jill unlocked the door, she stepped aside, and Fabiola walked in with a confident gait. She approached Annette and observed her with a squint. Cheryl walked in next, and then Jill. The sisters waited in silence as the mambo scrutinized their mother's comatose body.

Fabiola sat on the edge of the bed and touched Annette's hand. A few seconds later, she said.

"She is cold."

She mumbled the sentence under her breath and took Cheryl a moment to register that she was just voicing her thoughts aloud.

175

"Yeah, she's in a coma," Jill said.

Fabiola shook her head.

"No, this is not a coma. She is unnaturally cold. She has been taken by an evil spirit."

She said it so calmly that Cheryl didn't even consider the implications of her words.

"What does that mean?" Jill frowned.

"It means there is something in the house. Something evil." When Fabiola turned to look at the sisters, she had a grievous expression on her face.

She darted her eyes back and forth between Jill and Cheryl. When she didn't say anything else, Cheryl spoke up.

"Okay, but what should we do?"

"I need to look around the house, okay? I need to see where more evil is hiding, *oke*?"

"*Oke*," Jill nodded, much to Cheryl's glower.

"I need to check the whole house, okay?" Fabiola said.

"Yes, but you should probably see one room, first," Jill said.

"Okay, *cheri*. Show me, *tanpri*."

Jill stalked out of the room, with Cheryl and Fabiola closely behind her. Cheryl didn't even need to guess which room Jill wanted to show her.

Once they were in front of Mom's office, Jill put one hand on the doorknob and looked at Fabiola.

"You ready?" she asked.

"*Cheri,* I have seen many things in my life. Nothing can surprise me," the mambo waved a hand in front of Jill's face vigorously.

"Alright," Jill said, and pushed the door open.

The first thing Fabiola did when she gazed upon the room's interior was gasp. Her mouth hung open for at least a few seconds before she closed it and swallowed loudly. She walked inside and mumbled something in her language. Cheryl couldn't tell what she was uttering, but she could tell that it was the same phrase over and over.

176

"Your mother, she did this?" Fabiola asked with wide eyes, pointing to the *vèvè* and the WE HAD A DEAL message on the wall.

"Yes. I think so," Jill shrugged. "The *vèvè* was here when Cheryl and I arrived. But the message appeared only last night."

Fabiola glanced at the message and then at the *vèvè*.

"Oh, *Bondye*, why would she draw this *vèvè*? It is an evil *vèvè*!"

"That's not true. This is Papa Legba's *vèvè*, isn't it?" Jill insisted.

Fabiola shook her head. She looked around the room, and her focus was captured by one of the books. She went over to it and picked it up, continuously muttering in her language while flipping through the pages.

"Ah!" she exclaimed a minute later, and approached the sisters.

She turned the page so that both of them could see the book clearly. Cheryl saw the *vèvè* of Papa Legba with some text under it. It was the same as the one on the wall. Fabiola pointed to the *vèvè* in the book with her forefinger and said.

"You see? This is Papa Legba's *vèvè*, *wi*?"

"Okay," Jill voiced and nodded.

Fabiola slid her finger to the top line of the *vèvè* and then pointed to the *vèvè* on the wall. Cheryl noticed that the *vèvè* on the wall had just one short, inconspicuous line drawn diagonally across the top vertical line. The one in the book didn't.

Fabiola pointed to the *vèvè* in the book one more time.

"This is Papa Legba's *vèvè*," she repeated before pointing to the wall. "That is a trickster spirit *vèvè*."

Chapter 28

"Come again?" Jill asked.

"*Wi,*" Fabiola nodded. "Trickster spirit."

Cheryl and Jill looked at each other incredulously. Cheryl had a look of dismay on her face. Whatever this trickster spirit was, it was evidently not good, especially given how Fabiola reacted.

"So, what exactly is a trickster spirit?" Cheryl asked.

Fabiola licked a finger and continued flipping through the pages of the book. A minute went by—or it could have been minutes.

"Ah!" the mambo exclaimed triumphantly and turned the book so that the sisters could see it.

A moment later, Jill realized that Fabiola was actually handing the book to her. Jill took it, feeling its immense weight as she glanced over the open pages.

There was a title on the top that said '*BE CAREFUL WHO YOU INVOKE*' with some text under it. Jill focused as she read the words.

Summoning a loa can be a difficult process. Vodouisants who wish to summon one must first perfect the drawing of the vèvè. Oftentimes, Vodouisants who practice invoking the loa need to repeat the process many times until the loa decides to show up to them. Remember what we mentioned earlier in the book—the loa can choose if they want to present themselves to us, depending on the nature of our summons.

You need to be aware not only of the drawing of your vèvè, but you also need to do extensive research to find out which loa to summon. For example, you will have much more luck tending to your garden if you invoke Azaka Medeh, the loa of harvest and agriculture.

Sometimes, the wrong loa will show up to you, and it will be up to you to determine who it is. This is especially important because some loa enjoy riddles and pranks, and will therefore not tell you who they really are. In the worst-case scenarios, your ignorance will offend them.

However, while you should be careful not to summon the wrong loa who you may disrespect unknowingly, you should be even more careful of summoning trickster spirits.

These malevolent beings prey on innocent people—especially ones who have recently lost a loved one and are trying to get in touch with them. They are almost never summoned with an intention because they have no other purpose than to wreak havoc on one's life, but unfortunately, they often find their ways into the lives of those who practice Vodou, as well as other spiritualities.

That is why it is important whenever you are summoning a spirit of any kind to ask it many questions in order to determine if it is a trickster spirit or not. Most often, trickster spirits will pretend to be the spirit you desired to summon, through lies and vague answers and will almost always ask permission to enter your home. While spirits cannot physically enter your home without permission, they can do so once you have given them the go-ahead.

Once a trickster spirit is in your home, getting rid of it is a long and difficult process.

Jill looked up from the book. Fabiola had an expectant stare. Cheryl was still reading so Jill handed the book to her to finish the page.

"I don't understand," Jill said. "It says here that trickster spirits are never summoned on purpose."

"*Wi*," Fabiola nodded, but offered no explanation.

"Well then, what do you suggest happened? Did our mom accidentally summon a trickster spirit?"

"You must understand, Vodou is complicated. Drawing a *vèvè* is very hard. Mambos and houngans must practice

179

drawing *vèvè*s over and over until it is perfect. Your mother was not a mambo, was she?"

"Not for all we knew," Jill shrugged. "So I guess Mom tried to draw Papa Legba's *vèvè* for protection, but ended up messing it up, right?

Cheryl finished reading the book. She flipped back and forth through the next pages.

"There's nothing here on how to get rid of trickster spirits," she said.

"*Non*," Fabiola shook her head. "Getting rid of trickster spirits is a difficult process. Come."

She waved one arm for the sisters to follow her out of the room. Cheryl closed the book and put it back on the shelf. Fabiola led them back to their mother's room, where she knelt next to the bed and grabbed Annette by the wrist.

"Your mother visited a Haitian cave, that's what you said, *wi*?" she asked.

"Yes, that's what our neighbor told me. The one… the one who died," Cheryl retorted.

"*Wi*," Fabiola nodded.

She slowly pulled up the sleeve of Annette's pajama, revealing a marking on her forearm. Jill leaned closer, and indeed, there was a mark there, similar to a *vèvè*, as if done as a crude tattoo in black ink.

"Your mother was marked by Kalfou," Fabiola said ominously.

"Kal-who?" Cheryl frowned.

"Kalfou is the most dangerous loa in Haitian Vodou. You do not want to summon him. Instead of summoning him, you want to tell Kalfou, *'Leave me alone'*."

"I don't understand. What does this Kalfou have to do with our mother?" Cheryl asked.

"Your mother, she visited the cave in Haiti, *wi*?"

"Yes."

"She trespassed there, and Kalfou saw her. There is a reason why the cave is not entirely open. And your mother, she went to the forbidden place."

"So, she walked somewhere where she shouldn't have, Kalfou saw her, and then what?"

"He marked her. See?" she pointed to the mark on Annette's forearm again.

"I still don't get how this trickster spirit comes into play. Is the trickster spirit Kalfou?"

"*Non.* Kalfou is a loa. Trickster spirit is a trickster spirit. When your mother returned home from that Haitian cave, she was scared, and rightly so. Kalfou can destroy people's lives very quickly. Most of the times he just causes some damage before he gets bored, but your mother didn't know that. She was scared. She tried to summon Papa Legba for protection, but instead, she summoned a trickster spirit."

"What are we supposed to do now?"

"In order to save your mother, you have to get rid of the trickster spirit. I can help you with that, but it will be difficult."

And costly, she probably wanted to say.

"What if we fail to save her?" Jill asked.

Cheryl jerked her head towards Jill.

"What do you mean?" Fabiola asked.

"I mean, can this spirit follow us home and ruin our lives if we don't resolve it?"

Cheryl's look of intrigue turned into one of judgment. Jill knew that her sister knew why she was asking this question, but right now, she didn't care what Cheryl thought. If a life had to be traded for another life, then Annette was at the bottom of the priority ladder, and that was not up for debate.

"The spirit usually either attaches itself to a house or to a particular person. In this case, it is attached to your mother."

"So that means that Cheryl and I are safe, right?" Jill asked with slight relief washing over her.

"We're not leaving Mom for this thing to torture and kill," Cheryl raised her tone.

"I didn't say we would."

"That's what you were thinking."

"Are we gonna go through this again, Cheryl?" Jill was tired of Cheryl's outbursts, and she didn't plan on taking her shit anymore.

"*Tanpri, mezanmi, tanpri*," Fabiola raised her palms, each towards one sister. "No need to argue. We will save your mother, *oke?*"

Jill and Cheryl stared at each other a moment longer with near-hostility. Jill was the first one who looked away. The only sound that remained in the room was the machine's beeping.

"Hey," Fabiola said softly but authoritatively. "You want to fight like children? Do it. But wait until your mother is saved from the trickster spirit. Now, what will it be?"

She angrily stared at Cheryl and Jill, placing her closed fists on her hips and her nostrils flared from her visible frustration.

"Fine," Cheryl crossed her arms.

Jill silently nodded.

"Good," Fabiola nodded, and her face instantly turned back to a less gloomy expression.

Without another word, she strode out of the room, leaving Cheryl and Jill alone. Jill nodded and followed, motioning to Cheryl to stay with her.

"Let's go after her, I guess," she said.

Fabiola went outside the house to her miniature car and opened the trunk. Jill remained a slight distance from her, mostly because she didn't want to breathe down the woman's neck as she rummaged through the things.

A short time later, she slammed the trunk shut, and when she turned to face the house, she had a dusty, tattered suitcase in her hand. It looked ancient, and it bulged on one end, indicating that it was filled with too many things that barely fit inside.

"What have you got there?" Cheryl asked, pointing to the suitcase.

"A shrunken skull, a voodoo doll, chicken eyeballs, and snake venom," Fabiola recited.

Jill wrinkled her nose while Cheryl gave the mambo a sour smile. And then, Fabiola burst into a cackle.

"I joke!" she said as her laughter died down, and made her way past the confused sisters into the house.

■ ■

Jill and Cheryl followed Fabiola back to Annette's office. Jill couldn't help but notice how the Vodou priestess made herself at home, exploring each corner of the house the way she liked, not bothering to ask the hosts for permission.

Once all three of them were in the room, Fabiola cleared a spot and placed her suitcase on the floor. She undid the clasps and the suitcase practically burst from the released pressure inside.

Fabiola widely opened it, revealing the contents inside. There were no chicken eyeballs, or snake venom, but there may as well have been. There was a dried chicken leg, very similar to what Annette had in the office, there was chalk, some candles, a miniature drum, and other trinkets that Jill couldn't recognize.

The mambo began cautiously, and with care, removing items from the suitcase, gently placing them on the floor in front of herself. By now, all three women were sitting on the floor, with Jill and Cheryl patiently waiting to see what Fabiola would do next.

As intrigued as Jill was by all of this, she couldn't help but feel uncomfortable, too. She couldn't shake the feeling that she and Cheryl were getting into something from which there would be no turning back.

When Jill glanced at her little sister, she saw a concerned look in her eye. Cheryl followed Fabiola's movements without blinking, undoubtedly sensing that something big was coming up.

Once Fabiola placed all the necessary items in front of herself, she clapped her hands together and smiled, glancing between the two sisters.

"Now, which one of you two will be the horse?"

"The horse?" Jill raised an eyebrow.

"Yes, you want to get your mother back, *wi*?"

"Yes!" Cheryl loudly stated before Fabiola even finished the sentence.

Fabiola looked at her with that same bland smile plastered to her face.

"To save your mother, we need to invoke a loa. And to invoke a loa, we need a horse."

"Mind explaining what that means, exactly?" Jill inquired, gritting her teeth.

She really wasn't in the mood for this shit.

"It means," Fabiola said calmly. "That one of you will need to let a loa possess you."

184

Chapter 29

For a moment, Cheryl and Jill stared at each other in confusion. Let a Vodou loa possess them? What on earth was this woman's game plan? For a moment, Cheryl contemplated the possibility of Fabiola actually serving an evil loa and doing its bidding. Maybe Fabiola's job was exactly that—to cause evil and destruction to unsuspecting victims.

"No. No fucking way," Cheryl blurted out.

"I don't understand," Jill calmly said. "How in the hell is letting a loa possess one of us going to help us in any way?"

Fabiola raised a hand and began gesturing.

"We summon a benevolent loa to possess you, and while you're possessed, you are able to traverse the crossroads," she said.

"Crossroads? What's that? Is that some kind of Vodou limbo?" Jill asked.

"In a manner of speaking, yes. Crossroads connect all our worlds and everything else. Papa Legba is the loa responsible for opening the crossroads to us. However, Papa Legba would not open to us the path that we want to travel."

"And what path is that?" Cheryl interjected.

"The one where the trickster spirit has your mother."

Silence fell on the room once more, deafeningly so this time. Cheryl looked at Jill. Jill looked down, visibly uncomfortable. One of them would need to allow the loa to possess them, and who knows what kind of risks that entailed.

"I'll do it," Cheryl said with alacrity.

Fabiola and Jill looked at her.

"Hold up, Cheryl, you can't just jump into this," Jill objected. "We don't even know what the hell this means, let alone what to do."

"We have no other choice," Cheryl shrugged.

Jill opened her mouth, but quickly closed it, not saying a thing. She turned to Fabiola and pointed a finger at her.

"Why can't you be the one to do it?"

"Someone needs to summon the loa, and someone needs to tell it to leave in case things go bad."

"Jill, it's fine," Cheryl interjected and looked at Fabiola. "I'll do it. But I need you to tell me everything first."

Fabiola nodded. She moved closer to Cheryl and began explaining, "Before I invoke the loa, you need to clear your mind. The loa needs to feel welcome to possess you. You must understand that unlike in Christianity, Haitians *want* the loa to possess them. It is a great honor. And the loa do not possess those who do not want it."

"And what exactly will happen after the loa possesses me?" Cheryl asked.

She had already come to terms with the fact that she would go through this. She had to—for Mom's sake.

"In usual rituals, the horse would have no memory of the time they were possessed. Depending on the loa that we invoke, your physical body will display those behaviors. But in the ritual that we will perform here, your spirit will be transported to the crossroads. There, you must find your mother."

"How do I do that?"

Fabiola shook her head, and it sent Cheryl's hopes crashing.

"Only you will know, *cheri*," the mambo said. "Follow familiar paths, don't wander into obscured areas, and ignore the dead."

"The dead?"

Fabiola nodded.

"The crossroads are full of spirits of the dead, those who angered the loa, or who simply got lost, and are now doomed to wander forever, always looking for their way home, but never finding it."

Cheryl heard the expression of blood running cold many times in her life, but she never attributed it to an actual, physical meaning. Now, as she listened to Fabiola, she found that she could feel herself becoming cold, and finally understanding where the phrase came from.

"And this trickster spirit you mentioned; what exactly is it doing to our mom?"

"Keeping her soul captive, feeding off it. Until there is nothing left to eat."

"And Kalfou?"

"Gone. If he ever was here, he left a long time ago."

Cheryl sucked in a deep breath. The thought of that black figure from her dreams came back to her mind. Is that what she would be facing off against? If so, how would she be able to win?

"What is the worst-case scenario that could possibly happen?" Jill asked.

Fabiola grimaced, her eyes fixated up at the ceiling, "There are many things that could go wrong. She could get lost and end up like your mother, trapped in a coma-like state. The trickster spirit could latch onto her. And if she spends too long on the crossroads, or possessed by the loa, she could die."

"Alright, that's enough!" Jill's raised voice echoed loudly in the room. "You expect me to let my sister put herself in such danger?! And for what?! A small, almost impossible chance of bringing our mother back?!"

She looked at Cheryl with pleading eyes.

"Cheryl, please. Don't do this," she implored.

Cheryl sighed and looked down at the floor. On the one hand, Jill was right. This was a huge risk. On the other hand, Mom was in danger. Cheryl remembered her childhood and how Mom took care of her. That gave her enough courage to make her decision.

"I'm doing this," she said.

"Cheryl…"

"It's risky, I know. And I also know you wouldn't do this for Mom, because you don't love her. But I do. You always said that you wished you had more time with Dad. I feel the same way about Mom."

Her voice quivered, and her vision got blurry from the tears that formed in her eyes. She noticed that Jill's lips started quivering, too.

"Cherry, please don't do this…" Jill said with a broken-up voice, tears streaming down her cheeks as she sniffled.

This caused Cheryl to break down, as well. She shot forward at the same time as Jill, and they embraced each other tightly, sobbing uncontrollably. Cheryl felt Jill's tear-stricken cheeks pressing against hers, and for a moment, she felt like they were kids again when Cheryl got bullied, and Jill came to her rescue.

"If something happens to me, tell Charlie I love him," Cheryl said.

Jill pulled back and gently grabbed Cheryl by the cheeks.

"No. You'll tell him that yourself once you're back. And then he can spend some quality time with his aunt and his grandma."

Cheryl cried a little harder as she leaned her forehead against Jill's. Cheryl suddenly didn't want to let her sister go, but she knew that she had to. Mom was in trouble, going through god-knows-what, and she had to rescue her.

Once Cheryl pulled away and scooted back to her spot on the floor, she wiped her tears, sniffled, and nodded resolutely at Fabiola. Fabiola nodded back. Jill wiped her tears, as well, and now retained a calm, almost tired expression on her face, her eyes puffy and bloodshot from crying.

Cheryl felt like it would be really easy to start crying once again if she allowed the flood of emotions to overwhelm her. But she wouldn't allow that fear to overwhelm her. Mom's life depended on her, and she was intent on bringing her back.

"Do you need some more time, *cheri*?" Fabiola asked with a motherly concern in her timbre.

"No. I'm ready, Fabiola," Cheryl nodded.

"Good," Fabiola said and grabbed a chalk from the suitcase. "For this ritual, we will invoke Ezili Freda, the loa of love, femininity, and luxury. Make some room, *tanpri*."

Jill and Cheryl gave Fabiola a little more space so that she could begin drawing on the floor. The room had wooden flooring, so Fabiola was able to draw on it with relative ease.

Each line she drew was elegant and artistic, which indicated that she must have done this a million times over. It soon became apparent that she was drawing a *vèvè* in the shape of a heart, with various meticulously drawn lines in the interior, and some lines that decorated the exterior of the *vèvè*.

She drew quickly. Once she was done, she placed the chalk back in the suitcase and wiped her hands against one another to clean the white dust off her fingers.

"Now, go ahead, enter the portal," she gestured to the *vèvè*.

Cheryl looked at her with a raised eyebrow and then at the *vèvè*. She glanced at Jill, just to make sure she wasn't stupidly missing something obvious, but her sister looked just as confused.

When Cheryl looked back at Fabiola, she had an expectant look on her face. With no idea what to do next, Cheryl reached forward for the *vèvè*. Suddenly, she didn't want to touch it. Her finger hovered above the center of the heart, but she couldn't bring herself to lower it any further. It was as if an invisible magnet was pushing her finger away.

And then—

Fabiola burst into a guffawing fit. She laughed so hard that she almost fell sideways as she slapped her knee hysterically in laughter. Both Jill and Cheryl stared at her in confusion.

"I *joke!*" she finally said through laughing tears.

This baited a smile out of Cheryl, but nothing more. Jill didn't look amused at all.

"Okay, I will be serious now. This is a serious matter," Fabiola said and exhaled deeply, calming herself down.

She was about to say something else, but she laughed a little more. When she realized she was the only one in the room laughing, she wiped her tears away and sighed deeply. Her face morphed from laughing to a more serious expression.

"Okay. I joke a little to ease the difficult task ahead of us. But now, we must be serious when summoning the loa. Ezili Freda is easily offended, and we do not want to offend her, *wi?*"

"Wait!" Jill raised a hand with a focused expression.

Cheryl heard it, too.

The sound of a car pulling into the driveway. And then a muffled, petulant, barely audible voice that she knew all too well.

"Is Mom inside?" the child asked.

Chapter 30

Jill couldn't believe it. She was overcome by a feeling of surprise. And then a mixture of anger and happiness. She jumped to her feet and stormed out of the office, raced downstairs, and yanked the door open so violently that she thought she might tear the knob out of place. She strode outside and stopped, putting her hands on her hips.

"Mommy!" Charlie yelled almost immediately, once he saw her.

He ran towards her with his arms spread. Jill knelt down and embraced him just as he collided with her, causing her to fall backward. She didn't even care about getting her shirt dirty from the grass.

"Charlie! Oh, I missed you so much, baby," she said as she rocked left and right, kissing Charlie's head and caressing his face.

"Hey, babe," Lee said as he took a step forward towards them.

Jill looked at him with wide eyes.

"Lee! What are you doing here?!" she meant for the question to sound hostile and accusatory, but she couldn't hide her exuberance.

"You know. Came to see what you were doing. Charlie kinda missed you. I didn't, but he did, so we decided to come."

Despite the danger of the house, she couldn't help but feel happy to see her family. But then it dawned on her.

The house is dangerous.

She gently pulled Charlie off of her and clambered up to her feet, the initial joy of seeing her family slightly wearing down, and anger and newfound concern forming inside her.

"Lee, I'm serious. What are you guys doing here? I told you not to come here!"

Charlie was buzzing around her, tugging her hand, excitedly telling her a story.

"Not now, baby," Jill shushed him.

Charlie looked towards the house and his eyes suddenly gleamed with even more excitement.

"Aunt Cherry!" he shouted and ran towards the house.

"Charlie, wait!" Jill reached out to stop him from approaching the house, but it was too late.

She turned around and saw Cheryl and Fabiola standing on the porch. Cheryl embraced Charlie in a similar fashion, minus the falling on her back part. Fabiola darted her eyes at the newcomers with a flippant smile on her face. Jill couldn't tell from the reticence of the mambo's face if she was impatient or not.

"Who's that?" Lee asked, jutting his head subtly towards Fabiola.

Jill refocused herself and remembered that Lee was there, and the worry of what might happen to her family increased. She noticed that Charlie and Cheryl were preoccupied getting to know each other—Charlie was telling Cheryl about something with excited gestures, while Cheryl responded to everything he was saying with exaggerated and patronizing phrases.

Jill pulled Lee aside so that they had some privacy away from the others.

"I told you not to come here, Lee. Do you realize how dangerous it is here? What were you thinking bringing our son here?!"

"Hey, I couldn't just leave Charlie alone for the whole day. And I couldn't let you deal with whatever crap you have here on your own."

Jill sighed and ran a hand through her hair.

"You have to leave the house, now," she said.

"Why?" Lee chuckled. "What's so bad about this house?"

"It's not just the house. I don't want Charlie seeing my mother in a coma. He could start thinking about death and other morbid things."

"We won't let him see her, alright?" Lee raised his palms towards Jill defensively. "I already told him grandma is busy, so it's not like he expects to see her."

Jill crossed her arms, and suddenly became aware that it was a gesture that Cheryl often made. She looked towards the house and saw Fabiola now speaking to Charlie while he listened with eyes as wide as saucers.

She better not be talking to him about Vodou rituals and other such things.

"Hey. Babe? What exactly is wrong?" Lee asked solicitously.

Jill sighed and looked down at her feet. Lee took a step closer and put his hands on Jill's neck. She suddenly felt the relief leaving her at his touch.

"Jill, come on. You know you can tell me everything. We're a team, right?"

"You wouldn't understand this," Jill shook her head.

"Try me."

Jill pondered that for a moment. Should she tell him? Was Lee going to believe her? Or would he think that she was going crazy like Annette? She already told him a million times how her mom was paranoid, so what if Lee started to see Jill the same way? What if one day he left her and took Charlie, just like Dad did with her? But she had Cheryl on her side. Cheryl could confirm the story.

So it's going to be two crazy sisters.

"Alright, I'll tell you," Jill said. "But I need you to be open-minded about this. I'm not going crazy, I swear. Cheryl can confirm what I tell you, too."

"Okay, I'm listening," Lee said with a stern look on his face.

Jill sighed, not even sure where to start, so she just started with whatever came to her mind first. As she spoke,

Lee developed a frown on his face. Anyone who didn't know him would think that he was silently judging her, but Jill knew after all these years that it was just his focused gaze. He didn't change his facial expression once, even when Jill went into the supernatural details of what went down in the house.

When she finally finished explaining that they were about to send Cheryl to the Vodou crossroads, she realized how outlandish her entire story must sound. She expected Lee to laugh, or worse, to patronize her.

"Alright. What can I do to help?" Lee finally asked.

This surprised Jill, but it also terrified her. The reason for that was because if Lee believed the story, that meant that this was all real, and that there really was something supernatural going on. A small part of Jill still wanted to believe that there was a logical explanation for all of this, but that part disappeared with each passing hour.

"You and Charlie can go home, is what you can do," Jill said.

"We drove all the way out here. We're not going home," Lee shook his head firmly.

"Lee, didn't you hear a word of what I just said? The house is dangerous! Look, if you don't wanna go home, then at least take Charlie and go to Medford. Just until this is all finished. Okay?"

"Actually, Jill, all three of you can go to Medford together," Cheryl stealthily appeared at Jill's side, almost startling her.

She had Charlie with her, holding a hand on his shoulder.

"I bet Charlie would love to visit the Rogue Valley Zipline Adventure. Right, Charlie?"

"Yeah!" Charlie exclaimed, the excitement palpable in his voice.

It would be hard to calm him down now.

"Can we go, Mom? Please?" he pleaded as he bounced up and down while holding Jill by her hands.

"Cheryl, what are you doing?" Jill glowered at Cheryl.

"Nothing," Cheryl shrugged aloofly. "You guys need some family time together. Let me and Fabiola take care of the house while you're gone."

As if on cue, Fabiola walked up to them and grinned. She must have heard what Cheryl said because she nodded fervently.

"Everything will be okay while you're gone, *cheri*. You have fun with your family," she dismissively waved with her wrist.

"It's okay, Jill. We got this," Cheryl smiled confidently.

Jill thought for a moment. Everyone was looking at her. Charlie was still tugging her hands and begging her to go to the zipline park. Jill's eyes met Cheryl's. They smiled reassuringly at each other. She looked down at Charlie.

"Okay, sure, why not?" Jill shrugged. "Let's go to Rogue Valley Zipline Adventure!"

"Yay!" Charlie triumphantly hopped around.

"But under one condition," Jill added.

Charlie stopped cheering.

"That you let Aunt Cheryl sleep over at our apartment once we get back," she looked at Cheryl with a satisfactory smile.

Charlie exploded in happiness and immediately started telling Cheryl about the cool video games he had to show her. Cheryl agreed to see everything he wanted her to see. Lee ushered Charlie—with great effort—back to the car and motioned with his head for Jill to also get in. Jill looked at Cheryl once more. There may have been a glimmer of fear in her eyes, or maybe not. Jill couldn't quite tell.

As she entered the car, she continued staring at her sister, hoping they would be able to start rebuilding their relationship, once this was all over.

Chapter 31

As Cheryl watched Jill, Lee, and Charlie leaving, she didn't feel sad anymore. For so many years, she had wanted to fix her relationship with Jill, even though she wasn't truly aware of it until their reunion. It was one of those things that had caused a void in her life—and no matter what she tried, she couldn't fill it up. What happened to Mom was terrible, but it had brought her and Jill back together, so it was also a good thing.

Cheryl wondered for a moment if Mom could see them right now and what she would think about it. She always talked about how sorry she was that Jill and Cheryl weren't closer and often compared them to siblings who had really tight-knit relationships.

Now, Cheryl had at least buried the hatchet with her sister. And with that came a strong will to live. She wanted to live for Mom, but even more potently, she wanted to live for Jill *and* for Charlie.

"Are you okay, *cheri?*" Fabiola gently stroked Cheryl's back.

"Yeah," Cheryl said, still staring at the car that was now a tiny dot in the distance. "Yeah, I'm good. Let's get this over with, huh?"

"*Wi,*" Fabiola nodded with a reassuring smile.
***
Cheryl's anxiety eased out of her when they sat back down in the office, in front of the *vèvè* drawn on the floor. Fabiola and Cheryl had scavenged any fancy items they could find in the house. Cheryl didn't know what 'fancy' meant until Fabiola explained to her that the loa they were summoning, Ezili Freda, loved gifts like lipstick, perfumes, candy, and jewelry.

Cheryl found some good candy, and Mom had lots of jewelry in her bedroom—rings, necklaces, and bracelets of both sentimental and monetary value. When she retrieved a perfume from the bathroom, Fabiola took it from her and scrutinized it before making a disgusted grimace and shoving it back to Cheryl.

"What?" Cheryl shrugged.

"This will not do. Ezili Freda prefers only the *finest* perfume. If we give her this, she will be insulted."

"My mom's been using this perfume all her life. There's nothing wrong with it."

"Yes, and in Haiti, some people save money for weeks to be able to afford a fancy perfume just to summon Ezili Freda."

Once all the items were placed on the *vèvè* drawn on the floor, Fabiola calmly looked at Cheryl and said, "We are ready to begin. Are you prepared?"

Cheryl nodded.

"Remember, if you get in trouble, or when you find your mother, chant these words aloud. *Papa Legba, get me out.* Or *Papa Legba, get us out.* Okay?"

"Papa Legba, get us out. Okay," Cheryl acknowledged while repeating the phrase back to her.

"Just keep repeating it until you are out of there, okay?"

"Okay."

Fabiola nodded.

"Then first, close your eyes."

Cheryl did so.

"Clear your mind of everything. You need to relax."

Cheryl inhaled and exhaled calmly, trying to blank out her mind. She quickly realized that is was impossible. Her mind repeatedly raced from thought to thought—from Jill, to Charlie, to Mom, to Erika, then to Erika's dead body splayed on the stairs—

"I can't clear my mind," Cheryl said dismally.

197

"Then try to imagine something peaceful, *cheri*. A time when you were relaxed or happy."

Cheryl thought about that. When was the last time she was happy—*truly happy*?

She wasn't a pessimistic person in general, and it didn't take a lot to make her happy. Her life in college was pretty relaxing. She had lots of friends (not counting the backstabbers), college wasn't overly hard or stressful, and she generally liked living in California. But she didn't have a feeling of immense happiness there. She was content, yes, but not happy. Even when she was with Tom, madly in love, that feeling wasn't present.

Her thoughts returned to when she was a kid, back when life was much simpler. She remembered a vacation the entire family had once taken to the Bahamas. She was only four back then, and this was before Mom had started losing her mind.

The family was on the beach; Mom and Dad were sunbathing, and Jill and Cheryl were building a sandcastle nearby. Cheryl didn't do anything to actually contribute to building the castle, but she tried futilely. She even accidentally caused a cave-in on one of the towers and shouted '*Oh, no!*' in dismay. She thought Jill would be upset about it.

To her relief, Jill simply told her that it was okay and fixed it. She then told Cheryl to take the seashells they found in the water and embed them around the castle as decorations. By the time they finished, the castle was large, with multiple battlements and towers, and even a bridge with a dug-in moat around it.

Cheryl was proud of the work she accomplished by settling the seashells around various spots of the castle. She was even prouder when Jill told her what a good team they made.

Cheryl opened her eyes.

"Okay, now what?" she asked.

"Now, we summon Ezili Freda. Please, try to stay calm. Do not fear, no matter what you see or hear. Ezili Freda is not an evil loa."

"What should I do?"

"Just relax and allow Ezili Freda to enter your physical body."

With that, Fabiola started chanting words of invocation intermittently in English and Haitian Creole. The words were simple, mostly focusing on calling Ezili Freda by her name and stating what gifts were being given to her.

Cheryl expected to start seeing things happening soon, but long minutes went by without any unusual occurrences. Soon, she had let her guard down. She no longer felt nervous. If anything, she was bored, and her ass was starting to hurt from sitting on the wooden floor. The entire time, Fabiola chanted the words tirelessly, over and over, until Cheryl memorized them—even in Haitian Creole.

And then, after an unbeknownst amount of time, Cheryl noticed something out of the corner of her eye.

There was a wisp of pink smoke swirling in the corner of the room...

At first, it slowly glided through the air. But then it increased in size, coming from an unknown source of the room, until the wisp coiled like a snake and gyrated in the air. The smoke looked almost as if it had come from a cigarette, except it wasn't dispersed out in various directions and uneven, but rather it continued to twist through the air as one giant wisp.

Fabiola's chanting grew louder and faster, repeatedly raising the gifts presented to Ezili Freda and lowering them as the smoke randomly slid through the air like a snake, drawing ever-closer to the *vèvè*. Cheryl didn't take her eyes off the smoke. She thought she saw a humanoid face there, but she dismissed it as her overactive imagination.

The smoke now slowly danced around her head, veiling her vision with a shade of pink. And then, just as Cheryl inhaled, the smoke violently entered her nose and her mouth. She felt a burning sensation sliding up her nostrils and through her sinuses, rushing all the way down her throat until it reached her chest.

She felt the urge to cough violently, but she suddenly realized that she no longer had any control of her body. She started shaking violently.

And then, there was nothing.

Chapter 32

Fabiola watched as the pink, odorless smoke entered Cheryl's mouth and nose. The girl gagged momentarily and then froze. She started convulsing, first slightly, and then it turned into epileptical-like shaking. Cheryl threw her head back, and the convulsing stopped.

She was frozen for a moment before jerking her head forward. She looked around the room in confusion, mouth slightly agape, shoulders relaxed. Her eyes locked with Fabiola's, and the mambo knew that she was no longer staring at Cheryl, but at Ezili Freda.

"Thank you for answering my call, Ezili Freda," Fabiola said. "You are even more beautiful than the last time we met."

Cheryl's mouth morphed into a brusque smile. Her eyes fell on the *vèvè* and the gifts in front of it, and her face lit up with fascination.

"Oh!" she uttered as she reached for the emerald-decorated ring.

She put the ring on her finger and outstretched her arm in front of herself, admiring how her hand looked with the ring on it. Fabiola noticed a drastic change in Cheryl's facial expressions and body language.

Fabiola had met Ezili Freda a few times in the past, and although she didn't like dealing with this particular loa due to her high-maintenance nature, Fabiola found that she was the best fit for Cheryl. Had it been Jill who decided to be possessed, then invoking Ezili Danto would have worked better.

The first time Fabiola witnessed the drumming ritual, she was only six years old and had found it bizarre. People were dancing and singing to sounds of drums, until one of the young male dancers began convulsing. His eyes rolled to the back of his head, and his dancing drastically changed. He got on the floor and started slithering like a snake—and he did it with such finesse!

Fabiola had thought originally that he was just faking it, but after some time, the young dancer lost consciousness. When he woke up, he claimed he had no recollection of what happened. Fabiola remained unconvinced, but continued practicing Vodou as per her parents' request.

At the age of thirteen, she experienced being the *chwal*—or horse—for the first time. She remembered dancing to the drum beat, and the next thing she knew, she woke up on the floor, with people cheering and praising her. She learned later that the loa they summoned was Ayizan, and they even showed her the video of her dancing. Sure enough, it couldn't have been her because the dancing was much more complex and elegant; something she had never learned in her everyday life.

She became more interested in Vodou after that, and went on to become an initiate, until she finally climbed to the rank of mambo. By that time, she had decided to move to America for a more prosperous future—something Papa Legba told her to do during one of her services to him.

Cheryl placed more rings on her fingers and admired her decorated hand from various angles, grinning at the shiny objects. Fabiola patiently waited until the loa got bored with the jewelry and moved on to the lipstick. Fabiola held up a small mirror in front of Ezili Freda as she watched her put on the lipstick.

She pouted and pursed her lips, swiveling her head left and right, examining how the colors looked from various angles.

"You look so beautiful, Ezili Freda. I admire your beauty," Fabiola praised.

She had to flatter Ezili Freda. She was one of the more demanding loa who didn't go for simple gifts—like Papa

Legba, who simply preferred roasted corn and tobacco for his pipe. No, Ezili Freda preferred flattery and expensive gifts, and she was also known for being jealous. That's why Fabiola always advised men who wanted to invoke her to never speak about their partners, or have any evidence of a potential partner in the room when summoning her.

Ezili Freda took the mirror from Fabiola and admired her own reflection. She giggled from time to time, something that looked so unnatural for Cheryl, despite the fact that Fabiola had only known her for a very short time.

"You are really beautiful, Ezili Freda. You are the most beautiful loa," Fabiola repeated.

Fabiola hoped that Cheryl would be able to find her mom in the crossroads soon, because all of this flattering was making her cringe.

Chapter 33

It couldn't have been longer than a few seconds since everything had gone dark. One moment, Cheryl was in the room with Fabiola, the pink smoke swirling around her, and in the next, she was standing outside somewhere, surrounded by a thick fog.

She carefully observed the area surrounding her. She was standing on a beaten-down dirt path, except it seemed like it was more than just a path. It was quite wide, at least as far as the part unobscured by the fog stretched. The ground was flat, giving it a feeling of a large dirt street, rather than a naturally formed pathway.

It was night, or so Cheryl thought. Everything around her was dark, but not too dark. It was as if she were standing under a starless sky, and yet some sort of light similar to moonlight came from somewhere.

"Fabiola?" Cheryl called out, her voice barely audible in the air.

There was no response. Of course not. What did she expect? To hear Fabiola's voice booming from somewhere like a celestial entity, guiding her through the crossroads? No, she was on her own here.

But what should she do? Wherever she turned, there was nothing but fog. In her mind, she repeatedly chanted the sentence that Fabiola told her, if only to avoid forgetting the words. The fact that she could use that as her ticket out of here gave her a sense of assurance. Besides, could something bad really happen to her at the crossroads? She wasn't physically here, right?

Just then, she saw a signpost, barely visible through the fog. It was pointing in one direction down the path, but whatever had been written on the wooden board was so badly scratched up that the letters were indiscernible.

Cheryl spun around once more, making sure to stay somewhat close to the signpost out of fear of losing sight of it. There was nothing else around. Cheryl didn't want to move. What if she walked into the fog, following where the old signpost was pointing, and ended up lost forever? Fabiola told her not to go into unfamiliar areas, and Cheryl assumed that the crossroads were vast.

She continuously spun around in circles, and when she realized that there was absolutely nothing else that she might have missed, decided that following the signpost was her only option. She took a deep breath and broke into a gait forward.

Almost as soon as she did, the fog began dispersing—ever so slightly. It retreated enough for Cheryl to see just how wide the road was—and it was surprisingly much narrower than she had originally thought. It stretched about eight feet in width before revealing walls that cordoned off the path on either side.

No, not walls. Houses. Old, dilapidated makeshift structures slapped together from wood, mud, and rusted metal, made in a way that they provided shelter from the elements, but not looking fit for living inside them.

She wasn't on a trail; she was on a street.

The alleyways between the houses were filled with an even thicker fog, and Cheryl did her best to stay in the center of the street to avoid those creepy alleys as much as possible. The fog was still somewhat thick ahead of her, but she was now able to see at least ten feet ahead.

Cheryl had no idea how long she walked for—it could have been five minutes or fifteen minutes—when she saw the outlines of figures not far ahead. She stopped dead in her tracks and held her breath.

There were three of them, and they stood close to each other, in the middle of the road. From here, they looked like their backs were hunched over and they faced away from her. Cheryl continued staring, but no movement came from them. Maybe they weren't figures at all, but some sort of statues?

Tentatively, she continued walking forward, not taking her eyes off the figures. As the fog retreated forward, she suddenly realized that there were many more than three of them. She watched as dozens of them appeared all over the street, some standing in the middle of the dirt road, others farther back near the houses, and she saw a number of them in the dark alleyways.

Cheryl observed the figure closest to her, which was only a few feet in front of her. It was a gaunt, cadaverous man with bones protruding tightly against his skin at every spot on his body. His head slumped forward in a droopy facial expression, his back kyphotically hunched forward, his arms lamely dangling at his sides. His knees were slightly bent, looking as if they would barely be able to withhold the weight of his own body. He wore some kind of tattered, dirtied robes that looked like they may have come from the middle ages.

Cheryl walked around the figure in a wide arc to the right, but kept her eyes fixated on it. She wondered if all these beings were imitations of humans or something more macabre—maybe a husk of a human long since gone. She looked forward at the army of statues—

A moan to Cheryl's left caused her to jump. She jerked her head towards it, eyes wide, heart leaping into her throat.

The gaunt man had moved!

Cheryl clasped her hands over her mouth, suppressing a terrified scream. The man slowly raised his head and raspily moaned once more, before letting it droop back down again. It was as if he barely had the strength to lift his head, even for that brief moment.

As if on cue, Cheryl saw the other figures on the street moving, too. How had she not seen it before?

Most of them stood still, with their heads, or one limb, occasionally moving briefly, in a near-futile manner. Some of them were shambling down the street or aimlessly walking in circles. Not all of them were as decrepit as the first figure Cheryl had laid her eyes upon. In fact, most of them simply looked tired. They had tortured expressions on their faces, their backs concaved forward, and they dragged their feet on the ground. A small number of them, however, looked like they had retained a lot of their energy—they rocked back and forth like junkies, their eyes darting in various directions with terrified stares, and some even muttered incoherent words.

The longer Cheryl stood in the middle of the street, though, the more she started to realize how harmless they actually were. One of the figures saw her—she was sure of it because its eyes met hers—and yet, it just continued wallowing in its own misery, whatever that misery was in this case.

Were these the dead that Fabiola warned her to stay away from? Have they been stuck here for so long that they became mere shells of their former selves? Is this what would happen to her, too?

Is this what was happening to Mom right now?

Cheryl pushed those questions away and looked ahead for the best route to avoid touching the people. They were densely converged in one spot, and Cheryl knew there was no way to circumvent them. She looked back and saw the foggy road, but to her amazement, the houses she passed by earlier had been swallowed up in a dense fog.

She could only go forward, and she would need to navigate around and sidle between the figures to make her way ahead. Without stalling any further, she started walking slowly forward.

At first, it was easy. All she needed to do was avoid the figures in a wide arc. But pretty soon, she got to the densely packed area, and she had to stop to examine where the widest gap was. She found one a few feet to the right—a narrow, two-foot-long gap between a young woman and an elderly man.

She sidled between them, step by step, holding her breath in the process. She flinched and stopped when the woman snorted, but once she was sure that she was safe, she continued walking sideways.

From there, Cheryl had to navigate in semicircles, eventually breaking away from the crowded area and continuing down the road. The number of people here was much sparser, but Cheryl still had to detour around them by getting close to one of the dark alleys. She did her best not to step close to it until she saw the silhouette of an elderly black man peeking from the fog, staring right at her. Cheryl quickly moved her gaze away and broke into a trot to get past the alleyway as soon as possible.

But then, the man spoke up with a heavily accented voice, "Pst. Child. Over here."

It came out as *'Ovah heah'*. Cheryl jerked her head towards him. She could now see the man's features a little more clearly. Although it was obscured by the darkness, Cheryl saw the creases and wrinkles that decorated his old face.

"Yes, you!" the man called out, when he realized that he had Cheryl's attention.

"What do you want?" Cheryl timorously asked before realizing that she probably shouldn't have spoken to the man at all.

He must be one of the dead, and Fabiola warned Cheryl to ignore them.

"Come closer, child."

Kom closah, child.

His accent sounded African, Cheryl thought.

"No. You can tell me what you want from there," she shook her head.

The man grinned, showing yellow teeth under pink gums. The fog somehow seemed to have cleared away, further revealing his form. Cheryl noticed an old straw hat on his head and a bushy beard that went nearly down to his stomach. He was wearing a cape of some sort, and under it, a shirt and pants. He was barefoot, sitting on an old barrel, holding a pipe in his hand.

"You are new here, are you not?" he asked.

"No. I'm not gonna stay here long," Cheryl said.

The old man threw his head back and cackled. This unnerved Cheryl. Once he was done laughing, he looked back at Cheryl and asked, "Say, child. You wouldn't happen to have some tobacco, would you?"

"No," Cheryl retorted.

She wished that the situation was less dreadful, so that she could give him a more ironic answer.

I don't go around carrying tobacco in my pockets when traveling to other dimensions, sorry.

The old man simply nodded with a disappointed look on his face.

"That's okay," he said. "You are looking for your mother, yes?"

That caught Cheryl's attention.

"Yes! How do you know?!" she almost took a step forward, before remembering not to approach the dark areas.

The man shrugged.

"I always recognize new faces."

"Tell me how to find her," Cheryl demanded.

She did her best not to sound too desperate. She didn't want the man to think that he had her wrapped around his finger.

"If you want to find your mother, all you need to do is look, child," he said.

He put the pipe in his mouth and pointed to Cheryl's right, even though he couldn't see the street from here. Cheryl followed his finger, and her eyes widened when she saw it.

209

The fog cleared up in one area, and Mom's house emerged a bit further down the street, incongruously towering above the slums surrounding it. Cheryl looked at the old man, wanting to express gratitude, but had no idea what to say. The man had a smirk on his face.

"Go on, child. But be warned. You might not like what you find."

Cheryl nodded to him and, without a word, broke into a jog towards the house. That was the place she needed to visit, no doubt about it. She didn't even care about the figures on the streets anymore. She narrowly avoided them—and once even brushed one with her shoulder—but continued running until she reached the house.

Once she was in front of it, she spent a moment in awe. It looked so strange to see it out here on this desolate road, surrounded by the other unfamiliar structures. There was no green lawn, no driveway, no paved walkway leading up and down the street. It was as if a giant crane had picked up the house and moved it here.

Cheryl climbed the steps of the porch and stopped in front of the door. What should she do? Knock? Go inside? Ring the doorbell? Suddenly, she felt something akin to dread building up inside her. It was a feeling that only intensified the closer she got to the house.

Something told her that no matter how she entered, the evil inside—whatever it was—would be alerted to her presence, and it wouldn't matter if she was stealthy or loud.

Without delaying any further than necessary, Cheryl grabbed the doorknob, twisted it, and firmly pushed the door open, ominously revealing the darkened interior.

Chapter 34

"Lee, make sure he's strapped in tightly!" Jill shouted.

She was standing next to a tree where the zip-line ended. The park was brimming with excited voices of both adults and children who had come for a zip-line adventure. There were various zip-lining challenges people could take, with some of them being as high as fifty feet, and going down in an almost vertical slant.

Lee and Charlie were on top of a hill about a hundred yards away. Charlie was standing on the wooden platform attached to the tree where the zip-line started, with Lee making sure that he was secure for the ride down.

A few minutes prior to this, the instructor had demonstrated to them how to use the equipment. Jill found it irresponsible to have the instructor buzzing elsewhere with all the kids around. Someone could very easily get hurt.

Sure, those who were under eighteen couldn't enter without parental supervision, but even after the age of eighteen, adolescents often did pretty stupid things. Eventually, when the instructor left, Lee decided to take Charlie up to the starting point, and Jill was supposed to wait where the line ended. Jill protested, insisting that she should be there to make sure Charlie was safe, but Lee assured her that everything would be fine.

He had an impatient look on his face, and Jill knew that this was one of the things they discussed a few times earlier—she needed to relax and trust that Lee wasn't going to let their son get injured or killed. Still, as she stood by the tree, nervously skipping from one foot to the other, she couldn't help but feel a sense of dread building up inside her.

She knew that she was overly protective of Charlie, and that she needed to back off a little bit. If she didn't, he might end up like Stella from middle school. Stella was one of those kids who had helicopter parents—or just one parent, in this case. Her dad was a relaxed man for the most part, but both he and Stella were terrified of Stella's mom, who was the one that called all the shots in the family.

Jill used to hang out with Stella from time to time, so she saw it all first-hand. Stella wasn't allowed to go from home to school, or vice versa, alone. Not only that, but she wasn't even allowed to visit Jill without her mom being there.

A very vivid memory Jill had of one of Stella's visits was when they were playing in the living room, and a movie played on the TV in the background while Annette and Stella's mom were talking.

At one point, there was a gory scene in the movie, and Stella's mom turned Stella's head away from the TV, ordering her not to look at it. Other memories included seeing Stella's father panicking because he forgot to defrost the chicken, and the mom being on her way home from work; Stella being rushed to the ER for waking up with a sore throat; Jill being reprimanded for talking to Stella about boys.

The last time Jill saw Stella, which was a few years ago, she was a completely different person. She had dyed her hair black, wore black clothes and black makeup, had piercings all over her face and tattoos all over her body, and was dating a guy with similarly questionable looks.

She claimed she had never been happier in her life.

"Alright, ready, Charlie?" Jill heard Lee shout.

Charlie nodded, and before Jill could say anything, Lee pushed Charlie forward. A loud *'Zzzziiiiip'* pierced the air. The sound caused Jill's heart to lurch, and then, when Charlie screamed, she froze, wide-eyed before realizing that Charlie was screaming in joy and excitement as he slid down the zip-line towards the tree next to Jill, a big grin on his face. The ride was over in mere seconds, and Charlie was safely on the platform next to Jill.

"So cool! Mom, did you see that?!" Only when Charlie looked at her for affirmation, speaking exuberantly, did Jill finally calm down.

She helped unclasp him from the zip-line. Even as she assisted him in climbing down, he continued talking about how incredible the ride was, not even taking a moment of pause between words and sentences.

"Can I go again?!" he asked with an excited hop.

Jill nervously chuckled and looked up at Lee. There were no other kids waiting in line, which seemed almost weird because most of the parents came here on the weekends.

"Yeah. Of course you can, sweetie. Go back over to Dad so he can strap you for the ride down, okay?"

"Yes!" Charlie ran off before Jill even finished the sentence.

Jill wiped her forehead with her palm. She hadn't realized until then that a patina of cold sweat covered her head. She enjoyed spending time with her family here, but a gnawing feeling of dread just wouldn't let her go.

She was terrified for Cheryl.

What was going on back at Mom's home right now? Was Cheryl already possessed? Did she already find Mom and rescue her? Or was she in a coma, just like Mom? That last thought sent a wave of panic throughout Jill's entire body.

She fished her phone out of her pocket, hoping to see anything from Fabiola or Cheryl... A call, a message saying she was okay, anything. But there were no notifications on her phone.

When she returned the phone back to her pocket and looked up, Charlie was already sliding down again. This time, Jill was much less agitated. She was still on edge, but less so than the first time. A part of her still almost expected the cable to snap, causing Charlie to topple down and injure himself.

No, no. Get those thoughts out! That will not happen, she told herself firmly.

213

She found it funny how she never thought about those things when she herself engaged in such activities as a child, but now, having a kid of her own, there were moments when she felt like everything in the world could harm her baby. She was getting better at controlling that anxiety, though, thanks to Lee. And she was determined to keep it up.

Charlie's ride ended, and his voice and tumultuous exclamations showed no signs of his excitement subsiding. He asked to go again, and Jill allowed him, with even less hesitation this time, but warned him that they would soon need to go back to Aunt Cherry. Charlie ran off to Lee to get ready once more.

Jill impatiently glanced at her phone's screen again. Still no notifications.

"Cherry. Please be okay," she nervously muttered to herself.

Chapter 35

As Cheryl stepped inside the house, she expected a freezing cold to envelop her. That didn't happen, and only then did she realize that there was no temperature in this world. Her skin didn't feel cold or hot, but that didn't mean it was pleasant. The lack of temperature was disturbing, kind of like opening your eyes in a dark room and not seeing anything.

The interior of the house was the same, and yet, somehow different. Just like the rest of the crossroads, the house seemed drained of life and hope, but unlike the outside street, there was a feeling of something bad inside.

The trickster spirit.

Upon entering, Cheryl spent a moment scrutinizing every spot in the foyer, partly mesmerized by the dark colors that she wasn't accustomed to and partly making sure nothing dangerous lurked nearby.

She thought she saw a shadow sliding across the wall, which made her gasp in terror. And then it happened again. Shadow after shadow danced across the walls in tall, slender, humanoid shapes, some of them refracting from the wall up to the ceiling, towering above Cheryl. Some of the shadows stayed for a second or two longer, as if curiously observing Cheryl. Others just walked past without even turning their faceless heads.

Cheryl walked over to the bottom of the stairs and looked up. The house was so dark that she couldn't see the top of the stairs from here. Even though Cheryl knew she should be scared, that feeling wasn't nearly as potent as she expected it to be. It was present, but only as a minor inconvenience. She likened it to the fear of speaking in front of the whole classroom.

When Cheryl reached the second floor, she realized just how incredibly dark it truly was up there. A part of her expected the darkness to disperse as she got closer, just as the fog had done, but that didn't happen.

She squinted towards the hallway and was relieved to see it partially illuminated by whatever source of light existed in the crossroads. She also noticed that the door of the office was half-open. She was even more surprised to hear muffled voices coming from inside.

Cheryl lurched forward, and once she reached the office, peeked inside. Her eyes widened at the sight in front of her.

She saw Fabiola sitting on the floor in front of the *vèvè*, staring at the corner of the room and mumbling something with a smile on her face. In the corner which Fabiola was transfixed on was Cheryl herself, standing ramrod straight, a lipstick in one hand and a hand-held mirror in the other.

Her lips were bright red from the lipstick that she had apparently put on, and she had an amused facial expression as she stared at her own reflection. It looked so bizarre, not only to see herself out of her body, but to see her making facial expressions that she rarely made. Or maybe she did make them; she just wasn't aware of them.

"Oh, Ezili Freda, your lips look so red and full!" Fabiola exclaimed, clapping her hands together.

Cheryl, or Ezili Freda, giggled as if amused, examining her face from various angles in the mirror, as she continued putting on lipstick. The Cheryl in the crossroads took a step inside the room and called out.

"Fabiola!"

Fabiola couldn't hear her or see her. But Ezili Freda could. As soon as Cheryl stepped inside and called out the mambo's name, Ezili Freda jerked her head to the source of the voice. For a moment, she looked shocked, almost even ready for a fight. But then she grinned and gestured to herself as if to say, *'Am I not beautiful?'*.

Cheryl opened her mouth to reply, but was interrupted by another voice. A small, meager voice that came from Annette's room.

"Mom?" Cheryl muttered to herself, instinctively jerking her head in the direction of the room.

When she looked back at Ezili Freda, she saw her briefly pointing towards Mom's bedroom. She then continued admiring herself in the mirror, brushing her hair from shoulder to shoulder, making facial expressions and continuing to act like a woman who was in love with her own reflection.

Cheryl no longer cared about Ezili Freda standing in the room. When she heard Mom's voice, her heart leapt into her throat and she suddenly felt the need to go see if it was truly her mother. She stepped out of the office and jackknifed towards Mom's room.

The bedroom door was slightly ajar, and she swung it open, not caring if all the trickster spirits of all the worlds were inside.

***

Ezili Freda finished admiring the lipstick and the jewelry, and had moved on to the candies. She unwrapped one of the miniature *Bounty* bars and took a small bite off the tip of it to see what it would taste like. Ezili Freda had a specific taste, and Fabiola hoped that the loa wouldn't be displeased with the sweets.

The loa spent a moment with the piece of chocolate in her mouth as if trying to figure out if she actually liked it or not. And then she wolfed down the rest of the chocolate, before voraciously moving on to the next one. She plucked a strawberry flavored one and tried it, taking a somewhat bigger bite this time.

Almost as soon as she did so, her face contorted into a grimace. She turned her head sideways and spat the half-chewed, saliva-covered bite on the floor. She dropped the rest of the candy in the wrapper and wiped her mouth, still grimacing.

"I apologize, Ezili Freda," Fabiola said. "We didn't know which ones you would like, so we decided to give you many kinds in hopes that you would find one that suits you."

Before Fabiola even finished that sentence, Ezili Freda already grabbed and unwrapped another *Bounty*. Fabiola glanced at her watch. It had only been five minutes since Cheryl entered the crossroads, but she didn't have much time left. Her physical body would grow tired soon, and Ezili Freda would leave, throwing Cheryl back to the world of the living.

She hoped that Cheryl would manage to find her mother before that.

***

The first thing that greeted Cheryl upon entering the bedroom was the familiar beeping of the machine. The room was dark, just barely illuminated by the faint light outside, but Cheryl saw everything she needed to see. On the bed was Mom, comatose, just as she had been since Cheryl arrived.

Another person was in the room, sitting huddled in the corner, with their arms around their knees, muttering something incoherent.

"Mom!" Cheryl shouted, unable to contain her happiness.

She dashed across the room and fell to her knees, wrapping her arms around her mom, tighter than she ever had before. Mom didn't hug her back. Cheryl observed her and realized that her mom didn't even look in her direction. She had a blank stare on her face, as she continued mumbling nonsensical words to herself, her arms wrapped around her knees. She was pallid and gaunt, just like her comatose body back in the physical world.

"Mom! It's me! It's Cheryl!" Cheryl repeated.

No response. Cheryl started to get worried. She listened to her mother and was able to discern only a few words.

218

Papa Legba...
He's after me...
The doll...
Vèvè...
Trapped...

Has she lost her mind entirely from being stuck in this world?

"Mom, come on! It's your daughter," Cheryl put a hand on Mom's cheek. "It's Cherry. Don't you remember me?"

Her mom stopped mumbling and turned her head toward Cheryl.

"Cherry?" she asked in a toneless voice.

"Yes! It's me!" Cheryl exclaimed, her eyes full of tears.

Mom continued staring at her for a moment in confusion and then—

She looked away, continuing to mumble the same words, over and over. Cheryl suppressed a new wave of incoming tears and contemplated what to do. She couldn't just leave her mom here, even if her mind was wholly ruined. And who knew? Maybe her mind would return to its old self once they were out of here.

"Mom, it's gonna be okay! I'm gonna get us out of here!" Cheryl cried as she wiped her tears away.

She firmly clutched her mother's bony wrists and began chanting the words Fabiola told her to chant.

"Papa Legba, get us out. Papa Legba, get us out."

Chanting the words suddenly seemed absurd. Were they going to teleport out of here or something? But then she remembered that she was teleported into the crossroads to begin with, and it suddenly didn't seem as absurd.

Cheryl chanted the words over and over, intentionally speaking over her mother's incoherent words. She felt something building up around her—some kind of tension in the air. The more she chanted the words, the more it seemed to grow, until it was all over the room. The best way Cheryl could describe it was a sort of invisible energy that permeated the room.

Along with that, Cheryl started to feel something else in the room, in equal quantity—a heaviness in the air. She instinctively turned her head towards the door and stopped chanting the words for a moment, her voice stuck in her throat.

A tall, dark figure stood in the doorway. It seemed to stare at Cheryl, even though she couldn't clearly see its eyes. As soon as Cheryl stopped repeating the words, the energy in the room seemed to wane. She immediately resumed chanting, faster and more panicked this time, but she refused to take her eyes off the tall being.

The figure—the same one from her dreams, she realized—tilted its head curiously and took a step forward. It had to stoop down to get under the top frame of the door, and as it did, Cheryl panicked even more.

She could see more features on the figure, including an inhuman mouth and sharp, jagged fingers. Its entire frame was strange, undefined, with some sort of mist microscopically surrounding its head, limbs, and torso, making it difficult to determine where its frame ended; like a drawing in which a child had colored outside the lines.

"Papa Legba, get us out, Papa Legba, get us out, Papa Legba, get us out!" Cheryl was practically screaming now, and her tone only increased when the figure took another step forward, drastically closing the distance between them with its stork-like long legs.

It now towered above Cheryl and she had to look up towards the ceiling to keep it in her line of sight. She still didn't see any eyes on it clearly, just dark holes that resembled two grey, cloudy orbs.

The heaviness in the air increased tenfold, but so did the invisible energy from before. It now manifested itself as a sort of a blur, enveloping both Cheryl and Annette.

"Papa Legba get us out Papa Legba get us out Papa Legba— you can't have her!" Cheryl screamed in protest as the figure reached towards her with one hand.

She felt its cold touch on her shoulder. No, not cold. Freezing. It was like she submerged her shoulder in icy water. Cheryl stopped chanting, and the blur became so pervading that she could see nothing else. She was overcome with a sense of weightlessness and vertigo. She could have fallen sideways for all she knew, and not be aware of it.

And then, just like that, her vision returned, and she felt her knees disappearing underneath her.

She hit the floor hard, slamming her head on the wooden surface in the process. She suddenly felt incredibly weak. Her body quivered in exhaustion, and she could hardly keep her head up. It took her a moment to realize that she was on the floor of the office, with Fabiola rushing to her side, asking her a flurry of questions. But Cheryl was focused on something else.

The dark figure stood behind Fabiola, towering above the two women, staring down at Cheryl.

"You... you're too late!" Cheryl muttered triumphantly. "I got her out! You lost!"

A slit of white appeared on the figure's face, and it took Cheryl a moment to realize it was grinning, showing rows of sharp teeth incongruously white compared to its blackness.

And then, Cheryl saw it. The images that the figure undoubtedly forced into her mind. She saw snippets, like a fast-moving reel, but she understood everything.

She saw herself with a young woman in a cave, and it didn't take long for her to deduce that the young woman was Erika, and Cheryl was actually Annette. She watched through her mom's eyes as shadowy movement flitted throughout the cave and she stalked after it. She saw her mom reaching a dead-end in the passageway. There was a complex drawing on the wall, portraying a slender, black figure in front of a *vèvè*.

221

She saw through her mom's eyes as the figure turned its head to face her, and her body felt frozen. She looked into the eyes of the figure and sensed unspeakable malice pouring from it. It saw her, and it hated her, just as it hated everything, and it decided right then that it would punish Annette for disturbing it.

She saw Mom being drawn closer to the figure without actually moving, and trying frantically to break away, but not being able to do so, despite the terror that enveloped her. She saw Erika touching her shoulder just as the figure lunged at her. She screamed and flailed like a lunatic, with a voice and body that weren't her own, even after the cave returned back to normal.

She saw herself coming back home and pretending to be okay, ignoring the towering black figure that continuously stood in the back of the room. And it was always there ever after, whether Mom stayed in the home, or went to work, or put Cheryl and Jill to sleep—the figure even peeked out from Cheryl's closet!

She watched her mom piling up books on various types of magic and religions, extensively focusing on Vodou, including the performance of rituals. She saw the figure fading at said rituals, only to return when their protection expired. She saw Mom progressively losing her mind, spending more and more time in the office. At one point, it was so cluttered with ritualistic objects that it became unrecognizable.

She saw her mistreating Jill, and she felt the heartache of it that Mom felt. She saw her putting Jill's doll, Lola, in the middle of a hand-drawn *vèvè* on the floor and chanting unfamiliar words.

She saw years pass, and Mom's health deteriorate more every year. She saw Dad taking Jill and leaving her, and Mom going crazy over it, telling Dad that he didn't understand what he was doing, and that he was ruining everything.

She saw Cheryl leaving for college and Annette pretending to be okay. She saw her drawing on Barbara's picture, and for some reason, she knew that she was trying to pass on this curse to the woman—unsuccessfully. She watched her running from the black figure in the house and into her bedroom. She heard her chanting more words while feverishly clutching Lola. She saw her dropping the doll and pulling a pen and paper from a drawer. She saw her jotting down *IM SORRY FOR TREATING YOU THE WAY I DID* on the back of the paper.

She saw her turning around and seeing the black figure standing right there, in her face. She saw the figure lunging forward with a caterwaul. She felt its icy touch all over herself and saw Mom falling sideways on the floor, with the paper sliding under the bed.

The flashbacks ended, and as Cheryl slipped out of consciousness, she could only conjure one thought.

The fucking doll.

Chapter 36

"Alright, let's go see Aunt Cherry," Lee said as he parked in the driveway of Annette's house.

It was dark outside already, and most of the lights in the house were on. Jill had been silent for most of the ride home. Charlie was naturally talkative, reflecting on how he slid down the zip-line, and how he couldn't wait to tell his buddies about it. Lee noticed the worry on Jill's face, so he took over the conversation and kept Charlie occupied until they arrived

"Hey, she'll be okay," Lee said as he killed the engine and put a hand on Jill's thigh.

Jill nodded with a smile. The truth was, she felt sick. The thought of coming home and seeing her sister dead sent daggers through her heart. She wanted to jump out of the car and dash towards the house right then, but she couldn't do it—not in front of Charlie. She didn't want to worry him.

"Can I go inside with you?" Charlie asked.

Absolutely not, Jill wanted to say, but Lee interrupted her.

"You and I can wait in the living room. Right, Jill?" he looked at Jill for confirmation.

"Sure. Your Aunt and I will be downstairs as soon as she's ready," Jill forced a smile at Charlie.

They stepped out of the car. Jill was in front of Charlie and Lee, and with each step she took, she felt a knot of dread forming in her stomach.

"Fabiola?" she called out expectantly as soon as she opened the front door.

There was no response, and the knot in Jill's stomach tightened further.

"Fabiola?!" she called out again, and she heard her voice cracking from the fear that had been building up inside her and threatening to seep out.

"Come on, Charlie, let's go to the living room," Lee said as he ushered Charlie towards the door.

As Jill started up the stairs, she heard an effeminate voice from upstairs.

"Jill! Up here!" It was Fabiola.

Jill raced up the stairs. She briefly heard Lee telling Charlie to go sit on the couch, but she was too panicked to worry about that right now.

"Where are you?!" she called out, once she was on the second floor.

"In here!" Fabiola's voice came from the office.

Jill rushed towards the office and peered inside, her heart thumping so loudly that she thought she was going to have a heart attack. There, she saw Fabiola kneeling in front of a supine Cheryl, laying right in the middle of the *vèvè*.

"Cheryl!" Jill screamed, too panicked to worry about alarming Charlie.

Fabiola looked at Jill and smiled. Even through that panic, Jill somehow found that reassuring. It meant that everything was okay.

"She made it," Fabiola said with a grin.

Jill saw Cheryl's face. She was pale, her eyes were closed, and her lips looked dry.

"What's wrong with her?" she asked with a crack in her voice.

"She is sleeping. The invocation of Ezili Freda has exhausted her. But she is okay."

"Are you sure? Maybe we should call a hospital. What if she's got—"

"Jill," Fabiola stood up and put her hands on Jill's shoulders. "Your sister is fine."

Jill looked down at Cheryl once more. Her face looked peaceful, and her chest steadily rose and fell in inhales and exhales. Seeing that calmed Jill down a little bit. She sighed, not even realizing that she had been holding her breath the entire time. She wanted to cry out from relief, but instead expressed her emotions by hugging Fabiola.

The mambo patted her on the back and said something in Haitian Creole. Although Jill didn't understand the words, they soothed her. Lee walked in and asked what was going on, and if Cheryl was okay. Jill would have answered him, but she couldn't speak right then. Just then, another question popped up in Jill's mind. She pulled back from Fabiola and asked.

"What about our mom?!"

Fabiola's smile drooped off her face, and she swallowed.

"Come with me," she motioned towards the door.

***

When Jill entered the bedroom, she couldn't believe her eyes and ears. The beeping of the machine was gone. It felt so surreal to enter the room and not hear that incessant sound.

Annette was awake and sitting up in bed, with her back pressed up against the hardboard. She looked haggard, almost corpse-like, her skin pale, the bags under her eyes heavy. She was staring in front of herself and mumbling something, but Jill couldn't discern the words.

"Mom?" she called out.

Her mother gave no indication whatsoever that she had heard Jill. She continued staring straight ahead and mumbling under her breath. Her eyes were bloodshot from a lack of blinking.

"What's wrong with her?" Jill asked Fabiola.

Fabiola inhaled deeply.

Jill immediately knew that what she was about to hear was not good news.

"I'm afraid your mother's mind has been destroyed by the trickster spirit. She has spent too long being hunted by it,

226

and then her soul was imprisoned by it. Whatever little sanity your mother had left is now gone. I'm sorry."

"What about the trickster spirit?"

"Chased away. Trickster spirits never stay when there's a loa in the house."

Jill stared at the person that was once her mother. Some of the words between the sentences were recognizable, specifically 'Papa Legba' and 'Vodou'.

This broken shell of a person was not Annette. As much as she wanted to stay angry at her—and as much as she wanted to be happy to see that she had woken up—Jill couldn't muster the capacity to feel anything more than pity.

"Did Cheryl already see her like this?" Jill asked.

"No. Well, probably yes, but in the crossroads."

"She's going to be heartbroken..." Jill said to herself.

What were they going to do with Mom now? They couldn't take care of her like this. She was catatonic. She would need twenty-four-hour care from professionals. Was waking her up really the better thing to do? A millisecond of a thought went through Jill's mind about ending her mother's suffering somehow. She would never do it, of course, because she wasn't a murderer, but if it were her instead, she would definitely prefer that her family pull the plug on her.

"Jill?" a male voice came from the door.

It was Lee. He was speaking softly, probably noticing the silence that permeated the room. Jill looked at him briefly. He entered the room and asked what was wrong with Annette. Fabiola filled him in with a few brusque words and then he went back to the office and carried Cheryl out of the room. By the time Jill and Fabiola exited the room, Lee was standing in the hallway alone.

"I carried Cheryl to her room. I think we should call an ambulance to check up on her. She could be suffering from something serious."

"Don't worry, *cheri*, I do this all the time. This is a normal process. Cheryl is fine. In fact, she should wake up any minute now."

Now that the panic and adrenaline were gone, Jill started to think more rationally.

"Lee, you left Charlie downstairs?" she asked.

"Yeah."

She suddenly felt another mini wave of panic blossoming inside her. He shouldn't be down there alone, not with the threat of that trickster spirit still around.

"I need to go check up on him," she said and started towards the door.

"I'm sure he's fine. It's only been a minute," Lee assured her.

Jill still had to see if Charlie was okay. She descended the stairs, entered the living room, and—

"Charlie?!" she called out. "Charlie!"

Charlie wasn't in the room.

Chapter 37

Charlie sensed that something was wrong. He could tell from his parents' apprehensiveness. His Mom was like that only once before, when Charlie fell out of a tree and hit his head. He was okay, but his Mom was so worried that she had rushed him to the hospital to make sure everything was okay. He walked out of the hospital with a smile on his face.

Now that they were at Grandma's house, he saw the same worried look on Mom's face, even though nothing visibly bad had happened. Was Aunt Cheryl in trouble? Or maybe Grandma?

Those thoughts kept racing through his head as he sat alone on the couch in the living room. Soon though, he started to get bored. He glanced around the room for anything entertaining. There was a big, box-shaped TV in front of him. Charlie had never seen such a TV. It was much smaller than the one they had at home, and it looked heavy.

He glanced under the TV to see if there were any video gaming consoles attached to it, but there were none. He thought about how sad a house looked with just a TV and no video games.

As he finished that thought, he heard the muffled patter of footsteps upstairs. It sounded like someone was running. What were they doing up there? Was someone playing? He wanted to play, too. He was tempted to go upstairs, but the only thing keeping him here was the fact that Dad told him to stay.

What if he just took a peek? He could always return downstairs.

With that determination, Charlie hopped off the couch and started towards the door. A sound behind caused him to stop and turn around. Charlie wasn't sure what kind of sound it was, but it immediately piqued his interest. It sounded like it came from the room in the back.

Curious, he followed it, wondering who could be in there. Upon walking through the threshold, he realized that the backroom was actually a kitchen. When Charlie looked around, he realized that the room was empty. His eyes fell on the fridge, and he suddenly felt hungry. He decided to go upstairs anyway to ask one of the adults to make him something to eat.

He turned around to leave when he heard that same sound from before again, this time much more clearly. It sounded like hissing. Charlie turned around, now a little bit on edge. He went over to the door left of the entrance to the kitchen and opened it. At first, he was greeted by nothing but darkness. But then he saw a switch on the wall on his left. He flipped it, and the ceiling light illuminated the stairs leading down to another door.

The hissing came again, and this time it was clear that it was coming from the basement. Charlie hated basements. There was always something scary in the dark down there. He didn't have a basement at home, luckily. This time, as he listened to the occasional hissing here, he didn't feel scared. If anything, he was curious. What could be making that sound?

He walked down the stairs, carefully taking each step since the stairs were too high for him, and he was still small. He opened the bottom door widely, letting the weak light inside the basement. As long as he stayed in the light, he would be safe.

The hissing resounded once more. No, it wasn't hissing. It sounded like someone saying 'Pssst!', like his friends did when they wanted to tell him a secret. It was coming from a nearby door. Charlie looked around. The meager light wasn't enough to illuminate the entire room, but he could still see the dust-covered shelves, and various objects covered with sheets, and an old pool table in the middle of the room.

"Pssst! Over here!" a petulant voice—no longer a hiss—said from somewhere in the basement.

"Who's there?" Charlie asked.

"I'm in here!" the boyish voice said.

"Where?"

"Here!"

Charlie felt his heart beginning to race, which was weird, because that only happened after playing, especially running. He also suddenly felt cold, even though it was really hot just a moment ago.

"I'm gonna go get my Mom and Dad," he said and turned to face the exit.

"No, wait!" the invisible boy in the room said. "I want to show you something!"

"Show me what?" Charlie faced the basement once more.

"Come here and I'll show you!"

Charlie looked around, but still to no avail. Nothing in the basement was moving. The voice sounded like it was coming somewhere around the pool table area. Charlie took a few tentative steps forward, looking around the basement for any children hiding and getting ready to jump out in front of him.

Maybe the boy who was hiding here wanted to give Charlie a good scare. He stopped right in front of the pool table and pivoted left and right.

"I can't see you!" he said.

"Here," the boy said softly this time—and it came from right under Charlie.

Charlie bent down and looked under the pool table and gasped.

There he was. There was really an actual boy under there.

He was pale and thin, with big, black eyes and long, unkempt hair; or at least it looked like that in the darkness of the basement. His clothes were as ordinary as Charlie's, but it's the look of seriousness on his face that Carlie noticed

231

first. He looked sad, troubled, maybe? The entire time, the thought of finding a boy squatting in the basement under an old pool table seemed weird to Charlie, but it was only at the back of his mind.

"Who are you?" Charlie asked.

"Just a boy. I live here," the boy whispered reticently.

"You've been living with my grandma?"

"Yes. For more than twenty years," he said.

"What? That's not true. You're not even twenty years old!" Charlie said.

"Shhh. Keep your voice down," the boy said with audible anger in his voice this time. "We don't want them to hear us."

"Who? You mean my Mom and Dad?"

"Yes."

Charlie looked behind himself, expecting to see an adult hovering above him. No one was there, much to his relief. He turned to face the kid under the table.

"Are you in trouble?"

"Yes."

The calmness of his voice scared Charlie.

"Why?" Charlie asked.

"Because I took this doll from your mom," he said.

He proceeded to whip out an ugly doll from the darkness and present it to Charlie. The doll looked like it had been made at home, and Charlie didn't understand why anyone would want to keep such an ugly toy.

"Can you please give it back to her in my name?" the boy asked.

"Why don't you just give it back to her yourself and say you're sorry?" Charlie asked.

"I can't. She's really angry with me. I need you to do it. Okay?"

Charlie hesitated. He could do it, but then another thought occurred to him. What if Mom then blamed Charlie for stealing the doll? He wanted to help this boy, but he didn't want to get in trouble for something he didn't do.

He had learned his lesson when Cindy ate a cookie Charlie's mom made, awhile back, and he took the blame. Cindy didn't even thank him and just bragged about how she managed to get out of that sticky predicament without getting in trouble.

"Take the doll," the boy said in a timorous tone as he outstretched the hand with the doll towards Charlie.

"Come with me," Charlie shook his head. "We can give her the doll together."

"No!" the boy shouted so loudly that it caused Charlie to recoil. "I'm sorry. It's just that your mom scares me. And I need to run back home."

"Where do you live?"

"Very close. Please, take the doll."

"I don't want to. My mom will think that I took it."

"No, she won't. You can tell her that you found it. And then you'll be a hero for saving her childhood toy," the boy grinned.

He was still holding the doll in the air, waiting for Charlie to accept it. Charlie glanced down at the doll once more. Maybe he could take it. Just bring it to Mom, and explain to her that he found it. She would be grateful to him, right?

A shriek from the upstairs caused Charlie to turn his head towards the sound.

"Lee! He's not here!" It was his mom.

"They're talking about the doll," the boy said. "Quick! Take it to her!"

Charlie looked at the boy just in time for the patter of footsteps upstairs to get closer. His parents would be here any moment. Should he take the doll or not? The boy looked like he really needed Charlie's help.

"Please, hurry!" the boy pleaded, his face now portraying impatience.

Charlie reached for the doll.

Chapter 38

Cheryl opened her eyes and gasped loudly. She felt as if she was choking when she abruptly woke up. The first thing she saw were the familiar objects of her room surrounding her.

I made it back! That was her first thought, and it was immediately followed by a million other thoughts that reminded her of everything that she saw just before passing out.

Shit, the doll!

Cheryl swung sideways and hopped off the bed. Her knees buckled, and she barely managed to stop herself from collapsing onto the floor. She was still in a weakened state from traveling through the crossroads. She wondered for a moment if she would have any long-term consequences from her astral projection, but right now, she didn't really care.

She also wondered if she had managed to save Mom, but there would be time to worry about that later. Right now, she had to destroy Jill's doll. As long as it lived, the trickster spirit would never let them go.

Cheryl propped herself into a standing position with a groan. Her legs felt like they were made of jelly, and she felt the urge to vomit. She swallowed and suppressed that urge as she made her way to the door.

As soon as she opened it, she heard a cacophony of voices downstairs. It sounded like Jill and... was that Lee? Yeah, Lee, and she heard Fabiola's voice there, too. Cheryl held one hand on the wall as she made her way towards the stairs.

"J... Jill..." she tried to shout, but was barely able to mutter more than a faint sound.

No use. She would need to go downstairs. And she knew that the doll was in the basement. She didn't know how, but she knew it. She had a connection with the trickster spirit; she knew that much. Again, she didn't know anything more than what she felt.

Cheryl walked past Mom's room. The door was open, and she saw Mom inside, sitting on the bed, muttering something to herself just as she had done in the crossroads. Sorrow would have overtaken her had she not been consumed by a sense of urgency to help Jill and Charlie.

The worried shouts of Jill and Lee calling after Charlie came from the living room, followed by frantic footsteps in various directions.

As Cheryl made her way towards the stairs, she started to regain her strength. Walking down the stairs was difficult, but step by step and holding on to the railing, Cheryl was able to climb down. She had three steps remaining to the bottom when she felt herself losing balance. Cheryl lurched forward, her body suddenly awake and ready, but it was too late.

She took a tumble down the stairs, each step that her body collided with sending sharp pangs of pain. Despite the fall being only a couple of feet, Cheryl's ribs and knee hurt like hell. She writhed in pain for a moment, trying to compose herself enough to stand up.

"Cheryl!" she heard Jill's voice from the door leading to the kitchen.

Cheryl looked at Jill and, through gritted teeth, muttered just one word.

***

It took Jill a moment to understand what Cheryl was telling her. Her sister was pale as she lay on the floor in front of the stairs, beads of sweat decorating her forehead.

"Basement!" Cheryl uttered with great effort.

Jill's eyes widened as terror surged through her. She spun on her heel and rushed past a concerned Lee and

Fabiola, not bothering to explain anything to them. She dashed through the living room and the kitchen, heading towards the basement.

The door was open. How had she not seen it before? So stupid of her not to notice such an important detail!

Jill didn't even bother slowing down before she began descending the stairs. Luckily for her, the lights were on, and she saw the outline of a child squatting at the bottom, right in front of the pool table.

"Charlie!" she shouted.

Charlie turned around at the mention of his name, his eyes as wide as saucers. And that's when Jill saw it.

A black figure was squatting under the pool table in front of Charlie. It almost looked comical, with its tall stature hunched, its knees on the same level as its head, its elbows touching the floor, with one hand limply splayed on the floor, and the other slightly in front of it. It was holding Lola in that hand, clutching it with sharp, elongated fingers.

"Charlie, get away from there!" Jill shouted as she skipped down the steps.

A line of white appeared on the figure's face where the mouth should have been, and it let out an inhuman shriek that made Jill's ears pulsate with pain. The ceiling light above Jill produced a popping sound, and the room was plunged into blackness. Somewhere in the basement, Jill heard Charlie screaming. Jill was overcome with a sense of déjà vu from last night as she froze, almost tripping and falling down the steps.

"Charlie! Charlie, where are you?!" she screamed.

"I'm right here!" Charlie shouted from somewhere in the darkness.

Jill couldn't see a thing. She heard footsteps upstairs and then voices.

"Jill, are you down there?!" It was Lee.

"Lee! We're here! Turn the lights on!" Jill shouted.

236

"I can't! They're not working! Hold on, I'll grab my phone from the car!"

Jill just then remembered that she still had her phone in her pocket. She pulled it out and fumbled with trembling hands until she found the torch. As soon as she tapped on it, the basement was bathed in a weak, pale light. As meager as it was, it was better than being in the dark, and for that, Jill was grateful.

"Charlie! Where are you?!" Jill screeched.

There was no response.

"Cha—" her words cut off when she saw something black and slender run past her torch's light.

Jill froze in her steps and moved the light in various directions, hoping to see what it was. She saw the slender figure's tall shadow against the floor behind the old sofa covered in a sheet. It was just sitting there, waiting for Jill, maybe to ambush her. Or maybe hiding from her. Jill suddenly became aware of the deafening silence inside the basement. Up until a moment ago, she wasn't even aware of her own panting, and now it was the only sound in the room.

"Charlie?" she called out timorously.

The adrenaline that ran through her muted the feeling of being overwhelmed by fear and panic. She had to confront the beast behind the sofa. Even if she didn't manage to overpower it, she'd hopefully be able to buy Charlie some time to hide or run away.

She kept the light trained on the sofa and the shadow that swiveled under her light with each step she took closer to it. The figure was still, she suddenly realized; it was only its shadow that moved under the refraction of the light. She saw its round head and the elongated torso. It must have been really flexible to be able to hide behind a sofa despite its tall stature. Or maybe it truly had no physical body at all?

When Jill was only two steps away from the sofa, she swallowed. It sounded alarmingly loud against the silence in the room, and she was sure that the creature was already alerted to her arrival unless it was somehow blind to the light. Maybe it was preparing to jump out in front of her just as she was preparing to jump out in front of it.

Jill inhaled through her nose as slowly as she could, ignoring her trembling breathing. With one swift step forward, she jumped in front of the sofa with her light pointed at—

Lola.

Her old doll sat on the floor, facing Jill. It stared at her with its black eyes and smiled in a morbidly jovial fashion not suitable for this situation. At first, Jill could do no more than just stare at the doll.

And then a clatter came from somewhere else in the basement.

"Charlie?!" Jill called out, the panic now threatening to supersede the adrenaline.

Quick footsteps resounded somewhere. Jill felt something brushing against her momentarily, just as the footsteps went past her. She screamed and fell on her rear, dropping the phone in the process.

She looked around the darkness, sure that the phone died when it fell on the concrete floor. But then she saw a small, rectangular glow. Realizing that the torch was face down, she scrambled to the phone and grabbed it, immediately shining her light around the basement once again.

There's no one here, she thought as she allowed her panicked breathing to take over as the only noise in the room.

She turned her phone to the right, and a face jumped in front of her. Jill screamed, flailed, and kicked against the assailant who grabbed her shoulders with his icy cold hands.

"Jill! It's me!" Cheryl shouted.

She must have shouted it at least three times before Jill actually heard the words, and once she did, she took a good look at the person in front of her. It was Cheryl, not the

238

trickster spirit or someone disguised as her. She was pale, but it was definitely her.

"Cheryl! We have to find Charlie!"

"He's right here!" Cheryl pointed under her arm.

Jill shone her phone's light down, and sure enough, there he was.

"Mommy!" Charlie leaped into Jill's arms and hugged her tightly.

He felt somewhat cold and was shivering. His eyes were wide as if he had just seen a ghost—which he had. Jill ran a hand through his hair to soothe him, but it ended up comforting her more, instead.

"We need to get out of here!" Jill said as she jumped to her feet.

"No, not yet! We have to find your doll!"

"Lola? Why?!"

"I'll explain later, just tell me where she is!"

Cheryl sounded desperate. Jill shone the light behind Cheryl and pointed a finger at the sofa.

"There! Stay with Charlie!"

She ran past Cheryl, and sure enough, the doll was still there, motionless—as it should be. Jill suddenly didn't want to go anywhere near Lola, not after seeing the trickster spirit touching it, but in the heat of the moment, she was on autopilot.

She bent down to pick it up, and just like that, something black and blurry grabbed Lola before Jill could and it scurried back out of sight in the blink of an eye. Jill screamed, and so did Charlie and Cheryl.

And so did the trickster spirit, with a shrill cry that pierced the air.

More screams came from the kitchen, and Jill realized it was Lee and Fabiola.

"What the fuck was that?!" Lee shouted.

There was a moment of commotion while Jill, Cheryl, and Charlie found each other in the dark again.

"Jill!" Lee's voice came from upstairs.

Jill looked up to see a strong beam illuminating the basement. It was the most divine thing Jill had ever witnessed, to see the darkness disperse in an instant. Lee stood at the bottom of the stairs with a bright flashlight, and was scanning the faces in the basement, a worried look on his face.

When he saw Charlie, Jill, and Cheryl, visible relief washed over his face, and he motioned for the three to follow him. Cheryl picked Charlie up and carried him up the stairs, with Jill running closely behind.

Fabiola was at the top of the stairs, urging them to hurry up. Her face was contorted into one of palpable fear, and it didn't suit the mambo one bit. It also instilled a primordial fear in Jill because it told her that Fabiola hasn't dealt with anything like this in the past.

The entire house was dark, Jill noticed as she ran upstairs and slammed the basement door shut, so the dark entity must have done something to kill the electricity.

"We need to get out of the house, come on!" Lee shouted.

"The back door!" Jill pointed to the door leading out of the kitchen.

Fabiola rushed to the door and grabbed the knob. A rattling sound ensued, but the door wouldn't budge.

"It's locked!" she shouted.

"Shit!" Jill cursed.

"Language!" Lee reprimanded her absently.

Cheryl put Charlie down, and the group huddled near the kitchen door, the visibility of the sky outside giving a sort of unreachable solace. A clatter nearby made everyone turn towards the living room. Charlie screamed and cried.

"It's okay, buddy. We'll be fine, alright?" Lee comforted Charlie as he pulled him closer and allowed him to hug him around the waist.

Another clatter, and then something sounding like glass shattering in the living room. And then a shriek.

"What the hell is going on?!" Jill asked in frustration in no more than a whimpery whisper.

"I don't know. I thought we banished the spirit!" Fabiola said defeatedly.

"No, we didn't," Cheryl exclaimed calmly.

Everyone turned to face her, visibly waiting for an answer. Even Charlie, who had no idea what was going on, stared at Aunt Cheryl. Another short screech came from the living room, followed by what sounded like bare feet running across the room. Jill and Lee kept the lights trained on the entrance of the living room. For some reason, Jill had the impression that as long as they did that, they'd be safe.

Cheryl sighed and shook her head. Everyone looked back at her.

"The trickster spirit was never supposed to be banished in the first place. We messed it up big time. When Mom returned from Haiti, something followed her here. She tried everything to get rid of that thing, including trying to transfer the spirit on to Barbara, but nothing worked. The only thing she could do was cast protection spells, but even they didn't last for long. As time went on, she started losing more and more of her mind."

"She couldn't cast the right spells and draw the *vèvès* properly anymore because of her memory, and then one day the spirit took her. Yeah, we already knew that," Jill said.

Cheryl shook her head.

"That's what we initially thought. But Mom didn't mess up in the protection spells and *vèvès*. She knew that her time was almost up, and that she had no way of making it out of this mess unscathed, so she instead purposely messed up the protection spells."

"Why? To make it quicker?" Jill incredulously asked.

Fabiola looked just as confused.

"No," Cheryl said. "To lure the trickster spirit and imprison the both of them in the crossroads. Don't you get

241

it? It was trapped there. It wanted us to go there. When I freed Mom, I also freed it from its imprisonment."

Silence fell on the room. It was interrupted by more footsteps somewhere in the house, followed by a muffled bang upstairs. Everyone instinctively looked up at the ceiling.

"Mom is up there," Jill said.

"She'll be fine. The spirit is no longer interested in her."

"How do you know that?" Fabiola asked.

"I saw it in a sort of vision. The trickster spirit latches on to a member of the family and feeds on them. When there's nothing left to eat, then it moves on to the younger generations in the same family. In this case, it's you and me, Jill."

Jill suddenly remembered everything from her childhood. The boy... there was never a boy. Instead, she suddenly saw something else in her memory. A black figure towering above her, always by her side, never doing anything, just gleefully watching. It was never a friend. The spirit had latched on to Jill from an early age like a parasite. It was her that it wanted.

As much as she wanted to protect Cheryl from this entity, she also wanted to protect Charlie. If the spirit latched on to Jill, then Charlie would be next in the line of succession. She couldn't let that happen.

"How do we stop it?!" she asked impatiently.

A loud bang, followed by scraping, and then another blood-curdling screech.

"The doll. We need to find it," Cheryl said.

Chapter 39

Everyone in the room stared at Cheryl incredulously. Their looks screamed the exact same thing Jill thought to herself.

Have you lost your damn mind?!

"You want us to go up there and retrieve Lola, right under the spirit's nose?" Jill asked with a sardonic, nervous chuckle.

"We have to. It's the only way to get rid of it," Cheryl said.

She was alarmingly calm, given the situation.

"Look, we can just get out of here. Let it keep the doll, right?" Lee shrugged.

"I told you," Cheryl frowned. "Running won't solve anything. The spirit attaches itself to family members. No matter where you run, it will find us."

"And I'm next," Jill put a hand on Charlie's cheek. "And then Charlie."

Charlie looked up in confusion. He obviously had no idea what was going on, but he was scared nonetheless. Poor kid. He was probably going to have nightmares for months after this. Might even need some therapy. Jill would make sure to let him sleep with her and Lee, with the lights on, if necessary.

"Okay, so we find the doll, and what then?" Jill asked.

"Then we destroy it," Fabiola said, and looked over at Cheryl, as if looking for confirmation from her.

Cheryl nodded in agreement.

"But do we know if that's even going to stop it?" Jill asked, with a timbre that turned more desperate by the minute.

"We do," Fabiola interjected. "Trickster spirits have difficulties staying in our world just by attaching themselves to a person. However, they can extend their stay if they transfer a part of themselves into a cherished object. Once a spirit attaches to an object in a manner like this one, its essence is tied to it. Destroying it will not destroy the spirit, but it will send it back to where it came from and cover your tracks, at least for a little bit."

"But it can return again?"

"Yes. You have to understand, trickster spirits can always find their way into our realm, but the odds of this happening are close to nil. I'll teach you some protection spells that you can cast to stay safe."

Silence fell on the room for a moment. Not even the ruckus upstairs could be heard anymore. For some reason, that caused Jill to feel even more on edge. When she heard the racket, she at least knew where the spirit was. When it was quiet like this, it could be anywhere, possibly even standing right behind her this very moment, just staring and waiting.

That thought caused shivers to run down her spine. She turned around and glanced at the torch-illuminated living room. Nothing was there from what she could tell. She didn't even realize that she'd been holding Charlie close this entire time with a hand on his shoulder.

"Okay, if it's the only way to get rid of it, let's do it, then," Lee said.

His shoulders tensed up with visible strain.

"I can't let you go up there, Lee," Jill said.

Lee shot her an annoyed smirk.

"She's right," Cheryl said softly.

Lee looked at her with the same annoyed look.

"It's our family. We are the ones who need to finish it. You need to stay here and protect Charlie," Jill said.

Lee laughed in disbelief.

"They are right," Fabiola jumped in to support the sisters. "This trickster spirit... I have seen many of them in my life, and most of them were harmless. Some of them were a pain to deal with, but you must understand that trickster spirits aren't usually this malevolent. They are like naughty boys and girls. But the spirit in this house... it is more powerful. That means that it will not hesitate to kill whoever it deems a threat to get to its new hosts."

"And that's why we need you to stay here with Charlie," Jill repeated.

Lee looked hesitant. For a moment, it looked like he was going to disagree, but instead, he caved with a terse nod.

"Wait," Fabiola said as she stepped towards the sisters. "Let me give you protection, *wi*?"

She put her hands on Cheryl's and Jill's shoulders, closed her eyes, and chanted something in Haitian Creole. This lasted for a dozen or so seconds, and then Fabiola kissed her palms and placed them on the sisters' foreheads.

"There. You should have at least a little bit of protection now, *wi*?"

"*Wi*," Jill nodded.

She briefly glanced at Cheryl and started towards the living room with a slow-paced walk, her phone's light pointed in front of herself. She wanted to look back at Charlie, too, but she was on the brink of tears and couldn't allow herself to break down.

Not now.

"Charlie, you stay close to me, okay, buddy?" she heard Lee say from behind.

"Mom, where are you going?" Charlie asked in a confused tone.

That made tears well up in Jill's eyes. He had no idea what was going on, and it would probably take a while for him to understand. And what if Jill tragically died tonight? Would Charlie spend years wondering what happened to his Mom, all the while wondering why he was the only one among his friends who had only one parent? Would he hate Jill because of that?

245

Jill turned around and faked a smile. Charlie's sheepish gaze was transfixed on her, which caused her heart to ache even more. He broke away from Lee and took a step towards her.

"Where are you going, Mom?" he asked with wide eyes just as Lee stepped forward to stop him from running off.

"Mommy will be back in a few minutes, Charlie. Okay?"

"I wanna go with you."

Jill knelt down in front of him and wrapped her arms around him tightly. She felt a bitter-sweet feeling as she held her son. She didn't want to think of this as a goodbye, even though at the back of her mind, there was a possibility of that actually being the case. She never wanted to let go of Charlie.

"I love you so much, baby," she said as she firmly closed her eyes and felt the tears flowing down her cheeks.

Charlie hugged her back, which strangely comforted her for a moment. Jill sniffled and wiped her tears away, hiding the fact that she was crying, before pulling away from the hug.

"You listen to Dad, okay? And don't run off. I'll be back in a bit," she had to work really hard to keep her composure and not break down.

"Okay," Charlie said as he tentatively took a step back under Lee's guidance.

Jill stood up and hugged Lee as well. He gently rubbed her back.

"You come back to us safely, okay?" he said with a commanding voice.

He handed the flashlight to her and took the phone from her hand.

"You'll need this more than we will," he smiled.

She wanted to argue with that, but Lee was right. Cheryl and Jill would have to scour the entire house to find the doll, and something like a phone's torch would only make the task harder.

Jill turned towards the living room and motioned with her head for Cheryl to follow her. Cheryl nodded and smiled reassuringly. For some reason, that confident facial expression made Jill feel better.

She sniffled one last time, and with a battle-ready frown on her face, stepped towards the living room.

Chapter 40

Cheryl was close behind Jill as they stood in the front of the living room. It was pitch black, and even with Lee's flashlight, it was difficult to see. The area where the beam was focused was illuminated immensely, but everything outside of that was black. Cheryl half-expected a horrid face to jump out in front of the beam, making both her and Jill scream in terror.

Jill scanned the living room slowly with the flashlight, the beam violently trembling in her hands. Cheryl felt her legs get weak when she thought she saw the creature crouching behind the couch. Her eyes adjusted to the scene quickly before she realized it was just the shadow of nearby objects.

"There's no one in here," Jill whispered.

As if in response, five steps came from upstairs, starting just above Cheryl and Jill, and advancing further down the corridor. Cheryl froze in place. She suddenly didn't want to budge from here. Being here on the first floor, surrounded by darkness was scary, yes, but at least they had Lee, Fabiola, and Charlie nearby.

Up there, on the second floor, everything seemed to be much darker and narrower. And there were no exits close by.

Jill broke into a confident gait across the living room, and that, in turn, gave Cheryl the confidence to start moving again. She stuck close to her sister, ready to push her out of the way at the first sign of danger. Once they reached the doorway leading to the foyer, Jill prudently peeked inside, vigorously shining the light around at every potential hiding spot for the dark spirit.

"It looks safe!" Jill whispered as she took a tentative step towards the foyer.

Cheryl was at her heels, trembling like a leaf in the wind. She looked back towards the living room. It was entirely black, not a single object visible, not even an outline. Cheryl imagined how easy it would be for the trickster spirit to just stand in the room and stare at them, and they would never even suspect a thing.

She imagined the tall, skinny figure peeking out from the dark and immediately averted her gaze back in front to avoid allowing the panic to overwhelm her. A rattling noise came from in front of her, causing her to freeze in terror.

"Locked," Jill said as she let go of the front door's knob.

Cheryl was once again enveloped by tentative relief at the realization that the rattling sound was Jill fiddling with the door.

"Geez, you almost gave me a heart attack," Cheryl said as she stuck close to Jill's side.

Jill giggled. It was a somewhat nervous, but genuine giggle, and that forced a smile out of Cheryl. She suddenly wondered how they got into this situation. Two estranged sisters who haven't spoken in years, fighting side by side against evil Vodou anomalies. It made her feel proud.

"Where is the doll?" Cheryl asked as Jill made the first step up the stairs.

The question was more directed to herself rather than Jill. She realized all of a sudden that she couldn't feel the doll's presence like she did when she first woke up.

"The spirit took it!" Jill slowly shook her head. "I guess we find the spirit, and we'll find the doll, no?"

"Okay, makes sense."

Jill nodded and continued leading the way, step by step. She was in front of Cheryl, with her hand sliding against the wall, the flashlight pointed at the top of the stairs. Cheryl kept her hand tight on the railing, her eyes fixated above her. She almost missed a step a few times, despite knowing every inch of the house by heart.

More clattering sounds came from upstairs, causing both Jill and Cheryl to stop in their steps. It sounded close, maybe just around the corner. There was nothing but silence after that. After just a few seconds, the sound of something shattering reverberated on the second floor.

It wasn't just unnerving hearing the sounds of items being smashed. It was the fact that it was unpredictable, with the silence that preceded between being full of palpable tension. And there was, of course, the fact that Cheryl expected something to jump out at them any moment.

After what felt like an eternity waiting near the top of the stairs, Cheryl decided to take the initiative. She took a step forward and then another until they came more fluidly. She tried not to step in front of the light and block it because the moment she did, blackness crept in, blinding Cheryl entirely. She assumed that her eyes would have gotten used to the dark by now, but the transition from staring at a bright flashlight to a fully dark area continually messed it up.

When she was at the second to last step, Cheryl looked back at Jill and silently outstretched her arm, motioning her to hand over the flashlight. Jill complied without a word. They almost dropped the flashlight, thanks to the the violent trembling coming from both of them.

Cheryl gripped the flashlight with both hands as she peeked around the corner and shone the light down the corridor. The place was a mess. The chest of drawers was knocked over, and the empty vase that once stood atop it was broken in countless pieces, scattered all over the floor. The flower pot that was on the windowsill at the far end of the corridor was on the floor, knocked over, with the wilted plant and dirt spread everywhere—it looked like it had been chucked across the hallway.

"See anything?" Jill asked haltingly.

Cheryl continued shining the flashlight to various spots of the corridor. Just to be on the safe side, she tipped it up and illuminated the ceiling, as well.

"Nothing," she finally said, still not fully convinced that she was right.

She climbed the final step to the second floor and stood motionless, wondering what to do next. Now that they were here, Cheryl wondered how the heck they were going to find the doll. It could be anywhere. In the best-case scenario, it would just be sitting somewhere, but that spot could be any place in the house—behind the couch, hidden in a wardrobe, on the ceiling fan above their reach...

And in the worst-case scenario, the trickster spirit had it, and would use it to lure Jill and Cheryl into a trap.

"Something tells me the doll is in my room," Jill said as she stopped next to Cheryl.

"What if it isn't?"

"Then we'll continue to look for it in other places," Jill shrugged.

Cheryl glanced over at her for a moment to see if she was joking. She wasn't.

That was the Jill she knew. Of the two of them, Jill was the more persistent one. If something didn't work out, she'd chip away at it until it did. Cheryl was the one who easily gave up. Unless someone told her specifically that she couldn't do something. Then she would find a way to do it just to spite them.

Seeing Jill's courage, Cheryl felt somewhat embarrassed and decided to swallow her fear. She stepped forward, still making sure not to make too much noise. The carpet here muffled their footsteps, so if the spirit hadn't somehow sensed them already—and Cheryl believed it did—then they might have been able to sneak up on it.

As they neared the open office, Cheryl slowed down. She was mustering the courage to peer inside. The room was already scary enough as it was, but if Cheryl looked inside and saw something else creepy in there, for example, a tall, dark figure...

She had to mentally brace herself for that.

She tried not to stop as she got closer to the door, but she couldn't help it. She needed a moment to prepare. Even though Jill didn't say anything, Cheryl felt like she was being rushed by Jill, standing so close, right behind her.

Before she could allow herself to think any further, Cheryl took the last step to bring her in front of the entrance and pointed the light inside. It trembled even more violently than a moment ago.

The room was empty. Cheryl darted the light in various directions, inspecting every inch of the room, hoping to god that she wouldn't run into something decidedly ungodly. The room was such a mess that nearly any object could easily be mistaken for a monster.

After scanning it three times over with the flashlight and even stepping close enough to check around the corners, she was content enough to tell Jill that there was nothing there. An invisible weight fell off her shoulders just for a moment until she realized she would need to inspect the rest of the roo—

When she turned around to face down the corridor, a dark figure stood mere inches from her face.

Cheryl screamed and dropped the flashlight before clasping her mouth with her hands. Jill quickly bent down and picked up the flashlight, pointing it at Mom's face.

"Mom! What are you doing?!" Cheryl whispered, her voice no more than a whimper.

Mom stood in one spot and stared at Cheryl. No, not at Cheryl. Just staring blankly in front of herself. Cheryl even looked behind herself to see what she was looking at, but there was nothing there.

The look of a zombie, Cheryl thought to herself with sadness creeping up on her, but not strong enough to overtake the anxiety and fear.

"Mom!" Cheryl called out again.

Even when Jill pointed the flashlight directly in her face, their mother didn't react—not even a flinch. The beam of the light cast ominous shadows across her face, making her look ten years older—and she already looked much older than her age.

"We can't worry about her now. Let's come back for her later," Jill said.

"We can't just leave her here," Cheryl protested.

"The spirit is no longer interested in her, right? We'll grab the doll, destroy it, and once we're done, we'll take care of her. Okay?"

Cheryl knew that it sounded much easier in theory and that Jill was just trying to convince her to set her priorities straight, but she had no other choice right now. She couldn't tug Mom by the hand wherever they went around the house. Not to mention she could put them even more at risk. No, Mom would need to stay here for now.

"Fine," Cheryl finally shrugged.

"Wait, look," Jill said.

"What?"

"Her hand."

Cheryl hung her head down and looked at Mom's hand. There was nothing remarkable about it. She thought that Jill might have been referring to a severe injury or something until she looked at her other hand.

Clutched in it was Lola.

The doll's eyes tantalizingly stared up at Cheryl, daring her to get closer. Cheryl looked up at Mom's face once more. She suddenly felt something that she never felt towards Mom ever before.

Fear.

She was afraid that trying to take the doll away from her was going to result in Mom going crazy and attacking her. Somehow, she came to terms with the fact that the person in front of her was no longer her mother, but simply an empty shell of the person she used to be.

"We have to get the doll away from her," Jill voiced Cheryl's thoughts.

"I know, just gimme a sec," Cheryl raised a palm towards Jill. "Mom? Can you hear me?"

Mom kept staring in front of herself with a blank look in her eyes. Cheryl just then realized she hadn't seen her blinking once since she woke up from her coma.

"I'm gonna take the doll, okay, Mom? I'm gonna take Lola, alright?"

To her amazement, Mom started speaking. Cheryl's hopes skyrocketed, and then dipped back down as soon as she realized that it was the same mumbling from before. Realizing that her mother was present only physically and not mentally, she slowly reached towards the doll in her hand.

Jill illuminated Mom's hand for Cheryl to get a better view. Cheryl saw just how much her own fingers trembled, and the more she tried steadying them, the more violently they shook. She decided to stop trying and just grabbed Lola by one stumpy limb.

As soon as her hand touched the doll, Mom's mumbling turned into a booming voice so loud that Cheryl's hands jerked as if struck by an electrical current.

"PAPA LEGBA, GRANT ME PROTECTION AGAINST THE EVIL IN MY HOUSE!" she shrieked and grabbed Cheryl by the wrist.

Cheryl screamed.

There was a commotion—Mom screaming the same words at the top of her lungs over and over, Jill's flashlight bobbing up and down, intermittently illuminating and plunging Cheryl's vision into darkness, panicked and incoherent words coming from Jill.

Cheryl was overcome with a sense of vertigo, and before she knew it, she lost her footing, and her back collided with the floor, knocking the wind out of her. She raised her head just in time to see a flashlight-illuminated hallway and Mom running off into her room and the door shutting—on its own.

"Cheryl! Are you okay?!" Jill was kneeling at her side as Cheryl remained on the floor in a recumbent position.

"Fine. I'm fi—"

Before she could finish that sentence, she caught something with her peripheral vision. It was fast, and entirely black, and the only reason Cheryl was able to see it was because a part of it stepped into the light—just for a split second.

It collided with Jill and sent her flying backward into the darkness. The flashlight flew from her hand and clattered to the floor before remaining there, its normally-potent beam snuffed by the wall it pointed at.

"Jill!" Cheryl shouted as she scrambled to reach for the flashlight.

Before she could even move a step, though, she felt something grabbing her by the ankle. She screamed and felt herself being dragged across the floor. Her shirt rose, and she felt her lower back getting scraped up by the rough fabric of the carpet, but she felt no pain....nothing except the everlasting fear and adrenaline that took the reins of her body.

"Cheryl!" she heard Jill's voice, distantly.

She saw the window at the far end of the corridor getting closer to her, and just in front of it, she stopped moving. The ice-like grip on her ankle that she hadn't even been fully aware of disappeared, and Cheryl lay on the floor motionless. The beam of the torch appeared somewhere above her, and at the same time, at the window through which she could see the sky disappeared, covered in blackness.

"Cheryl, watch o—" Jill's shout got cut off mid-sentence, and a familiar shriek echoed in the corridor.

Cheryl propped herself up on her elbows, but before she could do anything else, she realized why the window had disappeared.

Chapter 41

It took Jill a moment to orient herself. Something crashed into her and knocked her down. She pulled herself up with her hands and looked around the permeating darkness. She couldn't see anything because the flashlight was no longer in her hands, and that realization immediately caused a wave of panic to surge through her.

"Cheryl?" Jill called out frantically to her sister.

She then saw a sliver of light on the floor woefully pointing towards a nearby wall. She scrambled over to it and grabbed the flashlight more firmly in her grip this time.

"Cheryl!" she screamed and swiveled the light down the corridor.

Cheryl's screaming had stopped by then, and Jill feared for the worst. But then she saw Cheryl lying still on her back at the far end of the corridor, just in front of the window.

Just then, Jill saw the black figure creeping up from the corner in front of Cheryl. For a split second, she saw its demonic features, and even with the torch pointed directly at it, it was still abyss-black.

"Cheryl, watch o—" Jill's sentence abruptly got cut off when she felt something powerful collide with her on her left, sending her tumbling towards the wall, losing her balance, and falling down.

A shrill cry boomed in her ear, and she barely had enough time to point the light at the source of the sound when her mother jumped on top of her. More screaming ensued from Jill, Annette, Cheryl, and the trickster spirit, whose shriek drowned out all the others.

"Mom, stop!" Jill shouted as she held her arms in front of herself defensively.

Annette flailed and bashed at her like a rabid animal. Her face was contorted into an anger Jill had never seen before.

"Stop!" Jill shouted again, but Annette gave no indication that she heard her.

The flashlight got knocked out of Jill's hand once more, plunging her and her attacker into complete darkness. In a moment of confusion, Jill lowered her arms to defend herself, and that was all Annette needed.

Her mother wrapped her cold, bony hands around Jill's throat and squeezed. Jill immediately felt her throat closing up, and she was unable to inhale or exhale. Annette's strength was out of this world, Jill thought, as she futilely tried to pry the fingers off her neck.

That proved to be useless because she couldn't budge them even a tiny bit. The pressure on her throat intensified so much that she expected to hear a snap of a bone any moment. Her vision started getting darker, and her strength began to wane.

***

The trickster spirit lunged at Cheryl. Cheryl screamed and instinctively put her hands in front of her face. She couldn't see anything and only focused on one thing at that moment—blindly protecting herself.

She felt herself getting tugged and yanked by the arms while the creature screamed loudly, making Cheryl deaf to every other sound. Realizing that this wasn't going to work, Cheryl brought her knees up to her stomach and kicked. Her feet connected with something, and the creature shrieked somewhat differently this time—a shriek of pain, Cheryl hoped.

She flopped back down into a prone position and began scrambling forward. She saw Jill on the floor and Mom on top of her, the two of them locked in a wrestling contest. On the floor beside them, right next to the flashlight, was the doll.

Gotta get to it!

Cheryl planted her palms on the floor and propelled herself forward with her foot to save her sister. As she lunged forward, her other foot continued to dangle in the air, and she fell down on the floor, smashing her chin against the carpet.

She didn't have time to react before the grip on her ankle tightened.

***

"Cheryl!" Lee heard Jill shouting once more.

There was a commotion upstairs. Shouts, screams, something getting dragged, Jill shouting Cheryl's name. It sent a wave of panic through Lee.

"Shit, I need to go help them!" he said as he took a step towards the living room.

He was stopped by the African woman's hand on his chest. She looked far too calm, given the situation they were in.

"Out of the way, lady!" he said, but she wouldn't budge.

"*Non!* You cannot go there!"

"My wife is in danger!"

He tried to push past her again, but she was faster. She stepped in front of him with a stern look on her face.

"If you go up there, you will die! And then your son will be next!"

That made Lee stop and think. He definitely didn't want to leave Charlie alone in here, even in the presence of a Vodou expert. The woman calmly spoke, "You must understand. Jill and Cheryl are in no mortal danger. The spirit simply wants to latch onto them, not kill them. Why would it kill something that keeps it alive?"

Lee sighed in a defeated tone. He intermittently stared at the woman and the entrance to the living room.

He was about to shove the woman out of the way and bolt upstairs when he felt a small, soft hand touching his. Immediately, the adrenaline started leaving him.

"Dad? Are Mom and Aunt Cheryl okay?" Charlie asked.

Lee looked down at Charlie. He had a concerned look on his face, like the first time he went to baseball practice—only this time, the uncertainty on his face was amplified.

"Yeah, they're okay, buddy," Lee tried to give Charlie a reassuring smile.

Charlie didn't seem to believe him because he, too, glanced at the living room.

"They'll be back in no time, okay?" Lee put both hands on Charlie's shoulders. "When they do, we will need someone brave to lead us out of the house, and it will have to be you. Think you can do that for us?"

Charlie's look of concern was immediately replaced by one of readiness and determination.

"Yeah!" he said.

"Good. But I need you to stay right here and remain quiet until they return, okay? Can you do that?"

Charlie nodded.

"Good. We'll all be home safely in no time," Lee lied through gritted teeth.

***

Jill wanted to plead with her mom to stop, but she couldn't utter a single word. Even through the dark, she could see her vision becoming blurry. She didn't have long until she lost consciousness.

But hitting Annette proved to be futile. She didn't even budge, even when struck in the face. She barely flinched and then continued to choke Jill with that same crazed look in her eye. Jill felt the floor with her left hand, hoping to find something—anything—that would help her defend herself against Annette. She didn't care if she had to kill her mother right there, but she was not going to die.

Not like this.

Jill frantically felt around the floor, but there was noth—

She felt something different under her fingers, something hard, cold, and sharp. She clutched it in her hand and immediately realized that she was holding a piece of the broken vase.

No other choice.

Jill swung her hand towards Annette, and it connected with something. At first, she thought she didn't do any damage to her, but then Annette screamed and grabbed at her shoulder.

Immediately, the pressure on Jill's throat eased up, but she didn't waste any time recovering. She brought her knee to her face and then kicked out with her heel, as hard as she could.

The kick connected with Annette's jaw, sending her toppling backward.

Jill put a hand on her painful throat and wheezed, coughing and gasping, relieved to be able to breathe in even a whiff of the stale house air. She knew she had no time to waste; Cheryl was in danger. As Jill grabbed the flashlight from the floor and pointed it at Annette, she realized that her mother was motionless.

Unconscious, hopefully, she thought to herself with little concern.

When she pointed the light down the corridor, she saw Cheryl on her stomach, a terrified look on her face, and the black thing standing above her.

No, not standing. It was crouching, the knees on its elongated legs almost going above its shoulders. It held Cheryl under the chin with both hands as if ready to snap her neck. Even when Jill pointed the light directly at it, it didn't react. Jill saw a triumphant look on the creature's face as it stared down at Cheryl, even though she couldn't see its eyes—only the white grin. Perhaps it was savoring the moment before it decided to dig into its next meal. Cheryl's face was ghastly, drained of all color, and her eyes were wide with terror.

"Jill!" Cheryl reached out towards her sister with one hand. "The doll!"

Jill realized that Cheryl's eyes were transfixed somewhere on the floor. She looked down and saw Lola laying there, face down. She shot down and snapped it up.

"Hey!" she shouted as she victoriously raised the doll above her head.

The black thing jerked its head towards Jill. Its snarl left its face, perhaps in a moment of desperate realization that it had messed up.

"I got your thing!" Jill taunted the creature.

"We had a deal!" a horrid, guttural sentence left the creature's mouth.

It dropped Cheryl on the floor and caterwauled. With nimble motions, it began dashing towards Jill. Jill turned around to shield Lola, closing her eyes firmly and bracing herself for impact.

But the impact never came.

Instead, the creature shrieked even louder, and then Jill heard someone else hasty speaking. She opened her eyes and glanced at the white-clothed person standing beside her.

Fabiola!

The mambo was chanting something in her language with one hand in front of herself. The black creature cowered and shrank under the mambo's words. It no longer screamed but rather growled and hissed. It still looked threatening, although it no longer glared like a hungry wolf ready to pounce on its prey, but instead like a wounded and cornered fox.

Fabiola continued speaking the words, and slowly advanced towards the monster, causing it, in turn, to retreat further back. It screeched at Fabiola before running off into the darkness and disappearing.

Silence ensued, and it was the most pleasant sound Jill had ever heard.

"Cheryl!" she shouted, breaking the silence.

She was about to rush to her sister's side when she saw Cheryl running towards them instead. Fabiola touched Jill's shoulder.

"We do not have much time until it returns! We have to destroy the doll!" Fabiola said.

"Right!" Cheryl interjected and stepped in front of Jill. "Jill, give me the doll! I'll take care of it!"

Jill nodded and handed the doll to Cheryl. She snatched it away quickly and took a step back. She looked around and knelt down to grab the nearest shard of the broken vase. She pinned the doll on the ground and raised the shard above her head. With one swift motion, she stabbed the pointy end of the shard into the head of the doll with a cry.

Jill saw blood trickling between Cheryl's fingers, and she heard a ripping sound as she dragged the shard from Lola's head all the way down to her torso, leaving a big rip with the wool sticking out.

A blood-curdling cry resounded from somewhere in the house, and this time, it sounded painful and long. It must have lasted for at least ten seconds before it finally died down.

"We had a deal!" it repeated before silence took over.

And then, just like that, the lights came back on, bathing the room in the dim, sickly light.

"Jill?! What's going on up there?!" It was Lee.

"They are okay, *cheri*!" Fabiola answered.

Jill felt relief overwhelming her. She rushed to Cheryl, who was sitting on the floor, holding her wounded hand. Blood trickled abundantly from her palm where the vase had cut her. Jill ran into the bathroom and retrieved a white towel. She ran back to her sister and wrapped Cheryl's hand into it, pressing hard against the wound.

Cheryl winced, but didn't complain. The towel almost immediately turned red, which worried Jill. Cheryl took over pressing the towel against her own and nodded at Jill reassuringly. The sisters hugged in a fleeting moment of respite and held each other tightly. Jill started to feel the adrenaline subsiding, and with it, the knowledge that she was so very close to losing her sister intensified, instilling astronomical fear in her.

"We're okay. We're okay. We're okay," Cheryl whispered over and over.

They were both trembling violently. An eternity later, they stood up with Fabiola's help.

"Let's go, *wi?*" the mambo grinned fondly.

Cheryl glanced over at Mom's unconscious body before nodding. Fabiola ushered the girls downstairs to the front door. Charlie and Lee were already there. The foyer lights were not working from when they blew out the day prior, but the light coming from the rest of the rooms was enough to illuminate the foyer.

Jill rushed over to hug her son and husband, no longer caring about hiding her fear. Lee inspected her to make sure she wasn't hurt.

She had to first confirm to him that the blood was from Cheryl's hand, not from her, and Lee sighed in relief and held her close. He, too, was trembling—not as violently as Jill, but still, visibly so.

Fabiola tried the knob. The door opened, letting in a squall of the fresh night air.

"Everybody outside! Now! *Prese!*" she implored, and swung the door wide open.

She ushered Jill and Charlie out first and then waited until Lee and Cheryl were out of there before she, too, stepped out and closed the door behind her. The crickets chirped jovially, and the cold breeze has never felt so wonderful.

Jill stepped off the porch and took a moment to breathe in the fresh air.

"Cheryl, we need to get you to an amb—" when Jill turned around, she saw Cheryl standing on the porch.

263

Everyone else was in the driveway, staring at her in confusion. She no longer had a terrified look on her face, but a sorrowful one. She locked eyes with Jill and smiled forlornly.

"It's not over yet," she said.

Chapter 42

Cheryl suppressed the tears welling up in her eyes. She saw the flabbergasted looks on everybody's faces, silently demanding an explanation. Even Fabiola looked confused.

"Cheryl?" Jill asked as she stepped forward.

She was visibly getting anxious and ready to start berating Cheryl with a flurry of questions.

"The spirit has been chased away. For now. But it will come back soon," Cheryl said.

Jill looked nowhere in particular. She suddenly felt every bit as exhausted as she probably looked.

"Then we gotta... we gotta stop it. We gotta—"

"We can't," Cheryl shook her head. "The spirit always latches onto a member of the family like a parasite. When the final member of the family dies, the spirit dies with it."

"No, no, no, no, we vanquished it. We destroyed the doll!" Jill refused to agree.

"The doll was only an object used to transfer the spirit from one family member to another."

"Wait..." Jill raised a hand, her face contorting into a look of confusion.

"When Mom learned that the spirit latched onto her, she knew that there was no way to get rid of it. So, she had to choose which one of us would inherit it," Cheryl's voice started cracking.

"And that's why she gave me Lola," Jill's face looked like she just got slapped. "And that's why she was so mean to me my entire life. And that's why the bitch gave the house to me! Because she wanted me to stay so that I could expose myself to the spirit while you—"

Her furious tone cracked and turned into a whimper, and she failed to finish her sentence. Cheryl stepped off the porch and approached Jill.

"Whatever happened in the past is all over now, Jill," Cheryl said. "You protected me when we were kids. And now it's my turn to protect you."

"Wh-what are you t-talking ab-about?" Jill asked, trembling through sniffles.

"When I took the doll from you, I accepted the spirit latching onto me."

"No, Cherry, no, no, no..."

"It had to be this way. It was either you or me. And if it latched onto you, then Charlie would be next," Cheryl was sobbing now, as well. "And I couldn't let that happen."

Jill rushed to Cheryl and embraced her tightly.

The two sisters spent a long moment holding each other tightly and sobbing, not caring that Lee, Charlie, and Fabiola were staring at them silently on the side.

Despite knowing the hardships that awaited her in the future, Cheryl couldn't help but feel happy. She brought some evil upon herself, yes, but she had also saved the lives of her mother, sister, and nephew.

Not to mention that she had finally reconnected with Jill.

And that was a pretty good tradeoff.

Epilogue

"There, you're all set," Fabiola said with a smile, victoriously spreading her arms wide. "Now, remember what I told you, *cheri.*"

"I know, I know," Cheryl sardonically rolled her eyes. "Purify the apartment once every couple of months, recite the prayers, and always have sage nearby…"

"And?" Fabiola waited patiently for a response, like a teacher waiting for the student to give an answer.

"And… and that's it?" Cheryl shrugged in confusion, wondering what else she forgot.

"And eat more healthy foods!" Fabiola added.

"How is that going to help with the protection?"

"It won't. It will just help you stay healthy. You look like a mess, *cheri.*"

"Thanks, Fabiola," Cheryl chuckled.

Fabiola's visits made her feel much better. She always made sure to do everything the mambo taught her in order to protect herself from evil spirits, word for word, and so far, it had worked perfectly. Fabiola still insisted on visiting her every couple of months, just to make sure she was truly okay. Cheryl told her that she wouldn't have enough cash to pay her, but Fabiola insisted that a cup of tea would be more than enough payment. During her visits, she made sure to teach Cheryl more things so that she could continue to protect herself.

"Remember, *cheri*, you are like an HIV patient."

"That's uplifting."

"My point is, you can live a perfectly normal life, but you need to make sure to take care of yourself. Okay?"

"Okay."

"Okay," Fabiola repeated as she finished packing her things. "Then I am done today. Thank you for the tea, and I will see you in a few months, *wi?*"

"Sure thing. Are you sure you don't wanna come with me to Jill's house? I'm sure she would be happy to see you."

Fabiola shook her head and walked to the door.

"I do not want to remind her of the bad things that happened. But say hi to her in my name, *oke?*"

"Alright, I'll be sure to do that."

Fabiola hugged Cheryl tightly. Cheryl found herself wondering how this woman got her masculine strength. The life of a mambo was undoubtedly physically demanding.

"Oh, one more question," Cheryl suddenly remembered.

"*Wi?*"

"Is there like, any danger that I can unknowingly put Jill and Charlie into if I get too close to them?"

"We talked about this before, *non?* You do not need to worry about it. Protect yourself, and you will also protect them."

"Thanks again, Fabiola," Cheryl smiled.

"You take good care of yourself, *cheri.*"

Fabiola smiled one last time before opening the door and leaving. Cheryl felt lighter after every single one of Fabiola's visits. The mambo was a lot more experienced in this sort of thing anyway, so her Vodou protections were a lot more efficient than Cheryl's.

Cheryl would get better at it; she just needed time.

But right now, it was time to visit her sister and nephew.

***

"What took you so long?" Lee asked as soon as Jill stepped inside the apartment.

He was sitting on the couch with his laptop on his lap.

"Busy day at work," she exasperatingly sighed.

"You need to take it a little easy. I know you got promoted, but that doesn't mean you need to be there for everyone all the time."

"I know, I know. I'm already working on slowing down, I promise."

She dropped her purse onto the chair in front of the kitchen counter and gave Lee a quick peck on the lips.

"Is the little troublemaker in his room?" she asked.

"Yeah. Been there almost the entire day."

"You didn't pick out some clothes for him for when Cheryl arrives, did you?"

"Oh, crap."

Lee's face contorted into the familiar one that said, '*I messed up!*'. He immediately tried making an excuse about being too busy and forgetting, but Jill dismissed it with a laugh. She was too excited about Cheryl coming over to get irritated.

It had been a few months since she'd last seen her sister. Ever since their reunion at the house, they kept up with seeing each other at least once a month—they were only one state away, after all.

Jill walked over to the door of Charlie's room and rapped on it.

"Charlie?" she called out after Charlie didn't respond.

When there was still no response, she let herself in. As soon as she opened the door, she heard the sound of soft and steady scratching. She saw him sitting at the desk and facing away from her, jotting something down in a notebook.

"Charles," Jill called out.

He rotated in his seat, finally becoming aware of Jill's presence.

"Hi, Mom," he said with a grin.

He had his *Fortnite* t-shirt on and a pair of sweatpants.

"How was your day, sweetie?" Jill asked as she stepped inside.

Charlie's demeanor immediately changed from calm to excited as he started talking about his day.

"It was great! I played *Minecraft* with Kyle, and we finished building a castle on top of a mountain! And we have

269

a farm below, and there's a cave full of diamond nodes underground, and—"

"Okay, okay!" Jill patted him on the head. "But let's talk about that later, okay? Aunt Cheryl will be here soon. Go tell Dad to pick out some clothes for you, alright?"

Charlie hopped off the chair and started towards the door. Jill smiled to herself and shook her head. She was about to follow him out when her eyes fell on the notebook on Charlie's desk.

It was open, and a pencil lay on top of it. At first glance, the drawing looked depressing and crude. Jill hated thinking about her son's artwork that way, but she saw all the other colorful things he drew, and this one was—

It was a *vèvè*.

A fucking *vèvè*.

Jill pushed the pencil out of the way and raised the notebook with trembling hands. A *vèvè*. Papa Legba's *vèvè*, at that. No, not Papa Legba's. The one her Mom drew on the wall of the house.

"Uh, Charlie?" Jill called out, trying to hide the quivering of her voice.

"Yes, Mommy?" Charlie stopped in front of the door and turned around with rapt attention.

"What is this?" she turned the notebook for him to see and stepped closer.

Charlie shrugged. Jill knelt down and pointed to the *vèvè*.

"Where did you see this?"

"My friend showed me."

"Wh-what friend, Charlie?" Jill's voice was merely a whisper.

She felt a knot forming deep in her stomach. Thank goodness she hadn't eaten prior to that, otherwise, she would have thrown up.

"Charlie, what friend, honey? What friend is that?!" Jill raised her voice to a near frantic level.

Charlie was visibly taken aback, his eyes widening, and he hung his head down, just like he did every single time he did something wrong.

"Charlie, look at me. Who showed you this? Who is the friend who showed you how to draw this?!" Jill pointed to the *vèvè* even more vigorously.

Lee rushed inside the room to see what the commotion was all about. Charlie calmly looked at Jill in total silence for a moment more, as if contemplating whether to tell her or not.

And then he opened his mouth.

"The boy," he said...

Heart n' Home Hospice, OR

"Good morning, Doctor Greer," Violet faked a smile as she walked past the doctor.

"Oh, Violet?" he turned to face the nurse just as she walked past him.

"Yes, doctor?"

"Would you mind checking on the patient in room three? She's been a little agitated lately, and I'm worried about her."

"Of course, doctor. I'll do it right away," Violet said.

"Thank you, Violet," he smiled in return before proceeding back down the hallway.

Violet had a lot of things to do already, but she was happy to assist Dr. Greer whenever she could. She learned a lot of things from him, and she wanted to stay in his good graces in order to continue having it so. She started her career as a nurse by working in Reed Hospital for Special Care under Dr. Emily Torres for the first three years, and she had learned nothing. The doctor was not only a recluse who had no patience to teach newbies, but she was also extremely unapproachable.

For the next few years, Violet hopped from hospital to hospital, eventually ending up working as a home health nurse for the Heart n' Home hospice. She worked not just at the homes of the patients, but at the hospice, as well. It was rough, but Violet enjoyed the job.

In fact, she loved it so much that she constantly educated herself in order to improve in her job. She was, in a literal sense, a workaholic. She never even got married, even though she had the opportunities for it. She had many patients, male nurses, and even doctors who tried wooing her, but she wasn't interested.

Her parents always told her that she should get married and have kids, but Violet wasn't interested in any of that. She dated for a while, but her cold demeanor would always drive the men away. She was far too busy anyway, and life was too short to bother with such insignificant things.

Violet stopped in front of the elevator and pushed the button to call it. It opened almost immediately, revealing a stern, middle-aged man with a janitorial cart.

"Good morning, Mr. Stein," Violet coldly said.

Mr. Stein gave her a brusque nod and pushed the cart out of the elevator before making his way down the hallway. He wasn't very talkative, but Violet was okay with that. Back when she was younger, she tried to be polite to everyone at her job. Whenever someone didn't match her politeness by greeting her back or by being rude to her, she'd get offended and would end up spending the whole day replaying the encounter in her head.

Eventually, she learned how to detach from those things. She herself became desensitized to the patients' moans, complaints, and problems, until being a nurse became an automated routine for her.

"I'm just so scared of what's going to happen to my daughter after cancer kills me," Mr. Wilgrave would say to her almost on a daily basis.

"I'm sure she'll be fine, Mr. Wilgrave. Now, turn so I can give you your injection," Violet would coldly retort.

She knew that thinking about those things would eventually start gnawing at her. It happened when she was younger. So, she began treating the patients as inanimate objects rather than humans. Eventually, she found that she was no longer pretending, but actually no longer cared.

Violet entered the elevator and pressed the button for the third floor. The doors closed, and the elevator started ascending. It was an old, slow elevator, so it would take some time until it reached the desired floor. But Violet didn't mind. She patiently waited until the doors opened, revealing a pristine, narrow hallway. There were orderlies buzzing from place to place, and Violet ignored every single one of them as they politely greeted her.

"Hey, Violet! Have a good weekend?" Mark asked with a nervous grin as she walked past him.

She made a show of rolling her eyes and refused to answer him. Mark had been eyeing her from time to time, and she expected him to ask her out any day now. She didn't even care enough to ponder how to tell him no without hurting his feelings.

Mark was a bald, overweight, forty-year-old orderly in the hospice. He was never married, as far as Violet knew, and there was a rumor around the place that Mark was actually gay. Violet sure hoped he was. That way, she'd be able to avoid the inconvenience of being asked out.

Violet opened the door to the patient's room, not bothering to knock first. Why should she bother with that? The patient was pretty much a vegetable.

"Good morning, Annette," Violet said in a loud tone. "How are we today?"

No response. Of course not.

Annette sat on the bed, staring blankly at the floor, drooling from her mouth. Violet wrinkled her nose at the horrendous smell that permeated the room. The patient must have defecated in her diapers, and no one bothered to change her again.

As she entered the room, she glanced at the desk. There was a platter of untouched mushy food on top of it. Violet sighed and took a mental note to tell Dr. Greer about the neglectful behavior of the orderlies towards the patients.

"Still haven't had your breakfast, Annette? You need your nutrients. I suppose sitting in a room all day long, doing nothing but drawing takes a lot of strength."

She fed Annette, bite by bite. She still retained her chewing and swallowing reflex, but she often made a mess by forgetting to close her mouth or swallow. Feeding her was a long and tedious process, but it had to be done.

Once that was finished, she placed the platter of half-eaten food on the bed and began cleaning Annette and changing her clothes.

"You've been really messy lately, haven't you?" Violet asked.

She had a habit of talking to mentally handicapped patients. They never talked back, they never disagreed, and they never complained. Not like the terminally ill patients who were so negative all the time.

"All done. You look good enough for a ball," Violet said as she finished cleaning and dressing Annette. "And a good thing, too. I have my monthly meet-up tonight with a group of people, and they are *very* interested in hearing about you. I'll be sure to tell them how wonderful you look."

She took the platter of food and turned, ready to leave the room, when her eyes fell on the desk again.

There was a paper on top of it, with black crayons next to it. Annette was incapable of even the most basic functions, but for some reason, she would draw from time to time. That's why Violet insisted that they allow her to have a notebook and some crayons. She couldn't have pencils, of course, because they were deemed too dangerous for patients like Annette. She might end up severely hurting herself.

It wouldn't be the first patient to end their life like that.

Violet got closer to the desk and glanced down at the paper. There was a crude, and yet oddly precise drawing there, made with a black crayon. Annette only used the black crayon for some reason, and in rare cases, red.

"Hm. You're getting better. This is Papa Legba's *vèvè*, isn't it?" Violet asked, not bothering to look at Annette.

"Papa... Legba... Pa... pa..." Annette muttered.

"Hm," Violet pensively uttered.

She freed one hand of the platter and reached down for the black crayon.

"I'll be sure to tell everyone tonight how much your drawing has improved," she said as she stared in silent awe at the accurate lines Annette made.

She was able to draw the *vèvè* from memory perfectly.

Violet pensively tapped the crayon on the paper, observing the artwork for any irregularities. She shrugged a moment later and said to herself, "It's a good *vèvè*, but in the end, we had a deal."

She added one simple line on top of the drawing. She placed the crayon down and turned to leave the room.

"Have a good day, Annette. I'll see you tomorrow morning," she said as she closed the door softly behind her.

THE END

About the Author

Boris Bacic (spelled Bačić in his native tongue) was born in 1990 in Serbia, in a small Northern town called Subotica.

As a kid, he developed a passion for writing and drawing because it allowed him to dive into a world of his own. When he started going to high school, he stopped writing for a while and focused on fitness in hopes of becoming a police officer (or a soldier).

After serving the army, he worked as a fitness coach for a few years before becoming interested in Creepypastas (short scary stories found on the internet). He spent a long time reading horror stories and listening to Creepypasta narrations before deciding to post his own story on Reddit's Nosleep forum. He immediately got tons of recognition and praise from the frequent readers, having his stories narrated by prominent Youtubers (some of which include MrCreepypasta, MrCreeps, DarkSomnium, DrCreepen, etc.), translated into various languages, and his most popular Nosleep series, **Tales of a Security Guard**, is currently being made into a video game and short film.

Boris published his first book in 2019, titled **Scary Stories With B.B.**, and after that, he focused on writing novels. His first novel, titled **Radio Tower**, received a lot of praise and positive criticism and continues to sell well among readers of all horror and thriller genres.

Boris' motto is 'I plan to keep writing until I'm either famous or dead'.

In his free time, he enjoys going to the gym, reading books, playing video games, exploring topics for his next book project, and occasionally – going to escape rooms.

Message from the author:
Want to get in touch with me? Shoot me an email at:

authorborisbacic@gmail.com
I always love hearing from my readers.
BB

Final Notes

Huge thanks for reading my book. If you enjoyed it, I would appreciate it if you left a review on the **Amazon Product page**. Your reviews help small-time authors like me grow and allow us to continue expanding our careers.

Haunted Places Free Excerpts

Apartment 401

Stephen fished the keychain out of the pocket of his jeans. The keyring jingled jovially in his hand while he fiddled with it, looking for the right one.

"Hey, Steve. Busy day?" Marty asked in passing, flashing a pearly grin and winking playfully.

He was a man in his forties, with a balding head and thick-rimmed glasses. He wore a white shirt and red tie, with beige dress pants and shiny shoes – just like every real estate employee had to in the company. Stephen hated the red tie, so he at least tried to hide it partially with a blue jacket over the white shirt.

"Yep, you know it," he said to Marty with a cock of the head.

Stephen would have shot him a finger gun had he not been holding a folder full of papers under his left arm. As he strode down the corridor and past one of the cubicle offices on the fourth floor, the murmurs of the busy employees intensified. They faded only a moment later when Stephen turned right and entered through the glass door with the sign next to it that said *LiveBetter*. The floor in his company's office had a red Belgium carpet that muffled the employees' footsteps. It gave it all the more the impression that people needed to be quiet because, with the absence of the loud thudding on the tiled floor, voices and low shuffling of the papers and seats became the only discernible noise. It was like a library. Stephen clutched the keyring tighter in his hand to prevent it from jingling.

Luckily, this was only the waiting room, where only the receptionist Claudia sat. Sometimes, one or two people were waiting for an appointment with one of the realtors. Right now, the seats for the clients were empty.

"Afternoon, Claudia," Stephen nodded politely.

Claudia looked up from her phone behind the reception, flashing her white grin to Stephen.

"Hi, Stephen! Working hard?"

"No, hardly working," Stephen retorted.

Claudia guffawed at his remark. It was an exaggerated laugh, but he knew about Claudia. She was just a receptionist, and he was the top real estate agent for the company. Everyone knew how much he earned, and since the company wasn't big, the news spread quickly.

When Claudia first started working for LiveBetter, she barely even dignified Stephen with a greeting. And then, around two months later, when the CEO of the company personally congratulated Stephen for his hard work for the company – in front of Claudia – things changed. She began smiling at him more often, tossing flirtatious comments about him looking good in his pants, casually mentioning that she didn't have any plans for the weekend, etc.

Stephen ignored her and maintained a professional relationship. He already heard about her from the other coworkers. Claudia was apparently one of those bimbos that he only saw in movies, who made their way to everything in life over a bed. She definitely fit the description with her pumped-up lips, powdered-up face, one-inch long nails that made Stephen wonder how she was able to hold anything in her hand, and tight and skimpy clothes that she posted on social media (he skimmed through her profile on Instagram). She probably would have worn the same kind of clothes in the office had it not been for the company's dress-code policy.

The word was that Claudia slept (or did something sexual) with the HR manager, and that's how she got her receptionist role. There were talks from other employees that she was a real slut, and that made her all the more repulsive to Stephen. The last thing he needed was to catch some STDs or become the talk of the office – and potentially lose his job over it. And to think that could happen over some lowlife like Cladia, no fucking way!

He had hoped that Claudia would take the hint and back off, but she was persistent, flirting with Stephen with every chance she got – and with others when he wasn't around. He even tried lying to her about having a girlfriend, but she wouldn't let up. Moreso, she seemed even more interested in him afterward, becoming more direct by briefly talking about her lesbian and threesome experiences, etc. Stephen silently prayed that she would fuck another higher-up soon so that she could get transferred to a different department because having to stop and make small talk with her out of courtesy every single working day was exhausting. Making small talk meaning listening to her talking about shallow nonsense and throwing pathetic compliments at Stephen.

"Off so soon?" Claudia teased Stephen when he loped his way past her without stopping more than to briefly exchange pleasantries.

"Yeah, got something to take care of in the office," he stopped in his tracks and turned to face Claudia. "Uh, if anyone comes looking for me, tell them to wait here and let me know about it."

He gave her a courteous smile.

"You got it, busy man," Claudia said with a wide grin.

Stephen couldn't help but notice how she looked all plasticized, like a life-sized Barbie doll – more so than usually. He thanked her and turned around before she could start a conversation about something else with him. Stephen found the key to his office once more, allowing the keyring to jungle loudly now that he was away from the waiting room. As he stopped in front of the door with a thick, opaque glass pane that had the plastered grey letters *Realtor Steve Hicks* on it, he inserted the key into the keyhole.

"Hi, Steve. Did you find someone for the apartment we talked about?" the voice came so abruptly from his left that Stephen nearly jumped.

"Jesus, Charlie!" Stephen chuckled at his manager's jumpscare.

"Sorry, didn't mean to scare you. I guess that's easy to do in a quiet place like this one," Charlie glanced down at the waiting room.

"Yeah. Anyway, I was just about to sit down and look at all the candidates for the apartment. I'll give them a call as soon as I look over their info."

"Good man. Keep up the good work. Just don't overdo it. You know what it means if you do."

"Yep, we get another increase in the required norms. I'll make sure to take it easy."

Charlie gently patted Stephen on the shoulder before making his way towards the exit. Stephen made sure to follow him with his gaze until he was through the glass doors and out of sight. Only then did he turn the key – slowly. The lock clicked much louder than he wanted it to, but then he realized that doing things slowly would make him look all the more suspicious.

He pulled the key out and opened the door, stepping inside the dark office. He skillfully flipped the switch, already familiar with its location, and the room immediately got bathed in bright, yellow light. The office was small but cozy. Stephen wished he had more space, but he appreciated having his own privacy and silence. He couldn't imagine working in a cubicle like the IT guys on the same floor. His introverted personality contradicted his job description where he needed to communicate with clients daily, and Stephen himself was surprised at his ability to speak with clients for hours without feeling fatigued. However, five minutes of small talk unrelated to work caused him to burn out pretty quickly.

Stephen locked his office, leaving the key in the keyhole, made his way around the desk, and slumped into the rotating chair. He tossed the thick and heavy folder on top of the desk, feeling the immense stress slowly leaving his body.

He had been buzzing from place to place all day long, and the seat came as a haven for him. He leaned back in the chair, groaning in relief and grabbing at his painful neck. Stephen closed his eyes and allowed himself to enjoy the moment of respite.

"Stephen," someone softly whispered into his ear.

It didn't startle him but rather reminded him that he had work to do. As he opened his eyes and turned his head in the direction of the sound, he saw no one.

"Alright, alright. Can't a guy get a moment of rest?" Stephen jokingly asked aloud.

He rubbed his eyes and leaned forward with a groan. He opened the folder and sifted through the papers. He took out one piece of document that had a picture of a young man attached with a clip to it and placed it on the desk, all the way in the upper left corner. He then pulled out the next paper, also one with a picture of a person, this one a middle-aged woman. Stephen neatly placed the paper next to the one of the young man and continued rummaging through the folder.

Since a lot of the people there were not adequate candidates, Stephen put those people's documents aside while sifting through the rest. The entire desk was soon cluttered with documents of various photos attached to them. Stephen had to make some papers overlap since he didn't have enough room, but by the time he was done, the previously heavy folder was much lighter as it lay in his lap.

Stephen tossed the folder on the floor next to him and leaned on his knees, staring at the bevy of papers in front of him. He scrutinized each photograph, trying to understand what kind of person he was looking at. He had met with all those people, of course, but most of them were nice, for the most part. They always were. It was the face they put on when they wanted to buy a property. Even after all these years of working as a realtor, Stephen was horrible at reading people. He was great convincing them to buy things, yes, but he was never able to get past that underlying smile and first-impressions personality where everyone portrayed themselves in the nicest possible way.

He glanced at the photograph of Andrew Wasdin. He was a fifty-year-old Marine Corps veteran who wanted to buy the apartment, and Stephen didn't like him one bit. Not only was he bulky and intrusive in personal space, but he wouldn't shut up about his stories from the army days. Stephen tried to be polite for the most part, but he accidentally let out a chuckle when Wasdin told him about the time he and his five buddies beat up fifty police officers before getting arrested. Wasdin shot Stephen an angry look when he saw him chuckling, and for a moment, Stephen thought he was going to call him out on it, but he instead turned into the living room and asked some questions about the apartment.

If anyone from the list of people was the best candidate for apartment 401, it was Wasdin, Stephen thought. But that was not for him to decide, and as previous experiences showed – first impressions could easily be deceiving. He leaned back in the chair. It didn't squeak, a testament to how rarely it was used. Stephen placed his hands on the armrest and took a deep breath.

"Alright. Show me," he said as he stared down at the document-littered desk.

He tapped his right hand on the armrest, averting his gaze from the papers and darting his eyes around the room. It was silent, so silent that he heard the calm, steady beating of his own heart. He swallowed, and at that moment, it sounded annoyingly loud, even to himself. He continued glancing around the room, waiting for... something. For what, exactly?

He already knew. He just needed to be patient.

Stephen looked down at his lap, starting to feel his eyelids getting heavy. He closed his eyes for a moment, just to rest them briefly. He wished he could be in his apartment right now, on his sofa next to the electric fireplace, with some soft classical music playing, while his cat, Mr. Pickles, rested on his lap. He would be purring, sending low vibrations along-

The sound of the wind's gust startled Stephen out of his daze so suddenly that he jerked his head up. The whistle sounded more like a person's voice trying to mimic the *whooshing* sound. Instantly, the papers on the desk scattered and flew around the room, gyrating in the air before dropping on the floor. Stephen made no effort to catch them. He looked around the room but saw no one inside.

Of course not.

If he had a window in the office, he would have glanced at it to see if he left it open, but the office had no windows; therefore, no breeze could have blown the pages. Only five pages remained in front of Stephen on the desk, scattered out of their neat order. And then another whoosh came from somewhere in the room (maybe from behind Stephen), and this time he did jump because it felt like someone was blowing an icy breath into the nape of his neck, causing his hairs to stand straight. More papers scattered off the desk, flying around the room before joining their fallen brethren on the floor.

Stephen looked at the desk and saw that only one piece of paper remained on top of it. Two photographs were attached in the upper right corner – a young married couple. He remembered them. Brad and Julia Napier. They went to see apartment 401 just a week ago. Nice couple, very polite. Stephen tentatively approached the desk and picked up the paper, staring at the photographs.

Brad was grinning at the camera. He had a clean-shaven face and a perfect, pretty-boy smile. This was complemented with lush, hazel hair that made him look all the better. Stephen remembered speaking to him a week ago. He was down to earth, polite, and considerate. He even asked Stephen if he needed to reschedule their appointment since the realtor complained about having a busy day.

And then there was Julia. She was a brunette with curly hair, and although in the photograph she looked beautiful with blue eyes and an enchanting smile, Stephen considered her to be a little above average in person – which was refreshing, especially since he expected her to look like a model – like in the photo. She was friendly, but she and Stephen didn't talk much. She spent most of the time following him and her husband around while the two men talked about the apartment.

"You... you want them? You want me to give the apartment to them?" Stephen asked, looking around the room.

He was met with silence. The lights flickered, briefly and intermittently engulfing the room in total darkness before they stopped working altogether. It took Stephen's eyes a moment to get adjusted to the dark, and then he started to make out shapes in the blackness of the room.

Just in front of him, in the corner of his office, stood a figure, unmoving and staring somewhere to Stephen's right. Stephen felt a lump forming in his throat as he looked at the figure. He started to discern more and more details on it – a featureless face, slick hair tied into a ponytail, a tight, dark dress against a slim, feminine body. Stephen couldn't force himself to look away. After what felt like an eternity of staring at it, his eyes burned from the lack of blinking. His eyes unwillingly closed and opened, and -

The figure's head was now facing him. Or was it? Was he just imagining it? No, no, he wasn't. Stephen blinked again, and the figure was now facing him not just with its head, but its entire body, too.

The lights came on, and Stephen stared at... nothing. There was nothing in front of him, just an old coat hanger with his jacket hanging on it and a red baseball cap just on top of it. Stephen felt his heart beating a million miles an hour, and as he looked down, he just then realized that he was still clutching the paper with Brad's and Julia's documents, so firmly that he slightly crumpled it near the edges. He gasped when he saw the crude red letters on the paper that weren't there just a minute ago.

It said, *THEM.*

The Door

"Hello?" Daniella shouted into the darkness ahead of her.

It was pitch black and she couldn't see her hand in front of her face. She took her phone out of her pocket and turned on the torch. It illuminated the dilapidated walls of the narrow corridor in front of her, which by logic shouldn't even be in front of her. The temperature was much lower here than it was back in the apartment and Daniella found herself shivering; and not just from the cold. Something was terribly wrong here and she could feel it in her bones, but she couldn't leave just yet.

She forced herself to take a step forward and after that, each subsequent step came naturally for her. The light of her torch barely penetrated the permeating darkness ahead and the deeper she went in, the more she became overwhelmed by a feeling of unease. She had no idea where she was headed and it was impossible to tell how far the corridor stretched on for. She glanced behind, just to reassure herself the apartment door was still open there. The idea of being trapped in this corridor, surrounded by such darkness, terrified her.

Come on, Daniella. Come on, you got this. Your sister's counting on you. She did her best to motivate herself, feeling her own breath uncontrollably tremble with each harsh exhale.

She quickened her pace a little. The steps she took up until this point were timid and short, but they slowly broke into a more confident stride, as the sound of her shoes echoed in the corridor with each step she took. Despite feeling less uneasy now, she kept glancing behind herself to make sure the door was still there, afraid it would somehow disappear, despite the corridor only going straight in a narrow path. The light which came from the apartment was now a small rectangle and Daniella was amazed at how much distance she put between herself and it.

The end couldn't possibly be far, right? The building wasn't that big, so whatever was on the other side must have been-

Her thoughts were interrupted when she heard a sound in the distance. She froze in place and perked up her ears. She stared down at the ground, since it allowed her to focus better, plus she couldn't see anything ahead of her from the dark anyway. Was it just her imagination? No, there it was again. Quiet, barely audible, but without a doubt, the sound of creaking, resounded in the distance.

It discouraged her, because she realized she probably had a long way to go yet. But then another terrifying thought occurred to her. What if someone else was in here? It made her pulse speed up and in the eerie silence of the corridor, she felt her heart thumping against her chest violently, all the way up to her ears.

"Hello?!" She called out again foolishly, knowing that she could potentially be putting herself in danger, as her voice echoed.

She didn't care about that, though. Right now she simply wanted whoever was there to respond, so that she knew if someone either was or wasn't there. This anticipation was only making her more nervous. She waited a moment, trying to catch even the faintest noise, her tremulous breathing being her only response.

"Come on Daniella, pull yourself together." she said to herself aloud this time, giving herself a mental shake and put one foot cautiously in front of the other.

She looked behind her shoulder. The light which provided solace to her was now barely a dot, a meager glimmer of hope in the ever-present darkness surrounding her. She turned back in the direction she was going, exhaled deeply and continued walking. The creaking noise from before followed her occasionally, but she decided not to stop and listen to it this time. After only a few more agonizing minutes which felt like hours, she started to notice something ahead of her. At first, she thought her eyes were playing tricks on her from being in such overwhelming darkness.

She put down her phone and squinted through the dark. It *wasn't* her imagination. There was a dot of light far ahead, just like the one behind her. It reinvigorated her and she broke into a light jog, as the torch of her phone violently bobbed up and down. And then she heard something that sounded like a moan, far ahead in the distance.

She gasped loudly and stopped to listen, breathless. Silence. She waited. And then it came again. A barely audible, feminine scream. A very familiar one.

"Michelle?!" Daniella shouted and broke into a sprint, "Michelle, hold on! I'm coming!"

The scream became louder and echoed throughout the corridor, as the creaking returned, now much louder than before, permeating the air both in front and behind her. The thought of her sister being harmed filled her with such primordial fear, that she forgot all about her own safety and threw herself in the path of danger to rescue her sibling.

"Michelle, hold on!" she shouted between sucking in shallow breaths, her voice drowned out by the creaking which was now so loud, that everything else became inaudible.

The dot of light in front of her grew and grew, until it turned into a rectangular, vertical slit and then took a clear shape of a door frame. *Just a little longer now, come on.* As she got closer, the source of light was somehow becoming thinner and she realized with dread that the reason for that was the fact that the door was closing. Terror coursed through her blood at the utter realization that the creaking came from the door itself and that it was slowly closing with each passing second, bringing her closer to being trapped inside this place.

"No, no, no, no!" she chanted repetitively to herself, as she sprinted towards the door.

But she was far too late. Just before she bumped into the door, the last vestiges of light disappeared and the door clicked loudly with an echo, instantly leaving her in complete and utter silence, save for her own panicked breathing.

"No! Open up! Michelle!" Daniella shouted, banging on the door with her palm as hard as she could, hysterically calling her sister's name over and over.

She fumbled for the doorknob, but found none. It was just a plain, wooden door with no doorknob and no lock. She banged on the door until her hands started throbbing with pain and when she finally stopped banging and the adrenaline subsided from her body, the meager panic which was previously present, gradually started to overtake her, building up like slow-boiling water.

Okay, okay. I'll go back to the apartment and then return and find a way to open the door. Then I'll find and rescue Michelle. She was starting to hyperventilate as she made that thought.

Her thoughts were interrupted when she heard the sound of steady footsteps echoing upon the concrete floor behind her, slowly approaching her. She froze in place, trying not to even breathe. The footsteps stopped right behind her and Daniella heard her own frantic breaths through her nose, as tears flowed down her cheeks.

She mustered all the remaining courage she had and ever so slowly, turned around, pointing the torch of the phone in front of herself with a jerky motion. There was nothing there. She stared at the encroaching darkness and slowly moved her phone down, revealing a set of footprints of what looked like pointy shoes on the ground, ending right in front of her. Footprints which came from a different set of shoes than hers.

She moved her phone back up, but before she could process what she was looking at, a face leapt out in front of her.

Printed in Great Britain
by Amazon